The voice spoke to Sindri. It told him a secret. Sindri understood what everything he saw before meant. What *he* meant to the world. And Sindri felt a sense of joy and devastation all at the same time, a feeling that he never thought he could feel.

You are not meant to know any of this yet, the voice said, lapping against his unseen body in waves of warmth. *But dreams like these, they are a side effect of what you have become. Wake up, Sindri. Forget what you have seen. Begin your journey.*

But I can't! Sindri thought, knowing that somehow the voice could hear his thoughts. I have to remember this!

THE NEW ADVENTURES

SUNCATCHER TRILOGY

Volume One
THE WAYWARD WIZARD

Volume Two
THE EBONY EYE
(MARCH 2007)

Volume Three
THE STOLEN SUN
(SEPTEMBER 2007)

THE NEW ADVENTURES

SUNCATCHER TRILOGY

• VOLUME ONE

THE WAYWARD WIZARD

JEFF SAMPSON

COVER & INTERIOR ART
Vinod Rams

MIRRORSTONE™

Dragonlance®: The New Adventures

THE WAYWARD WIZARD
©2006 Wizards of the Coast, Inc.

Cover art by Vinod Rams
Cartography by Dennis Kauth
First Printing: September 2006
Library of Congress Catalog Card Number: 2005935546

9 8 7 6 5 4 3 2 1

ISBN-10: 0-7869-4163-4
ISBN-13: 978-0-7869-4163-6
620-95742740-001-EN

U.S., CANADA,   EUROPEAN HEADQUARTERS
ASIA, PACIFIC, & LATIN AMERICA   Hasbro UK Ltd
Wizards of the Coast, Inc.   Caswell Way
P.O. Box 707   Newport, Gwent NP9 0YH
Renton, WA 98057-0707   GREAT BRITAIN
+1-800-324-6496   Save this address for your records.

Visit our web site at www.mirrorstonebooks.com

FOR MOM

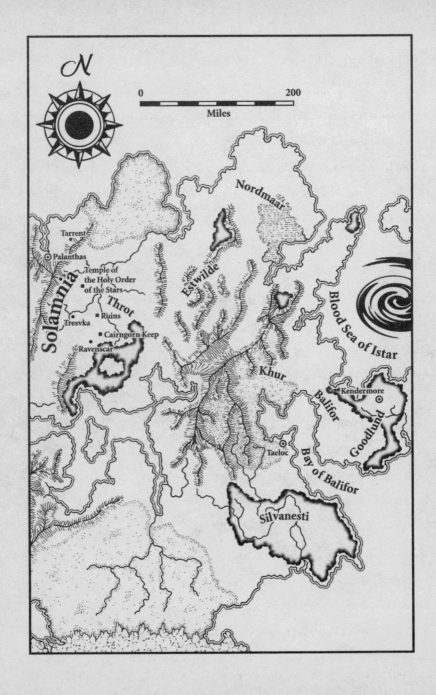

Table of Contents

PROLOGUE

Sindri Suncatcher, the inexplicable kender wizard, burst into his room in a flurry of shaggy black hair and billowing brown apprentice robes. Excitement jolted him from toes to ears. After six long months of doing nothing but studying magic with his mentor, Maddoc, he'd finally get his first real test the next day.

Best of all, after he succeeded in his test, he'd get his reward.

But first things first. Dressing in his nightclothes, Sindri put out the lamp in the corner and plopped onto his red velvet bedsheets. Digging his head into his pillows until finally comfortable, he closed his eyes. With images of magical battles swirling through his thoughts, Sindri let sleep overtake him.

And Sindri dreamed.

The dream began with darkness. Sindri walked through the dark, dirt crunching beneath his feet as blades of grass tickled his toes. A breeze brushed over his bare arms, sending fine hairs bristling.

Hmm, Sindri thought. This is interesting. I suppose this could be a world of nothing, but I can feel something, so it's a world of *something* at least. So maybe it's just really dark. Or maybe I've gone blind! Now that would be rather interesting.

Sindri sensed something—a presence, vast and powerful, somewhere close by. Blinking twice, Sindri looked to his left then to his right. He spun to look behind himself then leaned over to peer down at the bare toes he couldn't see.

Still, he saw nothing.

Only one place left to look.

Craning his neck, Sindri looked up toward the endless black sky. There, high above, was the presence. It was round and somehow an even darker black than that of the sky, a hole torn in the nothingness. Sindri knew that it was this thing, this presence, that had stolen all the light away. It was waiting to suck him into nothingness as well.

It had waited for this moment to devour him.

White light blazed, and Sindri found himself somewhere new. Though he still couldn't see himself, his surroundings were no longer nothingness. Floors of veined marble glared bright white in sunlight that filtered down through arched windows. Old men and women in embroidered robes of white, red, and black stood about in clusters around high-backed chairs. Peering at one another anxiously, their lips moved as they chatted noiselessly among themselves. Servants with trays of tiny edibles and goblets of wine darted between the groups.

Wizards, Sindri thought, and very important ones at that.

Though he should have heard the rustling of cloth, the tiny thuds of feet hitting stone as the servants bumbled about, the murmur of voices, Sindri heard nothing. He spun around, taking in the atmosphere. Along the walls, silver brackets shaped like leaves held unlit torches. Runic carvings decorated the molding, and intricately embroidered tapestries depicting ancient battles of magic hung heavy and somber.

A pair of voices approached behind him, the first and only sounds Sindri had heard since entering the place. He turned to see two men dressed in white robes. Strange symbols that Sindri thought he should recognize were embroidered in gold along their sleeves. One of the men was old, with wispy gray hair and black stubble shadowing a lined face. The other was young, seeming not too much older than Sindri himself, with flowing blond hair and inquisitive blue eyes.

"Master," the younger man said, "if the rumors are true, then this is beyond important. We must set out at once to capture this renegade and—"

The older man held up a hand and nodded his head as the younger's brow furrowed. "I agree, Wilden. I agree. But Raistlin, he's all anyone can worry about at the moment. We will have to handle this situation ourselves."

Arms behind his back, the older man scratched his stubbly chin and looked at the other wizards in the vast room, their voices still silent to Sindri even as they appeared deep in serious discussions. "Only you and I can capture the kender."

Another flash of white and the wizards were gone. Bark climbed along the stone pillars, turning them into towering trees, as the marble floor darkened and crumbled into leaf-strewn soil. As Sindri blinked to take in the sudden shift in scenery, he distinctly heard the sound of trees groaning in distress before thumping against the ground with resounding booms. Birds cawed in fear as the air screamed with a furious wind.

Sindri watched with interest as rabbits and a pair of deer darted from between overgrown bushes. Behind them the towering trees trembled in fear as the booms and groans grew louder. The wind roared, a feral, otherworldly screech. What little sky Sindri could see through the canopy darkened from blue to black, like a robin's egg drenched in ink.

In a flurry of leaves, another creature burst from the bushes. It stopped mere feet from Sindri, even as the sounds grew louder and the trees whipped as though caught in a tornado. The creature was like nothing Sindri had ever seen before; it was small, about the size of a house cat, with a triangle-shaped head very much like a dragon's, long limbs ending with tiny claws, and a thick tail. Despite its lizardlike shape, it was covered with coarse brown and black fur.

Its chest heaved as the creature stood on its hind legs and sniffed the air. Head darting back and forth like a bird, it looked to the left, then right, then directly up at Sindri. Wide amber eyes, with slit pupils like a cat, peered directly at Sindri's face.

Sindri tried to ask, "Can you see me?" But no words escaped his lips. The furry lizard tried to speak too, its scaly lips forming words, but Sindri was unable to hear it.

Finally, clearly startled, the creature darted one last look behind it and fled. Sindri looked up to see what was coming through the woods, catching a glimpse of something smoky and black and covered with eyes, dozens of eyes, and—

A flash. Sindri now saw a desolate plain of white sand. Wind blew around him, past what little scrubby brush made a go at growing in the endless desert. Sindri saw stony cliffs in the distance then nothing more but sand and a roiling, cloudy gray sky.

Sindri blinked as the air rippled, as though something large and invisible had disturbed the sky. Before Sindri could react, a giant lizardfish face appeared, its maw opened wide to tear into him and—

Another flash. A wizard stood at the mouth of a hall that seemed to stretch into endless darkness. All Sindri could see was the wizard's back, cloaked in a black robe. Tiny gnomes dressed in rags lined the hall, their flesh pale and their arms so skinny that they seemed little more than bones covered with papery flesh. They stared up at the wizard, fear clouding eyes that seemed much too wide on their starving, skeletal faces. Behind the gnomes, rusty gears churned along the walls. The only thing Sindri could hear was the aching screeches as the gears ground against one another. The wizard began to turn around and—

Flash. Maddoc, large, regal Maddoc with his cropped gray beard and black robes, was on his knees in the main hall of Cairngorn Keep, screaming in agony. Sindri ran toward him and—

Found himself in a plain of tall grass. A girl, her skin the color of freshly drawn sap and her black hair cropped short, raised her hands to cast a spell. Tears streamed from her stormy gray eyes even as the rest of her features were set with stern resolve. Behind her, hordes of red-faced goblins in piecemeal armor slashed at one another. Flames crackled over the girl's fingers and—

Sindri was at home. His family was there—his mother, Aunt Moonbeam, Cousin Dorny, everyone. They huddled in front of their huts and looked up in awe as something vast that Sindri couldn't see cast a large shadow over them. There were humans there too, and they looked afraid. Sindri called out to his mother and—

Flash.

Stop! Sindri yelled in his head. Closing his eyes, he stomped his foot.

How am I supposed to remember all of this if it goes by so quickly? he thought. I want to know more, but as soon as I see one thing, another takes its place! None of this seems like a normal dream. It all seems important, and—

A voice spoke, the sound of it like falling into a warm bath after coming inside from a snowy day. Opening his eyes, Sindri spun around to find himself in front of a wall of glimmering gold. It was all that he could see, the gold thing so vast, it seemed to stretch for miles in all directions.

The voice spoke to Sindri. It told him a secret. Sindri understood what everything he saw before meant. What *he* meant to the world. And Sindri felt a sense of joy and devastation all at the same time, a feeling that he never thought he could feel.

You are not meant to know any of this yet, the voice said, lapping against his unseen body in waves of warmth. *But dreams like these they are a side effect of what you have become. Wake up, Sindri. Forget what you have seen. Begin your journey.*

But I can't! Sindri thought, knowing that somehow the voice could hear his thoughts. I have to remember this!

He ran to the wall of gold and pounded his small fists against its side. I won't forget! he thought. I won't forget! I—

"Won't!"

With a start, Sindri sat straight up in his bed. The red velvet sheets had tangled around his ankles, and somehow he'd managed to spin around in his sleep so that he lay sideways on his mattress.

Daylight filtered through his white curtains and lit his room with a hazy brightness. Steaming water filled the golden wash-basin in the far corner, as it did every morning, and all of the portraits of great wizards on the walls seemed to smile down on him.

Someone rapped on the bedroom door. "You awake, Master Sindri?" a gravelly woman's voice called. "I heard you yell. You ain't dead, are you?"

"No," Sindri responded. Bouncing twice on the bed, he jumped down to the plush woven rug on his floor. "I'm fine. I think I had a dream that woke me up."

As Sindri walked to his wardrobe, the door opened and the old dwarf serving lady, Nitty, waddled in. In her plump arms she carried a tray of steaming food. Sindri's mouth watered.

"That smells wonderful!" Pulling on his brown apprentice robes over his underclothes, Sindri turned to give Nitty a big grin.

"Eh," the dwarf said as she shrugged. Hobbling past the bed, she set the tray on a little table in front of his windows. "Same ol' breakfast, if you ask me." Crossing her arms and tightening her wrinkled features, Nitty turned to give Sindri a hard look. "Leave it to a kender to get so excited by a dream it wakes him up," she said with a curt, disapproving shake of her head. "At least it must have been something important."

"It . . . " Sindri frowned. "Hmm, well, I remember it being interesting, at the very least. There were gold things with black eyes, and I think there were fancy people in robes drinking tea and turning invisible."

Nitty harrumphed. "Sounds like typical kender nonsense."

"I think I'm supposed to remember—"

"I don't particularly care, Master Sindri," Nitty interrupted.

Glaring disapprovingly at her gray hair in a nearby mirror, she scowled even further. "You said yesterday that you had some book you wanted me to send off with a messenger?"

"Yes, it's on the table there." Sindri straightened his robes, making sure every fold was in place.

Nitty walked to a table near the door and saw the brown, leather-bound book Sindri had prepared. A painting of a green dragon was embossed on its cover.

" 'A Practical Guide to Dragons,' " Nitty read as she picked the book up. "And you're having this sent to Kendermore? As if any kender would appreciate a practical anything."

Sindri shrugged. "I thought it was a good idea."

"If you say so," Nitty said, stuffing the book under her plump arm. "Oh, I almost forgot. Master Maddoc wants you to take breakfast in your room as quick as possible. He said to tell you that your test awaits."

"My test!" Sindri cried. With a yelp, Sindri raced across the rug and slid into his chair. He had a utensil in each hand and was diving into his meal before he was even fully seated. "I'll hurry as fast as I can," he mumbled through a mouth full of fried hens' eggs.

"Kender," Nitty muttered and quickly hobbled from the room.

Something nagged at Sindri as he ate. He was certain he was supposed to remember something.

Ah well, he decided after a moment. If it was really all that important, then I'd remember it, wouldn't I?

Sindri quickly downed his meal and raced to get to his test, the dream—and all its portents—completely forgotten.

CHAPTER

1   APPRENTICE'S TEST

R ight on time."

Maddoc stood tall and imposing in the doorway that led from the shady hall of the main keep to the open courtyard beyond. The edges of his gray hair and close-cropped beard glowed white from the overcast daylight streaming in behind him, but the rest of him was shadow.

"Of course!" Sindri's voice echoed in the high ceiling as he raced down the hall, his hoopak staff in one hand. He held up his new brown robes with the other hand so he wouldn't trip. He skittered to a stop right at Maddoc's feet, his head barely reaching the older wizard's waist.

Maddoc peered down at Sindri, a half smile on his lips. "Excited for your test, I take it?" Maddoc's deep, regal voice echoed in the rafters, the sound rich and booming.

Sindri nodded. "Well, more excited for the reward, but I'm sure the test will be fun too."

Maddoc let out a quick grunt of semilaughter and shook his head. "Well, then let's get to it. Follow me."

Black wizard's robes flowing behind him, Maddoc turned and

9

walked through the doorway. Sindri followed him out to the vast, open courtyard, paved in ruddy brown brick. Behind them rose the main tower from which they had exited. It thrust into the sky twenty times a human man's height, looking very much like a giant black gravestone. The tower's top was sheered flat rather than rising to a point, its edges surrounded by toothlike crenellations. Smaller, rounded towers encircled the main tower, their tops just as flat.

Other buildings, half as high, jutted up at different points around the courtyard like miniature versions of the main tower. Between these other towers were smaller, wooden buildings—the stables, the armory, and others—but it was too early for any of the servants to be around, and Maddoc probably would have made them stay away even if it wasn't. Surrounding everything was a twenty-foot wall, beyond which the darkened spires of fir trees rustled beneath the cloudy sky.

Collectively, the structures were known as Cairngorn Keep. Long before the great Cataclysm that forever changed the face of Krynn, an evil sorceress named Asvoria had built the keep as her main stronghold in the lands that were now known as Solamnia. Thousands of years later, spurred by an obsession with discovering Asvoria's secrets, Maddoc had purchased Cairngorn Keep as his home and place of study.

It wasn't that long ago that Sindri and a few of his companions had come to the keep for the first time to face Maddoc himself. At the time, the black-robed wizard had been their foe; he'd intended to release Asvoria's soul into the body of one of Sindri's friends against her will. To stop him, the companions had faced the hazardous forest outside the keep, the vast and mysterious caverns that coursed beneath its courtyard, and the many magical rooms inside.

They'd failed to stop Maddoc, and their friend Nearra was taken over by Asvoria's soul. Asvoria raced to begin her own treacherous plans—after first stripping Maddoc of his powers.

Ever since then, everyone had told Sindri, time and again, that he couldn't trust Maddoc. But after Asvoria's resurgence, Maddoc helped them find the weapons that would eventually destroy her. Maddoc had taken Sindri under his wing and taught him how to use magic, even while everyone else told the kender he could never be a wizard. And Maddoc, on regaining his own powers, had cast powerful spells that let Sindri and his friends dispense of the evil sorceress and finally free Nearra.

Maddoc had done bad things in the name of magic, sure, but Sindri was certain Maddoc had changed. The wizard wasn't just his mentor—he was Sindri's friend.

Striding in long, regal steps, Maddoc led Sindri toward the exact center of the courtyard. Stopping abruptly, the older wizard grasped his hands behind his back and looked up at the writhing gray clouds.

"Tell me, Sindri," he said. "What do *you* think is the first rule of magic?"

Fingering the smoothed wooden handle of his hoopak, Sindri bit his lip in thought. "I suppose that would be what everyone always tells me: 'Kender can't do magic.' "

Maddoc grunted a quick laugh, then spun to face Sindri, his lined features back to their usual serious expression. "Not just kender, Sindri. There are other races that are just as limited in magical abilities, but the people of Krynn are the most adamant about you and your kind. Why do you think that is?"

Sindri shrugged. "Everyone always underestimates kender. I think it's because we're so small."

"Not just that," Maddoc said. "Most, if not all, kender have an insatiable sense of curiosity and a low threshold for boredom. One could argue that even if kender had the capacity for magic, they simply don't have the necessary focus to become good at it."

Sindri scrunched his eyebrows. "Well, then they'd clearly be wrong because there's me."

Maddoc smiled. "Exactly. You are an anomaly, Sindri. You are the only kender wizard on all of Krynn. That is what makes you special. And that is what will make it all the harder for you to be accepted by all of your naysayers." Spreading his hands wide, Maddoc gestured toward the wide open courtyard. "That is why we need to have a test."

Sindri looked left and right. The brick courtyard was completely bare, save for the few spots where shriveled grass had managed to burst through cracks.

Scrunching his eyebrows, Sindri stared up at Maddoc inquisitively. "Is it an invisible test? I'm not sure I've mastered that."

"Not quite." With a flick of Maddoc's wrist, the bricks beneath Sindri's boots quaked. The red stone blocks jumped up and down at random, like the bubbles in boiling water. Startled and delighted, Sindri stood back to watch.

The bricks leaped from the ground, piling atop one another like a rickety tower of a child's building blocks. They formed a figure a little taller than Sindri that looked like a squarish, featureless human. An unusual statue, the block man stood perfectly still in the middle of the dirt that had once lay hidden beneath the bricks that now formed its body. Worms and bugs crawled over the soil that still clung to some of the stone.

"This," Maddoc said as he came to the block man's side, "is your foe. I will control its movements. Your job is to use the spells we've been studying along with the correct hand motions and spell components to stop its attacks. At first I will call out spells for you to use. Then I will expect you to figure out the spells on your own. Once you have proven to me that our studies have not been a waste, you will get your reward. I trust you have your spell components with you?"

Sindri felt his bulging robes and at the belt around his waist. Sands and knickknacks filled his pockets and pouches, ready to focus his powers. "I sure do. Let's go!"

Folding his hands into his flowing black sleeves, Maddoc nodded and walked backward toward the main tower. Thunder rumbled from a distant storm, echoing in Sindri's pointed ears. He imagined a roaring crowd of spectators, anxious to see his feats of magic.

Sindri rounded on the figure made of brick, passing his hoopak staff from hand to hand. The figure stood perfectly still beneath the swirling gray sky, nothing more than a rather ugly effigy. This was going to be easy.

"First spell!" Maddoc called from his new position near the tower's black stone walls. "Flare!"

Sindri tilted his head and looked past the block man. "Flare?" Sindri called back. "But he doesn't have eyes, wouldn't do much good to use—"

"Flare!" Maddoc called again.

The block man moved, its makeshift joints creaking. With seemingly great effort, it lifted one makeshift arm, then another. Red dust fell in little clouds as the bricks ground against one another.

"Wow, that's really—" Sindri started to say.

In a flurry of brick dust and dirt, the block man leaped.

Sindri scrambled backward, hoopak held in front of his torso and his fingers aimed forward. *"Pesona shirak!"* he yelled.

An intense, bright cone of light burst from Sindri's outstretched fingers. The light flared over the block man, its glare so bright that Sindri had to look away. The world turned bright white, the towering buildings shadows of black.

The spell faded away and Sindri lowered his hand. Blinking to clear the spots from his eyes, he turned his head back around and found the block man once again standing perfectly still.

Sindri pumped his fist and let out a gleeful shout. "Ha *ha!*" he crowed. Leaning to peer around the block man at Maddoc, he grinned. "Too easy."

Maddoc raised a bushy gray eyebrow. "Obscuring mist."

A screeching and crunching of stone against stone sounded as the strange little magic-made man crouched down. It moved slowly as it took one stealthy step toward Sindri, then another. Worms dangled from its knees, clinging to the soiled bricks.

Sindri smirked. Holding his hoopak high and moving his hand in slow, intricate motions, he mumbled, *"Tanda kendala."*

Tendrils of smoky gray mist curled from beneath the cracks at Sindri's feet. The tendrils braided together as they rose toward the sky, surrounding him with a hazy wall of fog. Satisfied, Sindri watched as the block man stalked near, the creature nothing but a shadow in the mist as it searched for him blindly.

Something beyond the shadow of the block man sparked bright orange. Sindri watched curiously as the orange spark came closer, not realizing until it was nearly too late what it was.

"Whoa!" he shouted, ducking as a fireball struck the fog. The magical flame consumed the fog, burning it into nothingness and revealing Sindri once more.

The wispy, ashy remnants of Sindri's spell drifted to his feet as he stood back up. Dusting himself off, he looked over at Maddoc. "What was that for? Did I do it wrong?"

Maddoc just smiled his unreadable smile. Only then did Sindri realize that he'd lost sight of the block man.

Strong, stony hands gripped Sindri beneath his shoulders. Before he realized what was happening, the block man held Sindri high above its head. His feet dangling, Sindri looked down at the block man, unsure what to make of this new development.

Then the block man threw him up into the air.

Trees and buildings, the gray sky dotted with black birds, the brick courtyard, Maddoc and the block man—everything swirled by faster and faster until the world was just a blur of gray and red.

Until, that is, Sindri's upward ascent slowed. It took him only a moment realize he was about to tumble to the courtyard below, and he grinned.

"Easy!" he shouted down toward Maddoc as he spread his arms wide and let himself fall. "I've done this lots of times!"

With the rush of air whipping his hair and his too-long brown robes, Sindri wiggled his fingers and called out, *"Pfeatherfall!"*

The air beneath him ceased to rush, instead billowing beneath him to form a giant, invisible pillow. His descent effectively slowed, Sindri swung himself up into a sitting position, crossed one leg over the other, and smirked down at Maddoc. "See?"

From where he watched below, Maddoc pulled his hands free from his robes and gave two large, sarcastic claps. "Impressive. What say we step it up a bit?"

Sindri placed a hand on his chest. His heart pounded from the adrenaline, and his breath seemed a little shaky from the effort. But there was no way was he going to fail this test.

"Of course!" he called back.

Ever so gently, the magic pillow of air lowered Sindri to the ground. With his boots once again upon brick, he nodded toward Maddoc then turned around to face the block man.

The brick creature stood still, its makeshift body devoid of any feature. But Sindri knew better than to be fooled. He tensed his free hand over his pouches, waiting.

The block man struck. Swinging one arm around, it flung free a brick, then another and another. A flurry of brick missiles whooshed through the air, headed straight toward Sindri's head.

With nimble fingers, Sindri unclasped a pouch. A crisp grasshopper's leg lay inside. Pulling it out and snapping the leg in two, Sindri shouted, *"Berlua itu!"* Sindri crouched, then he leaped into the air. The bricks flew beneath his feet. In a flurry of sparks, the bricks struck the main tower.

Trying to control the wild jump, Sindri landed in a roll behind the block man. He was on his feet in an instant and spun on his heels to face the creature. Its arms were gone now, having thrown all its bricks at Sindri, but at either side of the creature the courtyard once again bubbled. Bricks leaped one by one into the air, attaching to the block man's body.

"Oh no, you don't!" Sindri cried. Swinging his hoopak, he raced forward and slammed the sling end against what passed for the block man's back.

The block man spun, and to Sindri it seemed its once featureless face was now shadowed with dark shapes that looked like narrowed eyes and snarling lips. The creature strode forward, its brick arms flailing as it tried to strike Sindri. Sindri backed away, expertly blocking the blows with his staff while he dug through his pockets with his other hand.

"*Cerlang corak!*" Sindri tossed a handful of colored powder into the air. Tendrils of blue, red, and yellow light swirled through the air. The colors overtook the block man with a spell intended to blind it and give Sindri a moment to breathe.

Only it didn't work. The block man still came forward, its arms swinging like deadly clubs.

"Hey!" Sindri cried out in indignation. "If the flare spell worked, that one should have—whoa!"

With a surge of speed, the creature leaped toward Sindri, arms outstretched. Its brick fists hit him square in the chest, and Sindri flew backward. He landed with a *thud* and an *oof!* against the wall of a wooden building. Startled horses beyond the wall neighed in fear as Sindri slid to the ground.

His heart pounding faster and his lungs aching for air, Sindri knew he wouldn't be able to last much longer before passing out. A shadow loomed above him, blocking the hazy daylight. The block man stared down at him with its twisted, shadowy features and raised one fist in a killing blow.

"No," Sindri mumbled and shook his head. Then, louder and with both hands raised, he yelled, "No!"

Power surged within Sindri, a swirling sensation deep within his gut that filled him with a rush of joy and rage, and he focused that energy directly at the block man. Something strong and powerful burst from his fingertips, a rush of wind mixed with crackling blue energy that filled the courtyard with a feral screaming. The blast of magic hit the block man square in its makeshift chest, and the thing exploded backward in a cloud of ruddy dust and silt. Broken bricks scattered across the courtyard, the creature finally destroyed.

Lowering his hands and smiling in satisfaction, Sindri's eyes grew heavy. Ignoring the clomping hooves and whinnying of the horses in the stalls behind him, Sindri fell unconscious.

"Here we are," a voice said.

What felt like only seconds later, Sindri blinked his eyes open. Only it couldn't have been seconds later. He was in his bed and the sky beyond his curtains had grown dark. Somehow an entire day had disappeared on him.

"Huh?" Sindri asked. Sitting straight up and spinning to his right, he found Maddoc sitting at his bedside. The older wizard held up a cup of water.

"You should drink," he said. Nodding, Sindri took the cup and swallowed its contents in two gulps.

Wiping his lips with the back of his sleeve, he tilted his head and looked up at Maddoc. "Did I do all right? Did I pass the test? I didn't mean to pass out—I hate when that happens—but sometimes I just can't help it."

Maddoc nodded. "I know, Sindri. It's all right. You did well. More than deserving of a reward. I do have one question, though. The last spell. The one you used to destroy your foe. Did you use any spell components for it? Any words or hand motions?"

Biting his lower lip, Sindri turned away and thought. His fingers fidgeted at the red velvet bedsheets as he fought to remember. "You know," he said after a moment, "I don't believe I did. That's strange, isn't it?"

Saying nothing, Maddoc raised an eyebrow and picked up a small notebook Sindri hadn't noticed before. The older wizard scratched a note to himself, his eyes flashing with a familiar dark curiosity. Sindri was about to ask him what the notebook was for, but Maddoc finished his final notation with a flourish of his quill, placed a blotter between the pages, and clasped the book shut.

"You did well," Maddoc said again. Standing up, he gestured toward Sindri's bedroom door. "Why don't you get up and put on your boots? Your reward awaits."

Pushing the memory of the strange spell out of his mind and forgetting all about Maddoc's notebook, Sindri nodded in glee and leaped from his bed. It was finally time for him to earn the reward he'd been hoping for since he'd first entered Cairngorn Keep.

He was going to get to see the future.

CHAPTER

2   A Reward and a Warning

Sindri could barely keep from bouncing as he and Maddoc walked down the dusty, dark corridor that led to his reward. Maddoc carried a lamp lit with blue flame that did little to dispel the mysterious gloom. Its sapphire light cast wonderfully moody shadows all around them.

The corridor was in the little-used west wing on one of the upper floors of Cairngorn Keep. Sindri knew his prize lay at the hallway's end, beyond a door he could barely make out in the dim light. As they grew closer, Sindri was surprised to find that it seemed like an average wooden door, with the exception that it had neither handle nor doorknob with which to enter. Carved into the wood was an hourglass symbol, highlighted by the flickering blue light.

"This is it." Sindri's face split apart into a rapturous smile, and he couldn't help but clap his hands. "It has to be!"

Maddoc raised a bushy eyebrow and glanced down. "I will never get used to the endless excitement of a kender." With a shake of his head, the older wizard placed his free hand on the hourglass symbol and muttered a magical phrase. Its hinges creaked from disuse as the door swung open.

Unlike the rest of the keep, the room was covered floor to ceiling with perfectly polished white marble that reflected the blue light back at Sindri and made him blink. Once he got used to the glare, however, he gasped in wonder.

All manner of timepieces filled the room. Intricately carved grandfather clocks towered over the room, clustered together in a single corner. Stone sundials showed the hour despite the lack of sunlight. There were water clocks and hourglasses and counterweight clocks. A black globe twice as big as Sindri, glittering with dots of silver light, took up the entire right-hand side of the room.

In the center of it all, etched into the marble floor, was a looping figure eight that glowed with a blue light that stood out against the light from the lamp. A delicious, overwhelming power emanated from the symbol. Sindri's feet had started to race into the room before he even thought he might like to do so.

"Not so fast!" Maddoc clutched Sindri's shoulder and pulled him back. With Sindri pouting up at him, Maddoc shook his head. "This is the Chamber of Hours, Sindri. It's a powerful room that can manipulate time itself. If we do not enter together, we could cross into different time streams and be unable to communicate. You must stay close to me at all times. Understand?"

Sindri nodded eagerly. "Davyn told me all about what happened when you brought him here. I just forgot when I saw everything. It's better than I imagined!"

Maddoc raised an eyebrow. "Davyn told you about that, did he?"

"Well, of course. I wouldn't stop asking him until he told me everything that happened while Cat and Elidor and Ayanti and I were trapped in that painting that one time."

Maddoc let out a grunt. "Well. Shall we enter and proceed with the reward?"

"Of course!"

With Sindri clutching at Maddoc's robes and the wizard holding the lamp high, the two stepped into the room. It was like jumping into a white-water river, Sindri thought. The swirling and rushing and trickling of time flowed all around him. The roots of his hair tingled as though he could actually feel his hair growing even longer.

"Oh wow," he whispered. He stuck his hand out, stretching as far away from himself as he could. A rush like a sudden gust of wind overcame his fingers, sending icy tingles down his wrist. The fine hairs on his knuckles lengthened, his skin shriveled and wrinkled, and the edge of his robe unraveled.

Quickly Sindri pulled his hand back and it returned to normal. He could barely contain his smile. The Chamber of Hours was perhaps the most amazing room ever.

"So, Sindri," Maddoc said as they neared the shimmering figure eight symbol. "Which timepiece would you like to look into? They all have their own special properties, and any one of them will be able to show you something of the past or future that you never before imagined."

From here in the center of the room, the number of clocks and time measurers seemed even more abundant than from the hall. Sindri spun around, taking in the blue-tinted timepieces all around him, trying to decide. Their noise rushed at him—the steady drip-drip-drip of the water clocks, the gentle ticking of the grandfather clocks. Even the shadows of the sundials seemed to whoosh as they rotated, lengthening into skinny slivers before shrinking back into squat wedges.

In the corner, near the towering black globe sputtering with its dots of silver, was a little marble pedestal only half Sindri's size. A round, silver frame sat atop it. Nothing special really—until Sindri noticed a faint, iridescent glow shimmering from the glass within the frame.

"What's that do?" Sindri said. Already his feet had started carrying him toward it, his boots scampering over the glowing figure eight.

"Sindri, wait for—" Maddoc started to say. Sindri turned and saw Maddoc. The older man moved achingly slowly, as though he were a bug caught in molasses. His hand outstretched with fingers sluggishly unfurling, he reached for Sindri. His mouth and beard gradually twisted into a word that was taking a long time forming.

"Oops," Sindri said. It seemed they'd been caught in different time streams. Sindri tried to walk back toward Maddoc and take his hand only to find that he was moving slowly too, so slowly that it would take hours before their hands reached, which meant it would be even longer before Sindri would get to explore the shimmering silver frame.

"Sorry, Maddoc!" Sindri stepped back and shrugged. "We'll catch up soon, but I really need to see that frame first."

Turning back toward his original goal, Sindri hiked up his brown robes and raced across the room. The silver lights whispered as the dots sparkled over the black globe, filling Sindri with a strange, fizzy sensation that reminded him of a fancy drink his Uncle Bombaster had once given him.

But Sindri didn't have time for the globe. The frame was there, waiting for him to explore it. The entire glass center of the frame glowed a bluish green that pulsed like the ocean's waves. Flowing beneath the turquoise light was a pinpoint of red that swam around in lazy circles that grew bigger and smaller with each rotation. Certainly it was some strange, magical time device.

It was perfect.

Trembling with delight, Sindri gripped the silver frame and held it up at eye level. As he did, the red light shone brighter and spun around faster and faster until his eyes could barely keep up.

In a flash, the pulsing multicolored lights disappeared and the glass in the center of the frame faded into white nothingness. Sindri blinked, unsure what to make of it. But then vague outlines appeared. At first it was browns and greens and hints of blues, but rapidly the outlines filled in to reveal a forest path, as though he were looking through a window into another place. Towering trees swayed back and forth in a gentle wind, their star-shaped leaves rustling against one another. Birds twittered while bugs zipped beneath bushes.

Sindri stared at the serene scene, his eyes scanning every detail. Not the most interesting view of the past or future, but he supposed not every moment of every day of the past or future had to be interesting.

Somewhere beyond the edges of the frame, something rumbled. Something about the sound was familiar, though Sindri couldn't quite think what. He noticed the blue sky darken as gray storm clouds overtook the fluffy white ones that had meandered there before. The birds stopped singing, their calls turning into frightened shrieks as they burst from their hiding spots and disappeared into the sky.

Something appeared between the bushes, a strange little creature that Sindri at first thought was a house cat covered in brown and black fur. The thing trembled and limped forward, clearly scared for its life, and as it did, Sindri saw that it wasn't a cat at all. In fact, it looked almost like a lizard or a miniature dragon, with a triangular head and a long, thick tail.

The rumbling in the distance grew louder as the sky grew darker. The world beyond the magical frame was cast into a frightening gray and the little furry lizard yowled in fear. It leaped with its hind legs, half running, half wobbling directly toward the frame. Sindri cocked his head, unsure what to expect next. This was far more exciting that just a scenic forest view.

The creature ran faster and faster as it grew closer to the frame. It looked up as it scampered forward, its catlike amber eyes directly on Sindri's own.

Curious, Sindri thought. I wonder if it can see me.

That question was answered seconds later when the creature bunched its back legs, leaped into the air, and landed on the frame itself—directly between the real world and whatever time Sindri was looking into.

Quick as a snake, the creature grasped Sindri's cloak with its sharp black claws. Pulling Sindri closer with more strength than he would have imagined such a little thing could have, the lizard creature stared directly into Sindri's face. Its chest heaved in fear, and its jaw hung open as it panted for air.

"Kender man," the thing rasped. "You the kender man."

"You can talk!" Sindri said.

The furry lizard glanced over its shoulder toward the darkening woods, where the rumbling continued to grow, then back at Sindri. "Dark wizard lies to you. You not what been told. It comes for you."

"Huh?" Sindri asked. He tilted his head. "What do you mean? Who's lying to me? What's coming for me?"

The creature shook its head and let go of Sindri's cloak. Peering back over its shoulder one more time, it let out a gasp of despair then met Sindri's quizzical look with sad eyes.

"Run, kender man," it whispered. Behind it, a particularly loud thump shook the trees. "Run!"

With that, the creature darted back into the frame and disappeared from view. Enthralled, Sindri didn't let the frame go. The forest was almost completely shrouded in blackness, the trees flinging back and forth as though batted about by giant hands. The rumbling became a furious roar, and Sindri held his breath, anxious to see whatever it was that had the little lizard thing so frightened.

A strong hand fell on Sindri's shoulder, and he jumped with surprise. Looking up, he saw Maddoc glaring down at him with a raised eyebrow.

"Oh, hello, Maddoc," Sindri said with a grin. "Sorry, I just had to—"

"Yes, I know," Maddoc said. He wrenched the frame from Sindri's hand, destroying whatever connection Sindri had made. The blue and green light pulsed over the round glass once more, and the flickering red dot continued its circular course.

"Aw," Sindri said. "I wanted to see what was after the lizard thing."

Maddoc set the frame gently on its pedestal. "I told you we needed to stick together Sindri," Maddoc said, turning his back on the kender, "that being separated in here could be dangerous."

"I know," Sindri said. "It's just—"

"No." His gnarled hand held high to silence Sindri, Maddoc spun on his heels, his black robes whipping around his boots. "You are my apprentice, Sindri. You are to listen to my instructions. You cannot go messing with magical artifacts without me there to oversee. You have come far, especially for a kender, but you are not ready to just prance through magical rooms grabbing at things without regard for the consequences."

Frowning, Sindri lowered his head. "Sorry, Maddoc," he said. "I—"

"You cannot leave me incapacitated like that." Maddoc paced in his anger, as though not hearing Sindri's apology. The older man clenched his hands behind his back so tightly that veins bulged on his wrists.

"There is no excuse for what you just did. Every time you prove yourself a competent wizard, you go and pull a typical kender stunt. You're not supposed to be typical! You're supposed to be a wizard, for Nuitari's sake!"

Maddoc's pacing quickened, his eyes holding a rage Sindri had never before seen. It was a bit unsettling, and the lizard creature's words from moments before flitted through his mind.

Dark wizard lies to you.

"Sindri, I need to be able to trust you not to run off and act like a buffoon!"

"I know!" Sindri shouted. Quickly he slapped his hands over his mouth, ashamed of himself for yelling at his master.

"Sorry," he added quickly as Maddoc stopped midpace and glared down at him. "Sometimes I can't help myself. But I'm trying. Please don't be mad."

Maddoc sighed. Bowing his head, he rubbed his temples.

For a long moment, neither spoke.

"I apologize," Maddoc said finally. "I'm not mad at you, just concerned that we may not have made as much progress as I thought after our test."

"No!" Sindri said. Standing straight, he smoothed his robes. "No, we have. I promise."

Again Maddoc sighed. "I suppose there was no harm done, really." Running a hand through his gray hair, he shrugged. "We can talk about it later. It must be getting close to dinner. Shall we?"

Sindri nodded. "All right."

Maddoc gripped Sindri's shoulder and, holding the blue lamp high, steered the kender toward the door. "What did you see?" Maddoc asked after a moment.

Sindri peered up at Maddoc's lined, regal face, the man's eyes staring stoically ahead. What exactly was it that Sindri had seen? Was it something that had already happened or something that was yet to come? And as he thought of it, it wasn't just the rumbling in the trees that seemed familiar. The rapidly darkening skies, the fleeing animals, even the furry lizard creature—it was as though he'd seen it all somewhere before.

But if that were the case, wouldn't he have remembered?

"I'm not sure," Sindri responded as they passed a multileveled table stacked with hundreds of tiny hourglasses, different-colored sands running through them. "But I hope I get to see it again."

They passed through the hourglass-embossed door, and Maddoc took a moment to chant lightly. Again the hinges creaked as the door closed of its own accord. Sindri heard a click, like a latch falling in place.

The expression on Maddoc's face was all Sindri needed to see to know that he would not be allowed back in that room anytime soon.

CHAPTER

3   The Last Supper

Swinging his feet, Sindri sat in his formal, high-backed chair, waiting for one of Maddoc's servants to bring out the first course. To his right, at the head of the long vallenwood dining table, Maddoc sat with his elbows propped atop the table and his wrinkled hands steepled in front of his face. The older wizard hadn't said a word since they had sat down, and Sindri knew better than to bother him while he was lost in thought.

Sindri sighed. Propping his elbow on the table, he leaned his cheek against his fist and scanned the wide dining room. Like the rest of the keep, it was built of heavy black stone and had high ceilings supported by decorative arched beams. Ancient, fading tapestries hung between torches that lit the room with a cozy orange glow.

The table itself took up the entire center of the massive room, surrounded by enough chairs for at least several dozen people. But, as always, despite all the mostly unseen servants in the keep, it would just be Maddoc and Sindri having dinner that evening.

Maddoc's silence was almost deafening. Looking at the unlit

candles at the table's center, Sindri suddenly longed to see his old friends again. Brooding, stealthy Davyn. Kind, determined Nearra. Serious, loyal Catriona. Clever, tortured Elidor. And all the other friends they'd made along the way: Jax, Set-ai, Shemnara, Mudd, Ayanti, Vael, Adyn, Rina, Jirah, Rohawn, Kaja, Kelenthe, and countless others. He imagined a table filled with all these brave, interesting people and smiled at the thought of their conversations.

But no, this was Sindri's life now. Just him and Maddoc, studying magic. All work with no time for adventure.

Like he'd wanted.

The wooden doors to the kitchen banged open and the dwarf Nitty burst through, the gray hair of her bun unraveling. Behind her two dark-haired young girls followed, the eyes of both cast toward the floor. They carried trays with steaming bowls of soup and baskets of bread.

"Master Maddoc," Nitty said in her gravelly voice. With a slight sneer, she glanced at Sindri sitting on his chair, feet still dangling back and forth. "Master Sindri. First course is ready."

"Yes, I see that," Maddoc grumbled from behind his steepled fingers. Not moving his hands from in front of his face, he glanced from the bowls to the table in silent command. Smiling a gap-toothed and rather fake smile, Nitty nodded.

"Yes, Master Maddoc," she said. She snatched the two bowls from one of the frightened servant girls and set them in front of Sindri and Maddoc. Almost tossing a basket of bread from the other servant girl's tray onto the center of the table, Nitty shooed the two girls toward the kitchens.

Again the dining room fell into silence. With slow, deliberate motions, Maddoc snapped open his cloth napkin and placed it on his lap, then picked up one of the polished silver spoons and sipped at the hearty-smelling soup.

Sindri did the same, slurping the thick soup if only to hear the sound. He was anxious with boredom, but Maddoc had always told him a wizard's greatest attribute was patience. He'd force himself to be just as silent and just as patient as Maddoc, even if it killed him.

Only it did feel as if it were killing him. Between each slurp of the soup, and the occasional dip of the fresh rye bread into the broth, Sindri wondered what Maddoc was thinking about. He was definitely still mad at Sindri for leaving him in the time room, but Sindri couldn't understand why. It wasn't that big a deal, was it?

But then, that was how Maddoc always was—quiet, moody, mysterious, only helpful when he wanted to be. Sindri knew him better than anyone.

Dark wizard lies to you.

Sindri tried to shake the memory of the lizard creature's words from his thoughts, but it wouldn't go away. Something about the words made him uneasy, and he *never* felt uneasy.

It was then that he remembered words of warning from another friend, the last time he'd seen any of his original traveling companions. The memory was of when he and Catriona had parted ways at the end of the previous autumn, after she'd brought him to Cairngorn Keep.

They'd just survived an exciting adventure during which their recently resurrected friend, the elf Elidor, had been hunted down by an undead king called the Defiler. The Defiler had been desperate to destroy Elidor so as to regain a magical crown that Elidor wore. It was that crown that had awoken Elidor from death, and it was Maddoc himself who had placed the crown upon Elidor's brow.

"There it is," Catriona had said as they rode horses through the dark woods outside Cairngorn Keep.

Sindri rode on a steed following her, holding on to the muscular waist of Cat's traveling companion, the good-natured and imposingly large young squire, Rohawn. Rohawn's expansive back was all that Sindri could see, so he had to lean all the way to the side to see what Catriona was talking about.

At first all Sindri had seen was Catriona herself, riding in the lead with her mail shirt poking out from under her forest green tunic and her flaming red hair flowing behind her on the wind. But beyond Cat he finally saw the towering black structure atop a hill that Sindri immediately recognized as the keep itself.

Rohawn let out a low whistle and ran his hand through his unruly brown hair. "That thing looks like a giant tombstone. Sure this is the right place, Sindri?"

"Oh, I'm definitely sure!" Sindri had said. "Last time we were here we were chased through the woods by evil hounds and the ground collapsed into underground tunnels that I had to hold up with my magic. I think you can see where they filled in the holes over there. Wow, those were good times."

Cat peered over her shoulder and shook her head. "Yes, I think we can consider that some of the most fun we've ever had on our quests."

"Definitely!"

Pulling back on her reins, Cat slowed her steed to a stop and Rohawn followed suit. Not waiting for anyone else, Sindri let go of Rohawn's waist and leaped from the horse's back, his newly replaced purple traveling cloak flowing behind him like the wings of some exotic bird. He landed on both feet, grabbed his pack and hoopak staff from where they were strapped to the horse's side, and strolled toward the woods.

"Hey," Cat had called out to him. "Sindri, wait up." Throwing one leg over her own horse's back, Cat, too, jumped to the forest floor. Sindri hopped from foot to foot in anxiousness as he waited.

Cat kneeled in front of Sindri and put one of her gloved hands on his shoulder. She studied his face with concern. "Are you sure about this?" she asked.

Sindri sighed. "Yes, of course I am. Why do you always ask me that?"

Cat clenched her eyes closed and shook her head. A tendril of red hair fell across her cheek. "Sindri, it's just that I still don't know if we can trust Maddoc. He told us he called on Gieden when he realized Elidor wasn't entirely dead, and that's how he transported Elidor's body to the Jade Tower and put the crown on him. But he didn't mention anything about it until after we beat Asvoria. And he never explained how he could have contacted Gieden, or why he would have trusted a clearly evil elf wizard like him in the first place. I just don't know if going off to study magic with someone like Maddoc is the best idea."

"Maybe it's not," Sindri said with his head raised in defiance. "But it's my idea, and I think it's a good one. You'll see."

With that, he turned and stormed off toward the woods. Maddoc's letters said he would have servants waiting to guide him to the keep's entrance, and Sindri didn't want to waste another moment. He had nearly reached the main path through the gnarled, dark trees when he suddenly felt guilty about stomping off without saying good-bye.

Dropping his pack and his hoopak, Sindri turned and raced back toward Cat. His arms hugged her waist before she knew what hit her and, laughing, the red-haired warrior turned around and returned the embrace.

Shaking his shaggy black hair out of his face, Sindri met Cat's eyes. "I'll be all right, Cat," he said. "Even if Maddoc does turn out to be evil, which I highly doubt, well, he'll just end up sorry he ever messed with us. Right?"

The warrior let out another laugh, the sound so rare from her that Sindri drunk it in with a broad smile. "Right," she said. "Now don't forget to write, understand? You know where I'll be."

"Of course!"

"And if you ever do start to question Maddoc," she said, the laughter suddenly gone from her eyes, "I want to be the first to know."

Sindri nodded. "Of course," he whispered.

Behind them, one of the horses snorted and whinnied, and Sindri and Cat turned to see large, burly Rohawn scratching at his head and looking a bit uncomfortable. With a proper good-bye to him as well, Sindri turned back to the woods to resume his journey toward Cairngorn Keep and his new life with Maddoc, certain that everyone's fears about the black-robed wizard were completely unfounded.

Dark wizard lies to you.

The kitchen doors thudded open, and Sindri snapped back to the present. Shoveling the remainder of the soup down his throat, Sindri let Nitty wrench away his bowl and shove a plate of steaming roast in its place. In moments the servants disappeared back into the kitchen as quickly and silently as Maddoc preferred.

Sindri looked up at Maddoc, studying the man's wizened face. Maddoc caught Sindri's eye, and the corner of his lip twitched into a slight smile. His blue eyes glimmered with pinprick reflections of torchlight.

"I apologize," Maddoc said after a moment. "I have been a horrible dinner companion."

Letting out a quiet sigh of relief, Sindri shrugged. "You were just thinking, that's all. I was too. When there's absolutely nothing else to do, thinking is as good a way as any to keep busy."

"Glad you think so."

The two of them dived into the roast with their forks and knives, cutting off bits of the tender meat and taking small bites as they began polite chatter. As Maddoc spoke about inviting Arvin Derry—one of Maddoc's acquaintances whom Sindri had once met—to come visit, Sindri smiled. Maybe he was overthinking things. Why would a weird little creature from the future—or the past—warn Sindri about *Maddoc?* Cat's warnings, everyone's worries, they'd always proven unfounded before. Maddoc was simply worried about him in the time room, that's the only reason he'd yelled. Maddoc wanted to teach him magic the best way he could—that's why he was taking notes, nothing secretive about it.

Maddoc and Sindri, they were a family. Everything would be absolutely fine from now until he finished his training, as long as they were together.

Distant sounds echoed in Sindri's ears. Sindri dropped his fork and stood straight up on his chair, tilting his head so his pointed ears aimed in the direction of the main hall. He'd heard something, something that was most definitely not part of the normal sounds of the keep—a scuffling, a clang of swords.

"Sindri?" Maddoc lowered his fork and knife. "Sindri, what is it?"

Sindri held up a hand, listening closer. There was definitely something going on in the great hall. A fight, it sounded like. But it was much too quiet to be a proper fight.

There was a heavy thud, so loud that Maddoc heard it too. Then there was a toe-curling scream.

The kitchen doors burst open, and one of the serving girls ran through. Stumbling, she fell to her knees with a loud crack and screamed again.

"Girl!" Maddoc roared. He stood abruptly, sending his chair crashing backward. "Get to your feet! Explain yourself!"

Trembling, the skinny girl clutched at the table and pulled herself up. Her straggly black hair fell to cover her eyes.

"M-master M-Maddoc," she whispered. "T-there's a g-ghost in the great h-hall. I was downstairs, bringing the guards their meals . . . it was attacking them. I th-think it may have killed Goodwin."

"Go," Maddoc said with a wave of his hand toward the girl. "Hide in your quarters." To Sindri, he said, "Come on."

Excitement rushed through Sindri as he leaped down from his chair and raced to keep up with Maddoc's long, regal strides. They burst through high wooden doors, turned down hallways of gilded mahogany, and climbed down spiral staircases until finally they reached the great hall. Maddoc flung open the doors.

"Maddoc—" Sindri started to say, but the older wizard held up a hand to silence him.

Together, Sindri and Maddoc stepped into the great hall. Sindri clung to the back of Maddoc's robes, peering around his legs to study the room. The staircases behind them led to balconies on the upper stories, where doors led to other areas of the keep. Pillars lined either side of the great hall like towering tree trunks. Intricate runes and moon symbols were carved into the arches that connected the pillars and supported the high ceiling. Tapestries hung between the arches, fluttering high above, and torches lined the walls.

The two of them walked down the exact center of the hall, along the thin red carpet that led to the double entrance doors. Their footsteps and the crackling fire echoed in the silent room. But Sindri was certain only moments ago he'd heard the guards fighting someone or—

The guards—they were gone.

Out of the corner of his eye, Sindri saw something move. Still clutching Maddoc's robes with one hand, he spun and pointed. "There!"

Maddoc, too, spun, hands held high to cast a spell. But the thing that had moved had been someone's arm falling to the floor. The arm belonged to a guard who lay unconscious, tucked in the shadows between a pillar and a wall.

"What happened here?" Sindri whispered.

Maddoc said nothing. Shoving Sindri behind him, he backed toward the door from which they'd entered.

"We have to get out of this room," the older wizard said, his ancient blue eyes darting to study their surroundings. "We're too exposed."

"But Maddoc—" Sindri started.

"So this is the legendary kender wizard."

The echoing voice was deep and male and distinctly jovial, as though the speaker were on the brink of telling a joke. Both Maddoc and Sindri stopped moving when they heard it. Their eyes scanning the shadows on the ceiling, they strained to find the speaker. Sindri saw no one.

Then, as though forming from the shadows themselves, a man dressed completely in black appeared between the runes and carvings on the arch directly above them. The figure flipped through the arch, leaped toward the nearest balcony, and swung himself up to crouch on the oak railing. Balancing expertly, the black-swathed man stood to his full height and turned to face them.

Sindri could hardly speak from the surprise of it all. Not an inch of the man's skin was uncovered, and his clothes clung tightly to his slender body for mobility. A mask covered his face and hair, revealing only his penetrating blue eyes. At either side of his waist hung a handheld scythe, a weapon shaped like a crescent moon that shimmered as silver as Solinari in the torchlight.

"Who are you?" Maddoc demanded, again trying to shove Sindri behind him. "Tell me why you are in my keep!"

"Oh good," the man called down. "The easy questions first."

The man leaped forward and flipped through the air as though diving into water. Silent as a cat, he landed on both feet in a crouch directly across the hall from Maddoc.

"I have been sent by the Wizard's Conclave," the man said. Pulling free the two scythes with slow deliberation, he stood to his full height. "And I am here to capture a renegade magic-user."

The man's eyes darted past Maddoc, directly at Sindri. "I am here," he continued, "for *him.*"

CHAPTER

4   FIGHT FOR THE RENEGADE

Before Maddoc could stop him, Sindri leaped from behind the older wizard's back. "Me?" he asked. "Why would the Wizard's Conclave want *me?*"

The black-clad figure twirled one of his scythes expertly between his fingers. "Oh, I don't know," he said from behind his mask. "Might have something to do with the fact that not only are you a kender using magic, but you are a kender using magic *illegally*. That would make you what we like to call a *renegade*."

"You're a renegade hunter," Maddoc spat, clenching his hands and stepping forward. "Were you the best the Conclave had to send? Look at your eyes—you can't be more than a few years older than Sindri himself. And just one of you, against a whole keep protected by magic, and owned by someone like *me?*" Holding his head high, he let out a derisive snort.

"No offense intended, Maddoc," the renegade hunter said with a slight bow of his head. "You are indeed a fully sanctioned wizard of the Conclave. But you know full well that Sindri isn't, and he has to be stopped before he causes any more harm than he already has."

"You could have just asked," Sindri said with a shake of his head. Shoving past the startled renegade hunter, Sindri walked beneath the fluttering tapestries toward the guard they'd seen hidden behind the pillar. "I don't know if it was entirely necessary to do a surprise attack on all of Maddoc's guards. Although those flips you did were amazing!"

The renegade hunter tilted back his head and crossed his arms. Orange torchlight cast flickering shadows across his eyes. "We did ask," he said. "And we were flatly denied access to the keep. So here I am, to take what needs to be taken."

"You will only take him over my dead—" Maddoc began to growl, his hands raised and ready to cast a spell.

"Hey now," the renegade hunter interrupted. "No need for death to be involved."

"Fool," Maddoc sneered. "*Anak!*"

In a flare of red light, a magic dart bigger than any Sindri had ever seen flew from Maddoc's fingertips, straight toward the renegade hunter's chest.

The renegade hunter didn't try to get out of the way. Instead, he stood perfectly still, watching the dart fly toward him with complete calm. When it was only feet from striking him, he raised his hand, muttered his own arcane phrase, and watched calmly as the dart stopped mere feet from hitting him. The red dart hovered in the air, pulsing with deadly magic like a small river of lava.

"Nice try," the hunter said. With a flick of his wrist, the dart spun around and whooshed toward Maddoc. The older wizard dived for cover, hands over his head, as the dart burst against a pillar. Black shrapnel flew through the room in an explosion of sparks, and Sindri dived out of the way.

"Now you can see why they deemed it necessary to send me," the renegade hunter said as he sauntered toward where Sindri lay splayed on his back. "Wizards like Maddoc always demand we do it the hard way. Not that I mind."

"Sindri!" Maddoc called. He lay at the bottom of a staircase, black dust clinging to his gray hair. "Run! Do not let him touch you!"

"But, Maddoc, he'll hurt you!" Sindri cried.

"Go!"

Not wanting to anger Maddoc further, Sindri shoved himself up and leaped to his feet. Hiking up his robes, he raced toward the keep's main entrance. He tried to ignore Maddoc's shouts as the wizard and the renegade hunter once again cast spells at one another.

Not far from the keep's main entrance, Sindri saw something he hadn't before considered: one of the servant doors. He'd be able to go get help from elsewhere in the keep, then sneak back around and surprise the renegade hunter. He skidded to a stop on the black stone, then stumbled for the door, leaping once he got his footing.

Behind him, Sindri heard the renegade hunter giving chase. The man called out something Sindri couldn't hear, but Sindri didn't have time to make out what he was saying. Instead he gripped the doorknob and screamed in surprise when he found it to be blistering hot.

"Hey!" Sindri cried as he spun around to face the man chasing him. Smoke drifted up from his stinging hands. "That's cheating."

"You call it cheating," the renegade hunter said as he made two giant strides toward Sindri. "I call it doing my job." This close to him, Sindri could see that all sorts of magical symbols were sewn into the cloth of the man's clothes. He recognized a few of them—they were warding spells of some kind.

"Sindri!" Maddoc called again. His voice sputtered as though his mouth were full of liquid . . . like blood.

Shaking his head to rid it of curiosity, Sindri turned to race to the left. There was a flash of silver, and one of the renegade hunter's scythes flew an inch from his nose. It embedded in the soft wood of the door, quivering from the impact and looking very much like a fisherman's gutting hook.

"Not that way, then," Sindri muttered. Spinning around, he turned to race the other way, ready to duck as the renegade hunter's other scythe flew above his head. He was in such a hurry to escape that he didn't notice another unconscious guard hidden behind a pillar until he tripped over the man's bulky body and fell into a rather awkward position between the man's back and the craggy stone wall.

"This isn't good," Sindri said as he struggled to get back up. His leg had slipped beneath the heavy guard in his fall.

"I wouldn't say that." The renegade hunter loomed above him, both scythes back in hand. "Ready to go now, Sindri?"

Shoving at the guard's fat midsection to free his stuck leg, Sindri let out a grunt of frustration. "You know, all you had to do was send a letter, and I'm sure after a talk, Maddoc and I would have come to the Conclave willingly. See, I'm not a renegade, I'm an *apprentice*. I'm not sanctioned because I haven't taken my Test at the Tower of High Sorcery yet, but that doesn't mean I don't plan to. In fact, I even studied at magic school in Palanthas. Did you know that?" With another grunt, Sindri elbowed the guard's hamlike upper arm, which had now fallen over his head.

"We sent missives," the renegade hunter said as he watched, amused, as Sindri fought to free himself. "Maddoc declined them flatly, saying this was his business and we were to stay out of it. But honestly, Sindri, we've been hearing tales of you for months—reports of you and your so-called magic from everyone, from villagers to Solamnic Knights to other wizards. Yes, even from the school in Palanthas, though they didn't seem to take you seriously at first. Sindri, you aren't supposed to exist. The Conclave must study what has happened here." He tilted his head. "Say, do you want a hand up?"

"No, I'm fine, thanks," Sindri muttered between a mouthful of the guard's blubber. After a few more twists and turns and finding himself nowhere near free from his flabby prison, Sindri let out a sigh. "All right, fine, maybe I could use some help."

The renegade hunter placed one of his scythes back on his belt, then reached forward a gloved hand. Sindri took it and let the hunter pull him forward.

"Thanks," Sindri said. Then, flinging a handful of colored dust that he'd pulled from one his pockets, he shouted, *"Cerlang corak!"*

Swirling colored smoke burst from Sindri's hands, straight into the renegade hunter's face. Sputtering, the man stumbled backward against a pillar. Tugging at the fallen guard's belt, Sindri yanked free the man's sword. Holding the weapon high, he ran to attack the renegade hunter.

"Aaargh!" Sindri cried, and he thrust the sword.

Despite being partially blinded, the renegade hunter didn't miss a beat. He swiftly brought up both of his scythes, scissoring them together and capturing the sword's blade as though his weapons were a scorpion's pincer.

"Nice try," the hunter said, and he sounded like he meant it. Despite Sindri's determination, the much larger human man easily wrenched the sword from Sindri's fingers. He tossed the sword across the room, where it clattered against the stone wall beyond the pillars.

Sindri stumbled backward. Tripping over the hem of his apprentice robes, he tumbled onto his backside with a loud *oof!* The renegade hunter approached, shaking his head with surprise.

"You know, this has been a lot more trouble than I thought it would be," the man grumbled from behind his cloth mask. "I picked up another one of you renegades right before I came here, and let me tell you, I thought *she* put up a fight. But, by Solinari himself, you two—"

"Sindri!"

Maddoc's bellow was a cry of indignant fury. Both Sindri and the renegade hunter turned to watch the older wizard.

Clutching at the wall near the stairs, Maddoc pulled himself up with trembling arms. His hair was a wild, frayed halo of gray around his face, and a line of blood trickled down his forehead. Sindri gasped when he saw the rips on his mentor's fine robes.

"Managed to get back up, I see," the renegade hunter said. "Good for you."

"Go to the Abyss!" Maddoc spat. With a flick of his wrist, one of the tapestries directly above the renegade hunter's head burst into flame. Long shadows darted around the great hall, like the tendrils of some dark monster. Before the renegade hunter could react, Maddoc flicked his wrist again and the tapestry was flung down, enveloping the startled hunter in a shroud of fire.

Sindri leaped to his feet and ran past the flaming mound of

tapestry and man. He skidded to a stop at Maddoc's side.

"Maddoc!" he said. "Maddoc, are you all right? Did he just do this to you? What is he saying, that I'm illegal? That you told them that they couldn't see me? What's going on?"

"Doesn't matter," Maddoc grunted, his hands clenched and his eyes narrowed in hatred. He did not look away from the flaming mound. "We'll talk about it later."

"But Maddoc—"

"Aargh!"

Startled, Sindri stopped midsentence and turned just in time to see the flaming tapestry tear in half and fling to either side of the renegade hunter. One half slammed against the servant door Sindri had tried to escape through, the other along the center carpet that led from the main door to the back wall. Both the door and the carpet burst into flames.

The renegade hunter, however, was completely unharmed. And though all Sindri could see were his eyes, it was clear the man wasn't the least bit happy. Without a word, the hunter raced toward them.

Shoving Sindri out of the way, Maddoc raised his hands and shouted more magic words, sending dart after dart of deadly magic hurtling through the great hall. The renegade hunter didn't miss a step as he ducked some flying darts and flipped over others. Finally, only a few steps from reaching Maddoc again, the man spread his arms wide, muttered a phrase . . . and disappeared.

No, he hadn't disappeared, not exactly. Sindri wasn't sure what he'd seen. One second the renegade hunter was almost upon them; the next, a shadow had appeared in front of him and he wasn't there anymore.

Maddoc seemed just as surprised. Struggling to breathe,

45

the older man lowered his hand and let himself lean back against the wall behind him. From where Sindri had fallen on the nearby stairs, he crawled across the floor toward Maddoc. Both wizard and kender scanned the room, knowing their foe hadn't left.

Then, with another flash of shadow, the renegade hunter was back—on the balcony above Maddoc's head. Before Sindri could shout a warning, the renegade hunter mumbled a string of arcane phrases, the last one a word Sindri knew: "*Capik.*"

Paralyze.

Too late, Maddoc finally realized where the hunter had reappeared. As he turned to face the man in black, Maddoc's movement slowed. His arms stopped midraise. His head ceased to move midway in its tilt to look up. His legs stopped moving backward.

In one more swift, amazing flip, the renegade hunter leaped down from the balcony and landed directly behind Maddoc.

"All right, Sindri," the renegade hunter said. His black-clad chest heaved for air even as he tried to appear entirely in control. "Your master can't keep you from us anymore. This isn't his choice. We hate to take such harsh measures, but these days we have no other option. So will you come with me now, or do we have to fight until you and your mentor are both unconscious or dead?"

Shaking with anger, Sindri stood to his full height. Straightening his shoulders and clenching his jaw in defiance, he stared the renegade hunter directly in his eyes. "I won't go with you," he said. "I promised Maddoc I would never abandon him, no matter what. And I don't go back on my promises."

The renegade hunter looked down and sighed. "All right then," he said. "Fair enough."

The hunter shot out his arm, straight toward Maddoc's outstretched right hand. One of the scythes flashed as its metal edge sliced through flesh and bone. Maddoc's hand fell to the floor with a sickening, squelching thud, leaving behind a bloody stump.

"No!" Sindri cried. He started to leap forward to help Maddoc, but the hunter held up his free hand in warning.

"No sudden moves or the other hand goes," the hunter said, his voice strangely sad. "And you and I both know how important a mage's hands are for casting spells. With both hands gone, he'd be destroyed." As he spoke, his scythe glowed red with magical heat. He pressed the red-hot scythe against Maddoc's oozing stump. Black smoke curled up as the wound seared close.

Still trembling with rage for Maddoc's pain, Sindri stepped back. He looked up into Maddoc's frozen stare and saw the older man's blue eyes shimmering with tears of pain.

He couldn't leave Maddoc. No matter what the Conclave said, if Maddoc told them Sindri couldn't go, then Sindri had to stay—he just had to.

The renegade hunter pressed the scythe against Maddoc's other hand, the blood that had dripped from its edge now burned dark and black. "Make your choice, Sindri," he said. "We don't have all night."

Clenching his eyes closed, Sindri let out a deep breath and let himself plop down to the floor. Maddoc's pale, wrinkled right hand lay there on the carpet in a pool of red, never to be used properly again.

"All right," Sindri muttered after a moment. "All right. Take me with you. Just don't hurt him anymore."

"Good choice," the renegade hunter said. He sounded almost

relieved, but Sindri didn't care. Anyone who could ruthlessly attack innocent people couldn't possibly feel one bit of remorse.

While Sindri waited, resigned, the renegade hunter crouched down behind him. He pulled a small silver device, what looked to be a metal bar with four-pronged claws on either end, from his boot. Wrenching Sindri's hands behind his back, he clasped the clawed ends around both of Sindri's wrists, cuffing him.

"You made a good choice, Sindri," the man whispered in his ear as he made sure the restraints weren't going anywhere. "This will be better for everyone. You'll see. Now, *tidur*."

With that final word of magic, Sindri's eyes fluttered closed, no longer under his control. Darkness overtook him, and Sindri slept.

CHAPTER

5   The Filch and the Hunter

The world rumbled.

Not an unpleasant rumbling, like a ground-splitting earthquake—though Sindri thought it might be fun to experience one of those—but a steady bumping and jumping that reminded Sindri of something, though he couldn't think what. Too bad everything was completely black, or he could look around and—

"Whatgoinon?" Sindri mumbled as he realized he was no longer in Cairngorn Keep. It all came back to him in a flash—the shouts of the servants, the black-clad figure, Maddoc . . .

Maddoc! Sindri opened his eyes and sat straight up. Immediately he regretted the motion, for a particularly forceful jolt caused him to fly backward and slam his head against what felt like a metal pole.

Blinking to adjust to the sudden light, Sindri took in his surroundings. He was somewhere new, all right. The bumping beneath him was the motion of a small wagon rolling over a stony forest path. The wheels creaked as they rolled.

The wagon was open—except, of course, for the cagelike bars **49** against which he'd hit his head and the flat wooden roof above. Pressing his face through the bars, Sindri studied the scenery rolling by—leafy trees studded with fresh spring buds, fallen logs covered in fluffy moss, startled squirrels darting among the underbrush. Nothing seemed familiar—he could be in any forest, anywhere on Krynn.

It occurred to Sindri that the wagon was not propelling itself— though he thought it would be neat if there were some sort of spell that could make a wagon do that—and so he spun away from the bars. The wagon was hitched to a proud black horse, its heavy hooves clomping on the path as it flicked its tail at flies. Riding on its back was a man in a leather cloak. Long, unkempt blond hair brushed against his broad shoulders.

Only when someone who was neither the horse nor the blond man cleared her throat did Sindri realize that he was not alone in the little prison wagon.

Huddled in the front corner was a human girl, maybe around Sindri's age, dressed in a dirty green tunic and brown trousers. Legs pulled up to her chest, she peered over her knees at Sindri with wary eyes the color of a stormy sky. Her skin was a creamy reddish brown that reminded Sindri of a chocolate dessert he'd once eaten at Cairngorn Keep, and her black hair was cropped short and ragged.

"Hello," Sindri said. His head still groggy, he attempted to stand and toppled sideways instead. Finding standing near impossible—especially since his hands turned out to be clasped behind his back—he instead scooted toward the girl on his knees. Splinters from the wooden planks pierced his brown robes and stabbed his legs.

The girl continued to stare as Sindri came closer.

"Hello," Sindri said, a bit louder, for he didn't know if she could hear him over the clomping horse and the rumbling wagon. "Do you have any idea what—"

With a loud thump, the wagon shook violently from side to side, and Sindri fell backward. Wood creaked as what sounded like sacks full of heavy supplies smacked against the wagon's side.

"Whoa there!" the man on the horse called. He pulled the reins to slow his steed, then looked back over his shoulder. He looked surprisingly young, maybe twenty-one years, and something about his pale blue eyes was familiar.

"You all right back there? I think we hit a—" His eyes drifting past the glowering girl, the man finally saw Sindri. "Oh, you're up." He grinned and nodded in greeting. It was then that Sindri realized who it was.

"You!" Sindri cried. Thrusting his legs with all his might, he shot straight up and ran toward the front of the wagon. With his arms still stuck behind his back, he slammed chest-first into the wagon's bars. "You attacked us. You cut off Maddoc's hand! If he's not all right, I'll—"

"You'll what?" the man interrupted. "Cast a spell?" The man turned around and whispered in his horse's ear as he pulled its reins tight. The elegant beast slowed to a stop. The wagon rolled to a halt behind it.

Sindri's breathing quickened in his anger as the man turned as far around in his saddle as he could, crossed his arms, and raised his chin. "You'll notice, Sindri, that your hands are clasped behind your back. You are wearing cuffs specially created by the Wizard's Conclave to keep you from casting magic. Standard equipment for dealing with renegade magic-users. There is nothing you can do."

"I don't care!" Sindri stamped his foot, his hands clenched behind him. "You hurt Maddoc!"

The man shook his head. "I did what I had to do. I have a duty, and that duty is to hunt down and capture renegades. And if anyone gets in my way, I have to . . . well, you saw." With another shake of his head, he turned and kicked his horse's side. The horse resumed its journey down the bright forest path, the wagon bumping along behind it.

"Maddoc is fine," the man called back. "I made sure before we left." He looked over his shoulder once more. "The name's Wilden, by the way."

Defeated, Sindri let himself plop back down to the wagon's floor. The girl hadn't moved from her spot, where she studied Sindri with a raised eyebrow, a gesture Sindri took for wariness. Not finding her particularly interesting, Sindri leaned his head back to watch the golden light stream between the new spring leaves. Birds fluttered between their branches, calling out in twittering songs.

"Kender can't do magic."

Sindri peered over at the girl and cocked his head. She'd readjusted herself a bit so that he could see her whole face.

"Sorry?" Sindri said.

"Kender can't do magic," she repeated. "Everyone says."

Sindri sighed. This day was turning out to be fairly rotten, and it took a lot for him to think anything was ever not fun. First he'd been stolen from Maddoc, who could be lying dead for all he knew. Then his hands were tied back so he couldn't even touch or explore anything properly. Now this quiet, moody girl was telling him what everyone had insisted on telling him, over and over, his entire life.

No, this day was most certainly *not* a good one.

Leaning forward, Sindri narrowed his eyes. "That's true," he said. "They can't. But I'm not a normal kender. I was destined to be a wizard from the day I was born. My great-great-great-great-great-great-great-great uncle Mildred was a wizard of the sun, and Mother is a seer who had visions about me growing up to be an even more powerful wizard than our ancestor was. And she was right. So far I've blown up a god-forged sword, flayed an undead dragon, helped destroy an evil sorceress, and battled an undead king of thieves. I've been apprenticed to a powerful wizard for months and months now, so yes, while it is true that most kender cannot be wizards, I most certainly *am*."

Harrumphing, Sindri scooted back to lean against the bars and resume staring up at the birds fluttering in the clear sky. All he could think of was Maddoc, all alone without him, worrying about what the renegade hunter Wilden was doing with him. Maddoc had been like a father to Sindri the past few months. All the Conclave had to do was ask . . . .

"Well, all right then," the girl muttered. Retreating behind her knees, she looked away. "You're the snippiest kender I've ever met. Guess you're not normal after all."

Despite his frustration, Sindri suddenly felt guilty for being so rude. It wasn't his way. Sure, he'd been kidnapped, but that was no reason to forget his manners.

"Sorry," Sindri said. Shrugging, he met her eyes. "I haven't had a great day so far. Normally I'd find all this exciting, but my master—"

"Yes, I heard you," she said.

Sindri crawled toward her. "I'm Sindri, by the way."

The girl hesitated for a moment, glancing between Sindri and the renegade hunter on the horse. "Tayt," she said finally.

Sindri smiled. "Nice to meet you, Tayt. What are you locked up in here with me for?"

The girl sighed and shook her head. "Because I can't ever get a break."

From the direction of the horse, Wilden cleared his throat. "Actually, she's in here because, like you, she's a renegade. She spent years secretly learning magic, stole artifacts from a wizard, and has spent the past year using those artifacts and spells to steal from anyone and everyone in her path." He looked back over his shoulder. "She's what we call a spellfilch. You can see why the Conclave wants her."

"The wizard I stole from," Tayt seethed, "is a murderous wench who doesn't deserve the Conclave's sanction. I should have done a lot more than steal from her. Vile Black Robe."

Sindri tilted his head. "Hey, not all Black Robe wizards are bad. Maddoc isn't."

Tayt rolled her eyes. "Your master was a Black Robe? Maybe you're lucky the Conclave wanted you bad enough to send a hunter after you. Facing them has got to better than being some evil mage's pet."

"Hey!" Sindri shot up to his feet, stumbling as he tried to keep his balance while the wagon rumbled beneath him. "Maddoc is a good wizard! I mean, all right, so he did force an evil sorceress into the body of a friend of mine, and maybe he murdered my other friend's mother and made his dad a hideous beast, and he had those insane minions but . . . well, he's not bad now, and that's all that matters. He helped me learn magic when no one else believed in me."

"Sindri's right, you know," Wilden said without turning back around. "Despite harboring a renegade wizard, Maddoc is right in the eyes of the gods of magic and with the Conclave. As is *your* old master, Tayt."

"Hey!" Sindri spun toward the front of the wagon and scowled toward the back of Wilden's blond head. "I don't need you to agree with me. I don't particularly like you, you know. And I usually like *everyone*."

Wilden laughed as the spring breeze flowed past them, making his hair and cloak flow gently. "Well, it doesn't really matter if you like me or not. But for what it's worth, I have no reason to lie about your master, if that's what's taking away your kender spirit. I assure you, Maddoc is fine." Reaching down, he patted the horse's rump affectionately. "I love Thunder, but he's not the best conversationalist. It's a long journey, and I'd rather not have to spend it in complete silence. Tayt refuses to speak to me."

"Should have thought of that before you knocked me out and threw me in here, you psychotic acolyte." Tayt clenched her jaw and glared at Wilden.

Wilden smirked. "Hey, good, you're opening up."

Biting her lip so hard she drew blood, Tayt struggled to turn on her side—for she, too, had her hands clasped behind her back—and stared pointedly out of the back of the wagon. Sindri followed her gaze to see the pitiful trail they rode upon disappearing into an endless horizon of trees.

With a shrug, Wilden resumed guiding the black horse along the path. For a moment, the three of them rode in silence. Sindri fidgeted with his wrists, adjusted his sitting position several times, and was suddenly overcome with a desperate boredom.

"Tayt," he whispered, nudging her gently with his boot. "Hey, sorry, I didn't mean to upset you."

Still curled up in the corner and turned away from him, Tayt snorted. "You don't know anything," she muttered. "Neither of you." She glanced sidelong to meet Sindri's eyes. "Wilden is a blind follower of his institution. And your master? He's one of the Conclave's many, many corrupt members."

Shifting so that she was turned away even further, Tayt's voice grew quiet. "You may think you know what you're doing," she muttered, "but I guarantee you can't have learned anything good from a Black Robe. You're better off being dragged to prison."

With that, she fell silent. Sindri noticed Wilden looking back at them, his eyebrows raised and his lips cocked in an amused grin. "Well, I guess she's back to ignoring me again. Too bad. She's always so charming."

Sindri pointedly turned away from the renegade hunter and let out a deep breath. Tayt's words had stung. He'd been called many things, but one that stood out the most was *naive*. All his friends had warned him about Maddoc, Cat especially, and now there was Tayt, and even the vision of the lizard creature.

No, Sindri thought forcefully. My friends were wrong. Tayt is wrong.

Peering back toward the endless path behind their little wagon, Sindri clenched his jaw in resolution. No matter what happened, he'd eventually get back to Cairngorn Keep and continue his studies with Maddoc. Absolutely nothing was going to keep him from his goals, not even some cocky renegade hunter and his traveling prison. Even if the Conclave and every other wizard he'd ever met wanted to challenge him, he'd prove everyone wrong, once and for all.

CHAPTER

6 SEVERED

Maddoc scowled. The black-robed wizard sat upon a stool in front of a long oak table littered with bones and spools of wire. Spell books with yellowing pages were splayed between them in heaps, surrounded by spindly bottles and leather satchels filled with spell components.

In the middle of the table's mess lay Maddoc's hand. The shriveled skin of his rigid, severed hand was deathly pale, seeming all the whiter in contrast to the black velvet cloth laid protectively beneath it.

"Blast," Maddoc muttered.

The room in which Maddoc sat, known as the Ossuary, was one of the wizard's favorites. It was small, as the keep's rooms went, and every wall except for the one with the door was lined with tables and shelves. The walls rose high above him into the dusty rafters of an empty tower where once a giant bell had hung. The bell had long since been removed, leaving plenty of open room for an undead creature to soar up from the black stone darkness of the Ossuary, out through arched windows, and into the eternal gray sky beyond.

It was in that small room that Maddoc had performed his many experiments with necromancy, the magic of raising undead. And it was there where he intended to reattach the hand that the Conclave's renegade hunter had stolen from him.

But despite his efforts, Maddoc wasn't having any luck.

With a groan and a sigh, Maddoc stood up from his stool, straightened his black robes with his remaining hand, and began to pace. His footsteps echoed in the tower as he stared at the gray sky beyond the arched windows, their shutters open to let in daylight.

He'd had to watch, paralyzed, as the renegade hunter sliced off his hand. He'd been forced to watch as Sindri gave up and the man in black cuffed him, knocked him out, and dragged him out of the keep. Then, what felt like hours later, when his servants finally raced downstairs on smelling smoke, he'd been freed from the immobilizing spell.

Maddoc had collapsed immediately, having lost much blood. His servants tended him until he was finally well enough to cast healing spells on the burned stub at the end of his arm. The anger he felt toward the Conclave, the renegade hunter, and even Sindri had been so intense he did the only thing he could—he plotted. He'd need to find Sindri and bring the kender back to the keep to resume his study of Sindri's powers. And he'd capture that blasted renegade hunter and torture him until he felt the pain Maddoc was feeling.

But first things first. He'd resurrected hundreds of animals. Surely he could resurrect his own hand and regain full control over his spells. Maybe if—

"Ah, Maddoc. Looks like you lost something."

Maddoc stopped pacing. Holding the bandaged stub of his

JEFF SAMPSON

right hand behind his back, he tilted his head back and let out yet another disgruntled sigh. "Arvin. I see you still insist on stating the obvious."

The man behind Maddoc laughed, the sound throaty and manic, like a deranged animal growl. Shutting the door, the man shuffled into the Ossuary and came to Maddoc's side.

"It's what I do best, Maddoc. I was never very good at subtlety. Or much of anything, really." Again the man let out his deranged giggle.

Raising an eyebrow, Maddoc glanced sidelong at the short, stocky old man. Like Maddoc, Arvin was a black-robed wizard, though he was hardly in the same league—as Arvin was always the first to admit. His robes were dirty and disheveled, with spindly threads of embroidery dangling from the ragged sleeves. Age lined the man's face, his cheeks sagging into houndlike jowls that jostled with every twitch of his thin lips. His small black eyes gleamed like polished pebbles from either side of his wide nose, and what little gray hair he had left clung in patches to the scalp of his squarish head.

When Maddoc didn't speak, Arvin ducked his head and shuffled to stand before Maddoc's workbench. His dingy black robes hung too long past his feet, and a particularly large dust bunny one of the servants had missed found its way onto the hem.

"Ah, necromancy," Arvin said, his tone wistful. "I always wished I could be good at it. Or, well, at anything, really." He ran his gnarled, stubby fingers over the spines of the books and a few of the bones before finally resting them on the black velvet cloth upon which Maddoc's former hand resided.

"Oh my," Arvin whispered. "Oh my, my, my, my, my." The wizard's face contorted into a hideous smile, and for a moment

Maddoc saw Arvin's yellow teeth sharpen into ragged points and his skin flush with a dark red.

"You're drooling." Maddoc strode to Arvin's side and snapped the edges of the velvet cloth over the hand. Disappointed, Arvin backed away.

"There will be no eating of my appendages," Maddoc said. "You're here to help me reattach it."

Arvin shrugged. "Sometimes I can't help myself. It's the goblin in me."

Maddoc rolled his eyes. Arvin hadn't been flippant when he said he wasn't good at much. "Sometimes I wonder why I've kept you around so long," Maddoc said under his breath, out of Arvin's earshot. The two of them had met thirty-five years earlier, at magic school in Palanthas. Maddoc had excelled in his classes at such an early age that many assumed he'd be the kind of prodigy everyone proclaimed that golden-skinned, condescending Black Robe Raistlin to be nowadays.

Arvin had been languishing in school for years when the two of them met. The man had inherent magic power, that was clear, but he was—as many had said—simply too daft to figure out how to use it correctly.

Naturally Maddoc had befriended him. What better toady to have on his side than one so eager to be accepted that he'd do anything to be Maddoc's friend?

Over the years Maddoc had found a sort of detached fondness for his friend. They'd spent years working on various dark magical projects together long before Maddoc first learned of the long-dead sorceress who would become his obsession—Asvoria.

While Maddoc studied Asvoria inside and out, he gave the job of studying the sorceress's familiar, the shapeshifter Ophion, to Arvin. Arvin proved more than up to the task—going so far as to attempt to make *himself* a shapeshifter. Several failed experiments with goblins later, he had become the insane little creature standing with Maddoc—a reclusive, unkempt wizard with the essence of dozens of goblins flowing through his body, ready to emerge at the most inopportune times.

It was for that reason that Arvin lived in an isolated cave hidden at the base of the Vingaard Mountains. It was also the reason he'd become a bit of a local legend—he had become the Goblin Man.

Maddoc and Arvin had gone their separate ways when Maddoc first purchased Cairngorn Keep, but they'd kept in touch via the occasional missive. It wasn't that long ago that Maddoc had called upon Arvin to help protect a powerful weapon necessary to defeat Asvoria, who had turned against Maddoc despite his careful planning.

Maddoc had had many apprentices over the years. But as recent events involving a power-mad dark elf named Gieden proved, Maddoc was certain he couldn't trust any of them. So despite the Goblin Man's insanity and penchant for eating decaying limbs, Arvin was the one he called upon in this time of crisis.

Though seeing the way the man's beady little eyes stared intensely at the black velvet covering Maddoc's severed hand, the wizard was not entirely sure it had been the best idea.

"Well, Arvin, let's work on keeping that goblin part of you in check," Maddoc said as he maneuvered the stout man away from the hand. "We have work to do."

"Oh, of course, of course," Arvin said, bowing his head as he backed away. "We must focus." Peering up at him with a mischievous look in his eyes, Arvin tilted his head. "So sorry to hear about your kender. Did you at least get far in your studies before they took him from you?"

Maddoc sighed again. The past few days had been an endless string of frustrations. First Sindri still acted like a kender despite all the work they'd done trying to beat the vile kender habits out of him. Then the blasted Conclave sent the renegade hunter, and now his hand. But of course Arvin would be secretly gleeful at Maddoc's troubles. Hideous, mostly worthless men like Arvin were always pleasant to the faces of their betters while secretly harboring a deep hatred borne of jealousy. It was only natural.

"We were getting somewhere, yes," Maddoc said. Turning pointedly away, he slammed closed the books that lay open on the table and pulled new ones down from the shelves. Dust billowed around them and Arvin hacked out a cough.

"Sindri's powers are something I've never before experienced, something new. But, I think, something ancient as well." Maddoc stopped and stared up through the arches at the sky. "If I could . . ." Shaking his head, he turned back to the books. "Never mind. We'll just have to get him back. It's not safe for him out there."

"Can't be too hard," Arvin said as his stubby, sausagelike fingers dug through the books and bottles on another workbench. "I'd imagine the Conclave is much too busy with that Raistlin fellow and his Master of Past and Present business to really worry about your little kender. That Raistlin, he's quite the wizard." Again Arvin tilted his head and grinned, his yellow teeth glimmering in the dim light. "You heard about him?"

"Yes," Maddoc muttered. "I have." Slamming shut another book, he turned away from the workbench in exasperation. "Useless. All these books are useless! I can bring a deceased animal to life in an instant, but a hand? Look!"

Robes blustering behind him, Maddoc shoved past Arvin to

the other workbench. Atop the workbench sat bleached, curved bones that had once belonged to a falcon. The bones had been carefully reconnected with intricate, knotted wire. In fact, the reconstruction was almost ready.

Picking up a needle, Maddoc managed to thread it with wire one-handed and puncture the bird's left leg bones. He sewed in a frenzy, Arvin watching beside him with an expression between annoyance and awe.

Spitting out the excess wire from between his teeth, and awkwardly cutting it off with a pair of shears not made for his left hand, he managed to finish. He cast his spell by dumping bits of spell components from nearby bottles on the bones and muttering arcane phrases that came out in a flurry of words.

The bones shuddered. First one wing fluttered, then the other. Finally the falcon stood. Red light shone from its eye sockets, and it parted its decayed beak to let out a curious squawk.

"See?" Maddoc shouted as sweat poured down his forehead. "I have given life to the bones of a dead bird. And yet . . . this blasted hand!"

In his rage, Maddoc grabbed the nearest empty bottle and threw it against the wall. Arvin ducked and the undead bird screeched as the glass shattered into shimmering dust.

Trembling, Maddoc backed up and collapsed onto his stool. Rubbing his forehead, he tried to calm himself.

"Maddoc," Arvin muttered as he tepidly stepped forward. "Oh, Maddoc, I am so very sorry for all your losses. I've never seen you this angry before. I'm just sorry I'm a complete imbecile and not a normal wizard. I'm sure if I were, I would know the answer right away."

Maddoc waved his hand and looked away. "It's fine, Arvin.

We'll figure it out. But maybe it's enough for today."

"No!" Arvin leaned back and clutched his robes in horror. "Give up? You mustn't! You're the brilliant one. You'll surely find the answer. Look, I found this book hiding in your corner. Maybe it'll help."

Glancing at Arvin sidelong, Maddoc saw that the stubby wizard held a small leather-bound book that seemed to be decaying with age. From its size and design, Maddoc guessed it to be a diary. He'd never seen it before.

Eyes bulging and yellow, and ears sharpening into points, Arvin crept forward. Giggling under his breath, he set the book in front of Maddoc and opened it to a page in the center.

Maddoc scanned the page, shaking his head at his good fortune. "I knew there was a reason I called on you, Arvin," Maddoc said. "Good work."

Arvin's grin widened as his eyes and ears shrank back to normal. "I knew you'd be pleased, Maddoc," he said. "All I'm ever good for is my occasional luck in helping people as great as you figure out your plans." Pulling up another stool, Arvin sat down directly in front of the velvet-covered hand. "Now," he said, staring at the hand with another unsettling look, "let's get your hand reattached and go get your kender."

Maddoc nodded. Things could finally get back on track. He could go free Sindri from the clutches of the Council and from whoever else would dare steal Sindri from him. He had great plans for Sindri and for himself. They couldn't suffer any more setbacks.

But first things first. With Arvin at his side, Maddoc incanted the spells. His hand would be reattached soon.

Then no one would be able to stop him.

CHAPTER

7 THE DEVOURING DARK

The sun was well on its way toward the western horizon when Wilden slowed his horse—and, therefore, the wagon—to a stop. Sindri, who'd been stuck in the back in complete silence and felt he'd go insane soon if something interesting didn't happen, immediately snapped to attention.

As Sindri watched attentively, Wilden leaped from Thunder's back and strode to the side of the wagon. The renegade hunter dug through the sacks of supplies that hung there.

Curious as to why they'd stop traveling while it was only midafternoon, Sindri looked outside. More trees rustling in breezes, more fallen logs, more birds calling from their nests. Just the same old forest.

Tayt had also grown alert, and Sindri watched her with interest as she sat up from where she'd curled into the wagon's bars. She, too, watched Wilden go through the supplies.

"Hey," Sindri whispered as he scooted toward her. "What do you suppose is going on? Do you think the Conclave has secret entrances or portals or something hidden in the woods?"

Tayt gave Sindri a withering look but said nothing.

"Actually," Wilden said from behind him, "there aren't any portals, sadly. But I figured you two might be hungry, so we're stopping for a break."

Sindri's stomach gurgled in response, and only then did he realize that he hadn't had a thing to eat all day. With all the excitement, he'd forgotten all about any appetite he had before, but now he felt so hungry that he thought he could eat the robes off his back if it wouldn't leave him a bit too exposed.

Wilden unhitched Thunder from the wagon, then led the steed over to a small stream to drink. After tying the horse to a tree and patting its rump affectionately, the hunter came back to the path and unhooked one of the open packs from the side of the wagon. With a ring of silver keys jangling from his belt and one of the packs slung over his shoulder, he strolled around to the back of the wagon.

"All right," he said as he smiled through the bars. "This is going to be a bit tricky, but I've got to be careful. You understand. I need you both to sit absolutely still so my spell doesn't backfire."

"Whatever," Tayt mumbled. Scowling, she looked away.

"What are you going to do?" Sindri asked.

"Free your hands so you can eat," Wilden responded.

Wilden pulled back his sleeves and prepared to cast a spell. Intricate black tattoos in swirling patterns covered his forearms, Sindri noticed, symbols like the ones that had been sewn on his black hunting clothes.

Wilden muttered three quick phrases. Instantly Sindri felt his leg muscles spasm and seize up. It wasn't painful, but when he tried to move, he found that his entire lower body was completely frozen in place.

With a click of a lock and a creak of rusty hinges, Wilden opened the back door of the wagon, then jumped aboard with the same grace Sindri had seen him use the night before. "See, that wasn't too hard. Now we can get you out of those cuffs since you won't get very far even without them. Although, if you try to use magic on me, I'm supposed to use lethal force to stop you. Just so you know."

Sindri shrugged. "Fine with me. You took my spell components anyway, so I don't suppose I could get any really good spells off. Say, what're we eating?"

Though Wilden grinned in response to Sindri's enthusiasm, his eyes darted to Tayt. "You know, Sindri," he said while still appraising the scowling Tayt, "since you've been so exceedingly pleasant in comparison to our traveling companion here, I think I'll take off your cuffs and let you eat first. I can only release one of you at a time, you understand."

Narrowing her gray eyes and flaring her nostrils, Tayt shook her head slowly. "Go to the Abyss," she muttered under her breath. She jerked her head to the side and glared at the woods.

Sindri felt kind of bad for the girl. She had been kidnapped too, after all, and Wilden delighted in taunting her. Still, she had been awful moody, even toward him, so he didn't suspect she'd give the best dinner conversation. Even in comparison to Maddoc.

Wilden crouched behind Sindri. A sharp clicking sounded, and a tingling sensation raced through Sindri's wrists and hands, as though his hands had fallen asleep and were waking back up.

Snapping his hands forward, Sindri stretched his arms, then rubbed at his wrists. His skin seemed darker where the cuffs had clasped, leaving four curved marks on his flesh. The marks were tender to the touch.

"All right, here you go." Still crouched down, Wilden reached inside his sack and pulled out a piece of crusty bread and a chunk of dried meat.

His gut roiling with aching hunger, Sindri snatched both the bread and the meat from Wilden's hands and took two giant bites from both of them. Only when his mouth was full of the tough, spiced meat and the chewy bread did he remember his manners.

"Wenk wou," Sindri mumbled. Bits of bread crumbs flew from his mouth and landed on Wilden's white shirt.

Brushing off his shirt, Wilden let out a short laugh. "My pleasure. See, Tayt? This doesn't have to be all bad."

From her spot near the bars, Tayt trembled. Her brow furrowed and her lips curled into a sneer, the girl's head snapped back toward Wilden.

"Look here, you—"

Thunder whinnied, the sound full of so much intense fear that it stopped Tayt midword and Sindri midchew. All three of them turned to look at the horse tethered in the trees. Its eyes wide enough to see the whites from that distance, the creature shook its head and pulled back full force against its ties, its ears flattened back against its head. Again the horse whinnied, then reared, kicking its front legs.

Sindri swallowed and tilted his head. "What's gotten into him?"

Wilden's eyes clouded with concern, and he shook his head. "Don't move," he muttered. Leaving the pack behind, Wilden leaped out the back of the wagon and ran toward Thunder. Catching himself, he quickly turned back to clang shut the wagon's door and lock it.

The prisoners locked up, Wilden turned his attention back to his horse, who continued to rear and whinny in short, high-pitched bursts, tugging on the rope that bound it to the tree. Sindri gnawed absentmindedly at the bread as he watched the renegade hunter slowly approach the spooked horse, his hands held high. Near Sindri, Tayt watched as well, her look unreadable.

"Whoa there, Thunder." Wilden's voice was low and calm as he stepped carefully toward his steed. The creature lowered itself to all fours again and backed away, its tail still slapping at its sides. Its nostrils flared and eyes bulging, the horse shook its head, nipping at its tether. The end tied around one of the trees pulled tight, scraping at the bark and sending flakes of brown snowing to the ground.

"What's wrong, boy?" Wilden said. Carefully he came to the horse's side, his hand slowly running up the horse's neck and down its cheek to pat its nose. For a moment, it seemed Thunder's fear would pass.

Then the sound of a tree crashing against the ground somewhere deep in the woods echoed distantly in Sindri's pointed ears.

At the same time, Thunder's own ears perked to attention. With another terrified whinny, it reared again. Thunder's hooves met Wilden's chest with a hollow thud. Gasping in surprise, the renegade hunter stumbled backward and tripped over a fallen log. He fell on his backside near the stream, his breath knocked out.

"Whoa," Sindri said. He heard another thud and the sound of birds cawing as they flapped into the sky, the sound so distant he knew neither of the two humans could hear. Not that Tayt would have cared anyway—she was too busy laughing bitterly at their fallen captor.

"Ha!" she said. "That's what he gets."

Heart pounding with anticipation, Sindri ignored her. Dropping his bread, he stretched forward to grab the closest bars and pull himself nearer the forest. He tilted his head toward the sounds and listened. More thumps, more scurrying animals, more flocks of birds flapping into the sky. And there was something else too, something behind the sounds of the forest falling aside in terror—a constant whirring, screeching sound, like a tornado tearing through a metal shed.

"The vision," Sindri whispered. Tilting his head back toward Tayt, he met her eyes. "I think I saw this before. I think I know what's going to happen."

Tayt tilted her head as well. "What vision?" she asked. "What are you talking about?"

Off the path, Wilden finally caught his breath and climbed back to his feet. The ends of his hair dripped wet from where they'd fallen in the stream. Rubbing at his chest with a pained expression, he stepped over the log toward Thunder, who was biting at its tie again, its lips pulled back from its large, square teeth.

"Come on, boy," Wilden said, his voice just as calm as before, though it was now strained with a slight wheeze. "Come on."

Sindri couldn't pay attention to the two of them for long. The sounds grew closer, so close that even Tayt could hear them. Swallowing, she leaned back and pushed her lower half toward Sindri, and they both listened in the direction the sounds were coming from.

High above, the sky darkened. A liquid blackness seeped between the clouds, like a dark wine staining a bright blue dress. The tops of the trees swayed, new spring leaves clutching at their branches with all their strength. As Sindri had seen in the time room vision, all the nearby birds that had only moments ago

JEFF SAMPSON

sung trilling songs beneath the green canopy took wing as one, darting into the darkening sky and squawking.

The sudden bird calls and the thunderous sound of hundreds of flapping wings caught Wilden off guard. Stopping a few feet from the terrified Thunder, he tilted his head back to look up at the almost pitch-black sky.

"What the—" he started to say.

It was at that moment that Thunder bit all the way through its bonds.

With a triumphant, screaming neigh, Thunder reared back and shook its head, sending its black mane cascading over its muscular neck. The horse landed back on all four hooves and darted around Wilden to gallop furiously down the path in the direction they had been heading. A cloud of dust billowed in its wake.

"Hey!" Wilden called, taken completely off guard. "Thunder, come back!" Limping slightly, he nonetheless made chase, ignoring the dirt and dust that got in his eyes and clung to the wet ends of his hair.

"You two," he called over his shoulder, "don't move!"

"Funny," Tayt muttered sarcastically. Struggling with her clasped hands, she stared up at the sky, her stormy eyes clouded and wary. "Of course he'd just leave us here helpless. What's going on?"

By then the trees swayed so much that they seemed on the verge of tipping on their sides. The screeching of the wind was closer. Sindri blinked as a flurry of wind and dust hit him square in the eyes. His robes tugged at his body and his long, shaggy hair whipped around his face.

Helpless to do anything else, Sindri grabbed the bars and stuck his face through. Squinting and unable to hear Tayt over the shrieking wind, Sindri waited for what he knew was to come. To his amazement, he saw a tree deep in the woods completely uproot, swing wildly, and crash to the forest floor in a flurry of torn leaves.

Then near the log over which Wilden had tripped, a bush rustled. It could have been the wind, but the rustling looked a bit more manic, as though an animal were trying to burrow through.

Sindri held his breath as he waited. He didn't have to wait long. Ignoring the wagon, which creaked as it tilted back and forth from the force of the winds, and barely hearing Tayt's confused questions, Sindri watched as the creature he expected burst from the bush, sending broken twigs flying.

What emerged was just as Sindri had seen in his vision: It was a little lizard creature, about the size of a cat and covered in fur, though seeming more draconian than feline in shape. Except this time, the creature had something flat and the color of tea stains clutched in its triangle-shaped jaw.

Shivering in the wind, the lizard creature stood on its back legs. Tilting back its head, its amber eyes grew wide as they caught sight of Sindri.

It leaped, and in what seemed to Sindri like a blink of the eye, the creature was staring him straight in the face with eyes like a cat's. Clinging to the bars with its wide, lizardlike claws, the creature lashed its long, thick tail back and forth.

"Hello," Sindri shouted over the screaming of the wind. Behind the creature, another tree rose into the sky before flying off to land in a heap.

Trembling, the creature spat out the parchment clenched between its teeth. Sindri's nimble fingers caught it as it fell, and absentmindedly he stuffed it into one of his robe's pockets.

"Kender man," the creature gasped in a raspy, frightened voice. "You the kender man."

"That's what you said last time," Sindri said.

"Hey!" Tayt shouted over the deafening winds. Unable to do much else, she nudged Sindri's side with her shoulder. "What is that thing? What in the Abyss is going on?"

Sindri started to answer her, but the furry lizard shot out one of its claws and gripped Sindri's cloak. Pulling hard for emphasis, it kept its eyes locked onto Sindri's own and spoke the words Sindri already knew it would say. "Dark wizard lies to you. You not what been told. It comes for you."

"I know!" Sindri shouted, hoping the creature could hear him. "That's what you already told me! Who is the dark wizard? Is it Maddoc? What is it that's coming for me?"

As before, the creature only shook its head and let go of Sindri's cloak. Peering back over its shoulder at the quaking trees and blackening woods, it gasped in despair, then turned back to Sindri. Its wide amber eyes watered with impending tears.

"Run, kender man," it whispered. "Run!"

With that, it leaped between the bars, landed in a heap of fur on the wagon's wooden floor, and got back to its feet. It darted out the other side and into the woods beyond. Sindri craned his neck all the way around to follow its path.

"Hey!" Sindri shouted, though he knew there was no way the creature could hear him over the din. "Come back! You have to answer my questions!"

Then, though the wind still tore through the wagon and rocked it from side to side, the screaming sounds stopped.

"What is *that*?" Tayt shouted beside him, and Sindri darted his head to look at her. The dangerous winds tugged at her clothes, bunching them around her body. With her jaw clenched, she stared toward the woods.

Still blinking through the stinging winds, Sindri followed Tayt's gaze. His eyes scanned past the tarnished bars of their prison, across the dark path and trembling trees, toward the sky right above the woods. Something big hovered above the forest, a massive, seething shadow that Sindri at first couldn't quite see. It was like a black cloud, an even darker black than the stained sky above, stirring with an inner turmoil like waves during an ocean storm. A dark, misty aura wafted off it like a fog, shrouding the sky with nothingness.

But no, whatever this thing was, it was not a cloud. Dozens of perfectly round, dark eyes glimmered on its side, like black opals floating on a night sea. The eyes darted across the bulging cloudy surface of the beast, scanning the sky, the trees, and the ground for its prey.

Sindri watched in awe as Tayt struggled with her bonds beside him. A tendril of liquid blackness seethed from the creature's side. It wrapped around the trunk of a nearby tree, crushing branches and sending leaves falling. Unlike its stormy path through the forest only moments before, the creature slowed down, its motions deliberate. It twisted the ancient tree once, twice, then yanked it from the earth as easily as Sindri's mother used to pull weeds from her garden.

The shimmering black eyes swam to the lower left portion of the cloud-shaped creature. They studied the coiled roots of the tree with great interest. For a moment, nothing happened.

Then the whirring and screeching came back.

The tendril hefted up the tree and threw it behind the beast, where it crashed to the forest floor. In a whir of eyes and wind and teeth, the creature tore forward. More tendrils darted out from its body, shoving aside trees and writhing uselessly toward the sky.

The wagon bounced, the force of the monster's tornadolike presence too much for the transport to handle. As Tayt let out a startled cry, Sindri heard the cart's wooden supports snapping.

The beast was upon them. So stunned and amazed was he by this unknown creature, Sindri could do nothing but sit and watch. The writhing, cloudlike mass hovered close over the wagon, pressing down to surround it as opaline eyes swirled by. The deafening scream of the creature's rage hurt Sindri's ears.

Smoky tendrils slithered over the wagon, gripping it from above and beneath. Sindri saw the glimmer of sharp teeth appear in the beast's cloudy body as it lifted the wagon into the air.

But he didn't have time to stare at the creature for long. With one more particularly loud screech, the creature flung the wagon into the air. Sindri and Tayt found themselves spinning through the air, straight toward the ravaged woods. Wood planks tore from the wagon's side. Sacks of supplies burst open, sending food and papers flying.

As Sindri, Tayt, and the wagon descended toward the dark spires of the trees, the last thing Sindri saw of the creature that had tossed them so idly away was its cloudy back as it tore through the woods on the other side of the path, leaving a trail of destruction in its wake.

CHAPTER

8   THE MAP AND THE SCALE

Though it couldn't have been more than a few moments, the tumbling of the wagon over and through the trees seemed to take ages. As Sindri watched the sky and the underbrush fly by, he got dizzy, then nauseous. It didn't help that next to him Tayt muttered flatly that they were about to die, and though Sindri always found it strange when his non-kender friends talked about death as though it were something to be so afraid of (it was just the next big adventure, if you asked any kender), Sindri was certain he still had a lot to accomplish and couldn't leave the mortal world just yet.

As Sindri's stomach lurched with his hastily eaten meal, he thought that perhaps the wagon should slow down. That it would be nice if they somehow made it to a clearing, and especially nice if they made it in one piece.

As he thought it, something began to happen.

The feeling in Sindri's stomach went from vomitous to the strange stirring in his gut he'd felt the morning before, during the final spell of his test. He didn't incant any words or use any spell components or wave his hands around.

But the magic happened anyway.

First, the wagon stopped tumbling. It leveled out and seemed to glide, like a dragon that had spread out its wings and was coming in for a safe landing. Then a meadow came into sight between the evergreens, a lovely field of long, emerald green grass dotted with yellow daisies and split in half by a trickling blue stream.

While Sindri tried to catch his bearings as the ground grew near, Tayt took a deep breath. "Brace yourself, Sindri," she said between clenched teeth. "Brace yourself!"

The girl spread herself down as flat as she could get with her arms still behind her back, eyes closed as she prepared for impact. Feeling as though his stomach were boiling over, Sindri grabbed the bars and waited.

The wagon hit.

The force of the impact was enough to send both Sindri and Tayt bouncing into the air with a yelp of surprise. The wagon tipped over and slid on its side through the grass, gouging a path through the grass and leaving a trail of unearthed soil behind it. The metal bars rattled and the wood whined in protest as the wagon slowly lost momentum and, finally, came to a creaking stop.

Sindri found himself in a rather awkward position, stuck in a corner of the cage. Face squished between the bars into grass, he wasn't able to exclaim to Tayt that he was all right and that she should, perhaps, get off him.

Tayt meanwhile seemed to have no idea that they were in one piece. She lay sprawled atop Sindri with her arms still behind her back at an awkward angle due to the cuffs. Her eyes were clutched closed and her jaw was tensed. Her head lay right next to Sindri's.

The two of them lay there for a long moment. The wagon

rocked in its awkward position, and Sindri heard a creak and then a thump as one of the wheels fell off and landed in the grass. Close by he could hear the trickling of the stream and the calls of birds.

"Are we dead?" Tayt finally asked, her eyes still closed.

"I don' thwin swo," Sindri said, still stuck beneath her. Bits of gritty dirt slipped into his mouth as he spoke.

Tayt opened one gray eye, then the other. Since the dark beast had left, the sky had returned to normal, and the golden light of the setting sun fell over them both. A light breeze rustled their clothes and windswept hair.

Trembling, Tayt smiled. Sindri thought he saw tears forming in her eyes, but she quickly swallowed them back and rid herself of her happy expression. With an awkward twist, she managed to roll off Sindri. She landed on her back against the bars and winced.

"Thanks," Sindri said as he pushed himself up. Thankfully, the paralyze spell on their lower halves seemed to have worn off, and Sindri could walk again despite a strange numb sensation in his legs that felt as if he'd been sitting in snow. Once he was standing, he saw that the wagon was on its side and at an angle, so that the back of the wagon stuck up toward the sky and the wooden floor jutted beside him like a wall. Some of the floorboards had fallen away or cracked in places, but no opening big enough for him or Tayt to fit through.

Tayt shimmied up into a sitting position. "I can't believe we survived that," she said. "The wagon should have shattered into a dozen pieces, and we should have been impaled on trees. Maybe the Conclave enchanted the wagon so their prisoners couldn't die in it. Seems like something they'd do. They'd want the honor of killing us themselves." She glanced around, looking confused. "What *was* that thing?"

"I have no idea," Sindri said. "But it wasn't anything I've ever seen or heard of before. I'm not sure how we landed safely, but I'm glad we did."

Brushing his disheveled hair out of his eyes, he climbed up the bars toward the back of the wagon. He remembered the feeling he got as they flew through the air only moments ago, that power stirring within him, and wondered if it was he who had caused the wagon to land so well.

But that was impossible, wasn't it? He'd been studying with Maddoc, and Maddoc had made it very clear that wizards couldn't do things like that. They couldn't just *think* something and make it happen. Magic was very precise, based on combinations of words and spell components, even the positions of the moons. But maybe that's why Maddoc had been testing him. Maybe that's why Maddoc had that notebook where he jotted down information about Sindri.

Dark wizard lies to you. You not what been told.

A few bars from reaching the back of the wagon and the locked prison door, Sindri looked back the way they'd come and thought about the little lizard creature and its strange warnings. He wished he knew more about it and the strange cloud beast that chased it—and then he remembered the parchment in his pocket.

"Is it locked?" Tayt called up from behind him.

With his hand halfway to his pocket, Sindri stopped and glanced back. He found the spellfilch looking up at him expectantly, her hands still bound behind her back. In the golden light of the setting sun, her red-brown skin glowed bronze, and that combined with her look of hope at escaping made her seem different somehow, less angry.

"I don't know," Sindri called back. "But there's never been a door I couldn't open."

"That's right, I forgot," Tayt said, nodding with a knowing air. "You're a kender."

"No." Turning back to look up at the door, Sindri smiled. "I'm a *wizard*."

Sindri climbed the last few bars like the rungs of a ladder until he was as close to the door as possible. Reaching out one hand, he touched the bars of the door and tried to recall the words to his door-unlocking spell.

As his fingers met on the door's bars, however, the lock simply gave way. The door flew backward on its hinges and slammed against the bars with a jarring clang.

"Effective spell," Tayt said. "I guess kender can be wizards after all." Traces of a smile played at her lips, but the girl quickly hid it.

"Not a spell, but that works for me," Sindri said with a shrug. He reached for the edge of the open door to pull himself up and out, then realized Tayt was in a bit of a predicament. "Say," he called back over his shoulder, "do you need any help climbing? I could do a levitation spell, maybe. Those used to be my specialty."

"No, thanks," Tayt said. With a bit of shimmying and inching up the wooden floor at her side, the girl managed to get to her feet. Once standing, she crouched down and lowered her arms behind her back down to her feet. To Sindri's amazement, she simply stepped backward through her arms and straightened up again. She rotated both shoulders so her hands rested in front of her.

"Wow!" Sindri called down to her. "How did you do that? Didn't that hurt your arms? And why didn't you do that before?"

Tayt shrugged. "I didn't want that crazy hunter to know I could do it. And I was just waiting for the right moment anyway. It's not like I could have gotten out of the cage before."

"Good point."

While Tayt awkwardly climbed the bars with her clasped hands, Sindri pulled himself through the opening. Dangling his feet for a moment from the doorway's edge, he savored the cool evening breeze of the forest. It'd been months since he'd really been out of Cairngorn Keep, and he only just realized how much he'd missed being in a place like this, a place that wasn't covered in stone and hidden under an eternal gray sky.

Letting go, Sindri fell into the soft grass. Desperately thirsty, he crawled to the nearby stream. Cupping his hands, he took a huge gulp. Behind him, Tayt thumped to the ground, and Sindri peered back at her. Ignoring him, she walked around the wagon, studying the wreckage and probably looking for the remaining supply packs.

Brushing his sleeve across his mouth, Sindri felt a rustling beneath his robes. The parchment. In all his concern about the door and Tayt's ability to get out of the wagon, he'd almost forgotten about it.

Shaking with anticipation, Sindri reached into his pocket and pulled out the little square of parchment. He sat down cross-legged in the grass, his back toward the setting sun so the last of the rays would let him read the parchment. All around him the peaceful clearing grew quiet, as though even the trees and the flowers and zipping insects couldn't wait to see what the strange lizard thing had given him.

Fingers trembling, Sindri unfolded the square, then unfolded it again. Something that glittered in the sunlight fell from between the folds into his lap, but he ignored it.

The parchment was almost fully unfurled now. With a deep breath, Sindri opened it all the way . . . only to find that the page was completely blank.

Confused, Sindri flipped the page over to see if perhaps there was anything on the other side, then turned it upside down. Nothing. It was just a plain piece of parchment. There were no secrets written on it, no drawings of mysterious creatures, no map.

Disappointed, Sindri looked over the page and across the grass waving in the evening breeze toward Tayt. She had found some packs and leaned against the wagon's side, pawing through them with her cuffed hands. Grunting in irritation, she tossed aside one pack and turned to another.

With a sigh, Sindri looked down in his lap to see what had fallen out. It had been small, but if the whole point of the parchment was to protect it, maybe it'd be interesting.

At first, Sindri was annoyed to find that the little thing in his lap shimmered gold. Gold was pretty much useless, and no one really made anything important out of it. He was hoping that maybe the lizard thing had given him something to help explain the creature's warnings.

Still, the gold thing shone, so Sindri picked it up. Curved and triangular, it was just big enough to fit in the palm of his small hand. It was also warm to the touch, which definitely wasn't normal. Tracing it with his fingers, Sindri found that it seemed to be covered in slight lines, like the tiny grooves on his fingernails. Interested, Sindri lifted the gold thing up to his face so he could see it better in the rapidly dwindling light.

Sindri gasped as he finally saw clearly what the thing was. It wasn't just some random piece of useless gold treasure.

It was a scale from a gold dragon.

So amazed was he to actually be holding an artifact so rare, Sindri didn't notice the parchment at first. It had grown even darker as night fell, but when Sindri had picked up the golden dragon's scale, lines flowed over the blank parchment—lines that now glowed in greens and blues.

Amazed, Sindri picked up the parchment and watched as a map appeared on it, as though some invisible artist were painting on it in bright ink. The map started in the center and seemed to be of the clearing in which he sat. In fact, it *was* the clearing—there was the little stream coursing north through the middle. The wagon was a dark mark in the meadow's western side, and near the stream a pinpoint of golden light glowed like a star. That golden pinpoint appeared right in the spot where Sindri sat.

The map grew farther out from the clearing, revealing the surrounding forest and the path beyond. The detailed map even showed the trail of destruction left behind in the dark beast's wake.

As the map developed in the southeast corner, Sindri saw two things that excited him at once. The first was a massive black structure in the very bottom right corner of the map, which Sindri knew immediately was Cairngorn Keep. The other was another glimmering pinpoint of golden light, bigger than the one in the meadow, that lay almost halfway between where Sindri sat and Cairngorn Keep.

The map finished drawing itself, the final image a decorative compass in the lower left corner of the map. Sindri was about to jump up and run to Tayt—who still sat by the wagon, digging through packs—to show her the magic map, when he noticed dark black words written in scrawling, looping handwriting around the edges of the map. Squinting in what little light remained in the twilight, he muttered the words aloud as he read them.

Sindri:

Those you think of as friends are not. Those who at first appear enemies will help you. The beginning of your journey lies where the golden light glows. The truth of who and what you are will be revealed.

Swallowing, Sindri paused before he read the last part. "Do not look back."

His hands once again shaking, Sindri lowered the map. Something strange was going on, something bigger than just Maddoc's mysterious plans and the Conclave wanting to study him. The strange vision, the furry lizard's mysterious warnings, the map's scrawling message made out specifically to him—as in the time room, he felt something nagging at the back of his mind, something telling him that he knew more about this than he thought he did, if he could just remember . . .

He had to find out for himself. The glowing dot was midway between the clearing and home; it wouldn't be any trouble to stop there on the way. If people really were lying to him—though he wasn't entirely sure that could be true—and if his powers really weren't of the normal wizard sort, he'd have to find out. Maybe then he could tell Maddoc what he'd discovered, and the two of them together could solve this new puzzle . . . before whoever or whatever was after Sindri got to him first.

"Hey, is that a map?"

Tayt clomped toward him, her heavy leather boots crunching the grass as she made her way from the wagon to the stream. It was so dark that she seemed little more than a shadow in the scant light of the only moon in the sky, silver Solinari.

"It is!" Sindri said, bouncing to his feet excitedly. "That lizard thing gave it to me back on the path before that dark beast appeared, and at first it didn't show anything, but now it shows exactly where we are. And it shows Cairngorn Keep and someplace else that I probably should go first."

Coming to Sindri's side, Tayt stopped and gave him a strange look. "Hey now, slow down. Do you see any towns on that map? I didn't find any useful supplies in the packs that didn't rip off the wagon. We need to get away from here, get me out of these cuffs, get some new supplies, and get hidden before the renegade hunter finds us."

Sindri peered at the glowing lines of the map and shrugged. "I don't see anything but woods. The keep is near a town called Ravenscar, but it's not the nicest of towns."

Tayt laughed bitterly and looked off into the dark trees. "I'd fit right in."

"Hey," Sindri said. He stepped forward and looked up at her shadowy face. The edges of her short dark hair glowed silver in the moonlight. "I know we don't know each other well, but maybe I can help you. Maybe if you come back to Cairngorn Keep with me, Maddoc could help get you out of those cuffs. You could even stay there a little while so the Conclave won't find you. There's plenty of room."

Again Tayt looked at Sindri with palpable distrust. "I don't think so," she said. "Ravenscar is fine."

"Actually," a deep voice called from the wagon. "Ravenscar *isn't* fine."

Startled, both Sindri and Tayt spun to look back at the shadowy wreckage of the wagon. Wilden stood there, having crept toward them so silently, neither had heard his approach. His white shirt and leather cloak hung askew from his shoulders and his blond hair was a wild mess around his face. In the moonlight, Sindri saw a dark look cross the renegade hunter's face.

"You are both my prisoners," he said between clenched teeth. Stepping forward menacingly, his two handheld scythes glittered dangerously. "Neither of you are going anywhere."

CHAPTER

9   ON THE TRAIL

Tayt stepped forward and pursed her face into stony resolve. Her entire body tensed, looking ready to run at any moment. "I'm not going anywhere with you," she said through clenched teeth. "You won't take me back to her!"

Wilden twirled one of the scythes and took a few steps forward. "Oh really?" he said. "And how far do you expect to get with those cuffs? And without the belongings you stole?" Though his disheveled hair made him look like a wild man, his face creased into perfect calm as he gestured over his shoulder with his chin. "I have your pack. Found it in the woods while I trailed you. I know you need it."

Shaking her head, the short girl's chest heaved with anger. To Sindri's surprise, tears formed in her gray eyes. The watery sheen over her eyes shimmered in the moonlight.

"You can't take me back there," she said, her voice breaking. "I never did anything but try to survive. Why won't you just listen to me?"

Wilden sighed and shook his head. "It's my duty. I do what I must."

The three of them stood there in a tense silence. The night breeze flowed past them, rustling the grass and sending the shadowy spires of the trees swaying. Certain he'd soon need his hands free, Sindri folded up his map and placed both it and the dragon scale in a pocket of his brown robes.

Attracted by the crumpling sound of parchment being folded, Wilden's sharp eyes darted to Sindri as though noticing him for the first time. The renegade hunter took in a sharp breath. "I forgot," he said. "You're free!"

Sindri shook his head in confusion. "Of course I am," he said. "So is Tayt."

"No," Tayt said in realization. "Sindri, your cuffs. If you're really a wizard, cast a spell!"

"Huh?"

Wilden snapped to attention. Before Sindri could react, the hunter raced across the field, scythes swinging at his sides.

Tayt fell to her knees at Sindri's side. "He's going to disappear and reappear behind you," she whispered into his ear. "Cast a spell!"

Only two steps from reaching them, Wilden spread out his arms. A shadow flitted across him and then, as in Cairngorn Keep, he was gone. Only the silent, peaceful night remained.

Clutching Sindri's shoulder with her clasped hands, Tayt shook him hard. "Hurry!"

Sindri wasn't sure he could do anything, but Tayt was right—he needed to try. No way was he going to let the Conclave take him again, not after what they'd done to Maddoc and especially not since he had a new quest he was dying to begin.

Stretching his hands out and ready, Sindri spun on his heels. Just as Tayt promised, a shadow flitted between Sindri and the stream and Wilden reappeared. Before the renegade hunter could do anything, Sindri pointed and shouted, *"Pesona shirak!"*

A bright, white cone of light burst from Sindri's fingers, directly into Wilden's face. Sindri blinked and looked away, amazed to find that the entire dark meadow was lit up as though it were the middle of the day. Though Sindri couldn't see Wilden through the brightness, he could hear him call out in surprise as he stumbled backward and splashed into the stream.

As suddenly as someone snuffing out a lamp, the spell ended. Colored dots floated in front of Sindri's eyes, and he found that the clearing seemed pitch black. It took a few moments of blinking for his eyes to adjust. The renegade hunter stood in the stream with his eyes squinted, not moving. Water rushed over his boots, soaking the legs of his trousers.

"What is it with you and blinding spells?" Wilden asked as he stretched his arms out uncertainly. "You know this won't stop me, right?"

"Maybe not," Sindri said with a shrug. "But she might."

Unseen by Wilden, Tayt had leaped over the stream and stood silently behind him. Her boot met the back of the renegade hunter's right knee in a swift kick. His leg gave out from under him and he stumbled forward, landing on both knees in the water with a splash.

"What the—" he started to say.

Before he could finish, Tayt yelled and shot out her right leg. Her heavy boot met the back of Wilden's blond head with a loud crack. The renegade hunter fell unconscious face-first into the dirt, lying half in and half out of the stream. His scythes fell into the grass at his sides.

Tayt stood on the opposite side of the stream, a smile creasing her face.

"You have no idea," she said, "how much I've been dying to do that."

"Where'd you learn to do that?" Sindri asked. He crouched next to Wilden's side and poked the man's shoulder. He was still breathing, but he didn't react.

With another leap across the stream, Tayt landed at Sindri's side. "When you live on the streets, you learn to fight," she said. "Otherwise, you get dead fast. Where'd *you* learn magic?"

Sindri grinned. "Told you I was a wizard."

"A kender wizard," Tayt said with a shake of her head. "No wonder the Conclave wants you so bad." Her eyes scanned the fallen hunter for signs of movement as she, too, crouched at his side. Lifting his left arm, she found an unusually shaped silver ring on his middle finger. Holding his limp wrist tightly in her hands, she looked up at Sindri.

"Here," she said. "Take off his ring."

"You're stealing his ring?" Sindri asked with a tilt of his head.

"You're *concerned* about me stealing things?" she asked with a skeptical look. "You really aren't a normal kender, are you?" She shook her head. "The ring is what he uses to unlock the cuffs."

Nodding, Sindri tugged at the silver ring. Twisting it, he managed to yank it from Wilden's finger. Tayt let the renegade hunter's hand drop to the grass.

Knotted metal work formed an intricate design on the flattened metal top of the ring. Most people would think it was just a fancy accessory and not give it much mind, but as Sindri held it between his thumb and forefinger, he felt bits of magic energy zipping through his fingertips.

Tayt held out her bound wrists expectantly. On the metal bar between the two clawed ends that clutched at her wrists, Sindri saw an indent that matched the knotted design on the ring. Sindri stuck the ring into the indent and twisted. With a click, the clawed ends snapped opened.

The cuffs fell to the grass as Tayt sighed in relief. Rubbing her wrists, which were covered with dark marks from the claws just as Sindri's had been, she looked over Wilden's fallen form with stern eyes. Without a word, she reached down, picked up the cuffs, and stepped over Wilden to straddle his back. She hefted his arms and snapped on the cuffs.

"The ring, please?" she asked. Holding Wilden's arms back with one hand, she held the other one out expectantly.

With a shrug, Sindri tossed her the ring. Tayt caught it expertly in her right hand and locked the cuffs. Letting the renegade hunter's arms fall into what looked like a rather uncomfortable position, she stuck the ring into a hidden pocket on her tunic, then reached down and picked up the fallen scythes. With Wilden's weapons in hand, she strode purposefully toward the shadowy remnants of the crashed wagon.

Running to keep up with the taller girl (though she was short by human standards, Sindri noticed), Sindri looked up at her. "Are we just going to leave him like that?" he asked.

Tayt shrugged. "He'd do the same to us."

They reached the wagon and found a couple of new packs that the hunter must have found fallen in the woods. Tayt smiled and plopped down to sit cross-legged next to a leather one that was cracked with age. Setting down the scythes, she opened the pack. With a sigh of relief, she pulled out a silver necklace. Sindri couldn't help but gasp in awe when he saw the sparkling gemstone strung on the silver chain. It was a medium-sized stone shaped like a teardrop that seemed to change colors in the moonlight.

Tayt strapped the necklace around her neck then tucked the gem safely beneath her tunic.

"So," Sindri said as he sat beside her. "We should probably sleep here for the night. I've adventured quite a bit over the last few years, and traveling at night always leads to trouble. I don't think Wilden will be bothering us, so we've got some time." He looked over at the renegade hunter, barely able to make out his motionless form in the moonlight, still splayed in the grass and the water. "I've got a map now, so in the morning we can go back to the keep. That is, if you want to come. I don't think Ravenscar would be the best place to go with a necklace like that."

Tayt stopped rifling through her pack and looked up at Sindri. She bit her lip.

"That monster in the woods," she said, "and that furry thing that gave you the map. You said you had visions of them?"

Sindri nodded eagerly. "I did! And now there's some sort of place I'm supposed to head to. I'm not sure what's going on, but I intend to find out."

Tayt nodded slowly. "That place," she said. "You think it might have something valuable? Magical artifacts, maybe?"

"I don't know," Sindri said with a shrug. "I guess it could. Why?"

Not responding, Tayt pulled her pack close to her chest and scooted backward through the grass and flowers until she leaned against the metal bars of the wagon. Looking over the dark meadow, she, too, stared at the shadowy form of the fallen renegade hunter.

"I think," she said after a moment, "that I'll go with you after all."

Sindri smiled and jumped to his feet. "Perfect!" he said. "It would be awfully boring to have to go through these woods without a traveling companion. And you don't seem so bad, now that you're not tied up and locked in a cage."

Tayt snorted and shook her head. "Thanks," she muttered.

With their plans made, and after Tayt ran back to tie up Wilden's legs with some rope she found in one of the packs, the two fugitives settled in for the night. Curled near the wagon and using a pack as a pillow, Sindri patted his robe pocket to make sure the map and the scale were still there. They were, and he smiled.

Come morning, he'd finally be able to get to the bottom of this.

Midmorning light filtered through fluffy white clouds as Maddoc and Arvin Derry finally stumbled through the underbrush and made their way into the meadow.

Ahead of them, a thin, weaselly looking tracker peered at the ground with squinty eyes. "I do believe," the tracker called back in an irritating, high-pitched voice, "that this is where your kender ended up last."

Maddoc stopped at the edge of the trees. Crossing his arms, he raised an eyebrow. "How could you tell?" he said in a cool, even voice. "The shattered wagon or the trail of fallen trees behind us?"

The tracker looked back and nodded with an eager smile. "Both actually."

Maddoc rolled his eyes, then glanced sidelong at Arvin. "Where did you find this man?" he muttered.

Arvin shrugged sheepishly and ducked his head. "One of the pubs in Ravenscar. I think I may have vastly overpaid him for his services." He giggled in his deranged way.

"Perhaps just a bit." Maddoc clenched and unclenched his newly attached hand as he watched the tracker poke at the wagon then head toward the stream beyond it. His finger bones creaked, the sound enough to set his teeth on edge. They'd managed to reattach the hand after studying the book Arvin had found, but something about it didn't feel right. Before, when his hand had been cut off, Maddoc had felt as if it were still there, as though there were some sort of phantom hand at the end of his stump. But once the hand was back on, he could feel nothing. The appendage was completely numb and still just as pale and waxy as it had looked when it lay on his workbench. Unable to look at his ruined hand without feeling a surge of distracting anger, Maddoc kept both hands covered beneath black leather gloves.

Strolling alongside the trail in the grass gouged out by the wagon's apparent crash landing, Maddoc and Arvin followed the tracker. Behind them came the sound of a half dozen boots stomping through underbrush. Maddoc's guards trailed behind the two wizards, though most had volunteered to come, to avenge themselves on the renegade hunter.

The wagon was mostly intact, despite somehow having been flung halfway through the woods. Maddoc's limbs tingled with traces of the kender's unusual magic as they neared. Sindri had definitely been here. And since there were no bodies and no sign of anything having been dragged off by forest beasts, he was certain that Sindri was still alive.

Near the wagon even Maddoc could tell that the grass had been crushed in a formation that would imply that two people had spent the night here. Sindri and the renegade hunter? But why would the renegade hunter let Sindri sleep outside when he might have had a chance to escape?

"They went this way!" The tracker's shrill voice called out from the eastern edge of the meadow, across the stream that cut the grassy clearing in half. Maddoc looked up to see the spindly man gesturing wildly toward the woods. "There are three sets of tracks, and one of them is most definitely kender!"

"Hmm." Maddoc stood up straight and glanced over at Arvin. The Goblin Man's nose had upturned like a pig snout and taken on a reddish cast. He sniffed wildly at the bars of the wagon, like a mangy dog nosing through garbage.

Maddoc cleared his throat.

Snapped to alertness, the stubby little man jumped back from the bars. Grinning his yellow-toothed grin, Arvin's nose returned to normal. "Apologies," he said. "But I smelled something. The kender . . . and a human girl."

Rubbing his bearded chin with his left hand, Maddoc turned back to look at the woods from which they'd come. His guards had finally made it through, and they stood there, in full protective gear with their swords unsheathed, staring at the wagon tilted inexplicably on its front end.

"There is something going on here that I'm not aware of," Maddoc growled. "Something big tore through these woods and tossed aside the wagon carrying Sindri as though it were a toy. And I don't think their meeting with that entity was coincidence."

Ducking his head, Arvin came to Maddoc's side. "More Conclave trickery, perhaps?"

Maddoc shook his head. "No," he said. "I sensed a dark magic in the woods, remnants of whatever happened yesterday. It's powerful, as powerful as what I sensed of Asvoria when she first emerged, and . . . familiar, somehow."

"I'm not sure what you mean," Arvin said. "But, then, I am a bit dense." He chuckled.

Hands held behind his back, Maddoc turned to walk toward the irritating tracker. "I'm not sure either, Arvin," he said. "But I intend to find out. Absolutely *no one* is going to get their hands on Sindri."

As they reached the stream, Maddoc turned to look back at the shattered wagon, beyond which the guards were making their way forward.

Maddoc narrowed his eyes and looked down at his covered, dead right hand. "No one," he muttered under his breath, "except *me.*"

CHAPTER

10 SLAVES

Is he still back there?"

Sindri peered over his unfurled map and tilted his head. "Wilden?" he asked.

Ahead of him on the overgrown forest path, Tayt stopped and looked back. Her pack was flung over her shoulder and she held one of the renegade hunter's scythes high, ready to cut through any plants blocking their way. "Well, yes," she said. "Unless there's some other 'him' following us that I don't know about."

Sindri turned his head to the side and strained to hear. They were completely surrounded by towering evergreens. Scrubby bushes kept them from venturing too far off beaten trails, and vines snaked along their path.

At first all Sindri heard were the distant calls of wolves padding through the leaves and deer crunching through underbrush. Then he heard Wilden, distantly down the path. There was a heavy thud as something hit the overgrown forest floor, a pause, then another heavy thud.

"Yes, he's still back there," Sindri told Tayt. "He's gotten surprisingly far, considering he has to hop the whole way and can't use magic."

"No one can ever tell him he's not determined," Tayt said with a shrug.

She walked to Sindri. There was something different about her since she was no longer trapped in the wagon, Sindri thought. Despite the dirty tunic and the shorn hair, she held herself with a practiced regality. Shoulders back and chin high, her stride was long and determined. Tayt was definitely not as she at first seemed, Sindri thought, especially not with a necklace like the one she wore hidden beneath her shirt.

"What's the map say?" she asked as she came to his side. Though Sindri stood up straight, she had to kneel down to get a good look at it.

"Well, we're here," Sindri said, pointing at the portion of the woods that glowed with a pinprick of golden light. "And over there is the place we're heading, see that bigger glowing light? I think the dragon scale is how the map can tell where we are. That's really smart, actually. Whoever made this map knew what they were doing. I wonder—"

"What's that?" Tayt pointed at a place above the golden light that marked their destination.

Confused, Sindri followed her finger to the spot on the parchment. All that had been on the map the day before was the meadow, the location they were heading to, Cairngorn Keep, and lots and lots of woodland. But Tayt was right—something new had appeared in a clearing not too far from where they stood. Two dark, boxy shapes that looked similar to the drawing of the broken wagon in the meadow.

"That wasn't there before," Sindri said. He traced the location with his fingers, feeling the dried ink. "Too bad we can't just ask the map what these places are or—hey, what's happening?"

As Sindri and Tayt watched in amazement, scrawling text appeared beneath the drawing of the two wagons, as though some invisible person had come between them with a quill to write out the answer.

Sindri read the words aloud. " 'Slaver caravan.' Huh, I guess we *can* just ask."

With a sharp intake of breath, Tayt pulled the map from Sindri's hands and stood straight up. Startled, Sindri was unable to react, but all she did was hold the map close to her face, peering as hard as she could at the images of the slaver wagons.

"It can't be," she muttered.

"Hey!" Sindri cried. "What did you do that for?"

Shaking her head, Tayt lowered the map. "Sorry," she said. "I didn't mean . . . here, take it."

Sindri looked at the wagons on the map. As far as he could tell, they weren't anything special, except that they were probably carrying slaves, which was definitely not a good thing. Though once he looked closer, he could make out a symbol on the wagon's side—a black circle within a pointed oval. Some sort of eye?

Ahead of Sindri came the sound of scythes slicing through tree branches. Tayt stormed ahead without him, tromping through bushes and slicing through vines as she forged a path in the direction of the slaver camp.

"Hey!" Sindri called. "Wait up!" Folding the map and shoving it into a pocket of his brown robes, he lifted the pack of food he'd been carrying and made chase. Tayt didn't slow down.

"Hey," Sindri said again as he neared her. He had to weave between trees and duck branches, but he managed to keep close.

"Where are you going?" he asked. "This isn't the right way."

Anger pulled the girl's face tight; her eyes narrowed. "I have a question for you," she said as she swung the scythe, sending small branches flying. "You've been on the road a lot, right? Adventuring, you called it?"

Sindri jumped over a log and sidestepped to come closer. "I have indeed," he said. "Most kender wait till they're much older to go wandering, but I just couldn't stay at home any longer knowing I was meant to be a great wizard, so I left early. Mother was so proud that I got the wanderlust before the neighbor's children, so she and Aunt Toadwyn threw a big party and—"

"So you've traveled," Tayt interrupted. "You met a lot of people? You helped them out?"

"Of course!" Sindri said. "I mean, I always tried to stay focused on my magic, but when someone's in trouble, you have to help them, especially if you have abilities they don't. Why, if it wasn't for my friends and me, Nearra would probably still not have any memories, or the Beast would have killed everyone in Potter's Mill, or that dragon—"

"Good," Tayt said, interrupting again. Stopping abruptly, she turned to kneel in front of Sindri, staring him straight in the eye.

"Look," she said, "I'm not some sort of adventurer, all right? I don't travel to find damsels in distress and help them from their towers, I don't jump from town to town to help mayors recover their steel from bandits, or whatever it is you do. I just try to get by. But something's going on, and I don't like it. We both get taken by the renegade hunter, and then that beast appeared and you got a map, and now these slavers with her symbol. It just can't be coincidence."

Sindri tilted his head. "Whose symbol?"

Looking down, Tayt fell silent. Golden light streamed through the thick canopy above, highlighting her conflicted features in bronze.

"I don't—" Tayt started to say. She looked back up to meet Sindri's inquisitive eyes, shaking her head. "All right, look. We don't know each other well, but I'm going to ask a favor. You like to help people? Then help me. Those slaver wagons, I know where they're going, that's all. Whoever they have in those wagons, they're going to be tortured. We can't let the slavers get out of these woods with those people."

Swallowing, Sindri pulled out his map and unfolded it. Tayt watched intensely as he peered at the parchment's glowing lines. The golden dot that represented Sindri shimmered near what had been revealed to be the slaver caravan. It looked like the slavers had pulled off to the side of some other trail, setting up camp in a small clearing.

Biting his lip, Sindri didn't look up from the map. He agreed with Tayt—something really weird was going on. First he got the map that claimed to show him exactly the place he needed to go to learn secrets about his powers, then a caravan heading to a place Tayt seemed awfully familiar with just happened to appear.

Maddoc told him something about magic every day when they did their daily studies: To be a true wizard, to master the art of magic, to survive the eventual Test at the Tower of High Sorcery, one would have to give up everything in life except the study of magic. A wizard could focus only on furthering his own magical goals.

At the time, Sindri thought it seemed like sound advice. He found it difficult enough as it was to study his magic books and memorize his spells without having to deal with the distraction of an adventure, no matter how fun it was. But he knew Tayt was right. They couldn't just sneak by and let slavers take undoubtedly kidnapped people off to be sold and tortured.

"All right," Sindri said, lowering the map. He grinned up at Tayt. "Let's do it."

Tayt nodded, her eyes not losing their intense focus. She leaped up and resumed her thrashing course through the untamed forest, and Sindri followed at her heels.

They both heard the camp before they saw it. Boisterous laughter and guttural speech met their ears as Tayt slowed her pace and tried to quiet her steps. Sindri did the same, coming to her side as they tiptoed through the remaining trees.

The scent of charred animal flesh met Sindri's nose, wafting toward them on a midafternoon breeze. But with the aroma of the food also came a thick, wonderfully disgusting smell of unwashed men.

Holding her breath to avoid the stench, Tayt held one finger to her lips. Sindri nodded and they crept forward as one, he with the natural silence of kender and she with steps so precisely silent that she could almost be part elf.

Pushing aside fanlike leaves, Sindri and Tayt peered into the clearing. Immediately in front of them was the back end of a wagon. It was built like a long, low hut set on wheels. The walls were darkly stained oak, the roof a brownish red that reminded Sindri of the color of dried blood. Along the tops of the walls, beneath the overhang of the roof, were tiny, rectangular windows fitted with black metal bars, the only windows in the thing.

Strangest of all—about this and the other wagon, which Sindri saw partially hidden beyond the first one—was that they were decorated with fading, painted signs advertising a traveling vaudeville act. The slavers clearly pretended to be a performance troupe, which must have been how they managed to get through cities and towns without being challenged.

The slavers themselves were near the trail Sindri had seen on the map, sitting on logs around a spit set over a weak fire. They were large, burly men with calculating eyes, scar-mangled features, and scraggly beards that seemed to take up their entire faces. On a few of them, small tusks jutted from their jaws and propped their lips up into permanent sneers—half-ogres. Behind them, tied to the trees, a dozen or so horses pawed at the ground in boredom.

A woman stood there too, her red hair a tangled mess that hung to the middle of her back. Avoiding the groping hands of her companions, she leaned over the spit to rotate what looked like the charred remains of a rabbit. One of the half-ogres swigged from a flask then slapped at the woman's backside. All the men clutched at their sides as they doubled over with drunken laughter as though that were the funniest thing they'd ever seen.

"Disgusting," Tayt whispered.

Sindri turned to her to respond, but she met his look with her finger again at her lips. She shook her head and gestured toward the back of the nearest wagon. It was angled away from the partying slavers. They wouldn't see them.

With Tayt in the lead, they both crouched low. Making sure no one was watching, they slipped between the bushes and walked, still crouching, around the back of the wagon. They were about to round the corner when Sindri heard someone's voice.

"Making me guard," Sindri heard a man mutter. "Stupid gully dwarves. Stupid Org."

Tayt heard him too. Holding her back close to the side of the **103** wagon, she carefully sidestepped until she could peer around the corner. Tiptoeing in front of her, Sindri did the same.

There was a door on that side of the wagon, locked with an iron padlock. At the base of the heavy wooden door were two steps that led partway to the ground, to make it easier to step inside. Sitting on those steps was a short man who was so thin Sindri was certain he couldn't have eaten in weeks. The man was dressed only in trousers, boots, and a fur-lined vest. Gold hoops hung from both his drooping ears and from the left nostril of his rather large nose. Still muttering to himself, the man took a swig from a waterskin that Sindri was certain didn't contain water.

"Wait here," Tayt whispered to Sindri.

Before Sindri could protest, Tayt stepped out from behind the wagon. She got two steps away from the man before he noticed her. Swaying slightly as though he were having trouble sitting up, he stared at Tayt with bleary red eyes and his mouth slack.

Hands on her hips, Tayt tilted her head. "Drinking on the job?" she said with a cluck of her tongue. "What if someone came by and tried to free your slaves?"

The man closed his eyes, shook his head, and opened his eyes again. "Huh?" he said.

Reaching into a pouch at her side, Tayt pulled out a handful of sand. "Night night," she said. Pursing her lips, she blew into her palm. A cloud of dust billowed from her hands and into the man's eyes. As it did, Tayt said, "*Tidur.*"

Hacking through the lungful of sand, the guard tried to stand up. "You aren't . . . aren't . . . uh . . . " He took only one step before his eyes rolled back into his head, his legs turned to rubber, and he fell backward into the grass.

"What'd you do?" Sindri asked as he raced around the corner

of the wagon. He crouched at the sleeping guard's side and poked his stomach. The guard responded with a snorting honk of a snore.

"Sent him to bed," Tayt responded as she pulled her pack in front of her and dug through it. "Oldest trick in the book, but there are still people stupid enough to let one drunken idiot guard their treasures. Ah, here we go."

She pulled out a pair of iron lock picks and jumped up onto the steps beneath the door. Tongue between her teeth, she peered carefully at the padlock holding the door shut, then expertly slipped the picks inside.

Sindri stood from where he'd crouched near the fallen guard. "Wouldn't a spell be easier?"

"Maybe," Tayt said, not taking her eyes off her work. "But why waste the energy if I don't need to? There is such a thing as relying on magic too much, you know."

Sindri was about to protest, but he remembered an adventure he'd had once in Palanthas. There'd been a sea creature, one he couldn't use magic on. It had been a dagger—a simple iron dagger—that had ultimately saved his life. Maybe Tayt was right.

But he still thought a spell would be easier.

Behind them, a horse neighed in surprise and again the slavers exploded with laughter. Sindri inched closer to the wagon, his eyes drifting above Tayt's head to study the door. There, chiseled into the wood, was the same eyelike symbol he'd seen on the map—a black circle within a pointed oval. Curious.

The padlock clicked. "There," Tayt whispered. Unlatching the iron lock, she set it gently down in the grass. Holding her breath, she pulled open the door.

Sindri wasn't sure what he'd expected. Maybe two dozen

frightened men and women, pounding at the walls trying to escape. But that wasn't what he saw at all.

There were people sitting inside the wagon, but not humans. They were short, shorter than Sindri even, and dressed in rags—gully dwarves. Their bodies were flabby, pasty, stubby things that were covered in scabby sores. Whiskers stuck out from their dirty cheeks, and their hair hung limp and greasy.

Worst of all, Sindri thought, were their eyes. Those who were awake blinked at the sudden light with stares so devoid of hope that they might as well have been corpses.

Tayt gagged and turned away, hand over her mouth. Sindri didn't know why until he jumped onto the steps to enter the wagon. A stench of sewers and death met him in a wave, and even he had to admit that the smell of it was nauseating.

Swallowing, Tayt turned back to the wagon. She took a step inside and knelt down. None of the little creatures moved, and only a few seemed to have the energy to follow her with their eyes.

"We're here to rescue you," she whispered. "Do you understand? We're here to take you away from this."

One of the gully dwarves near the door—male or female, Sindri couldn't tell—coughed, nodding its head. "We help," it croaked between scabby lips. "Strong ones, we lift others. We get out."

"Yes," Tayt said, nodding. "Yes, we'll get you out."

"Tayt, I think I'd better—" Sindri started to say.

Behind them, from the forest, came the sound of someone running through the woods. "Tayt!" a voice called. "Sindri! I know you're there! You are my prisoners, and I will not stand for this!"

Tayt groaned and balled her fists. "No, no, no," she muttered.

To the gully dwarf that had spoken, she said, "We'll be back. Don't worry."

Grabbing at Sindri's arm and making sure her pack was firm over her shoulder, Tayt leaped from the wagon, shutting the door behind herself. As the two of them landed in the grass, Wilden burst from between the trees.

He stood there panting, his arms clasped awkwardly behind his back. His cheeks and nose were smudged with dirt, and his hair was once again a wild mess littered with bits of twigs and leaves.

"Very funny," he growled, "tying up my legs. But I got loose. You will unlock me at once. Don't think I can't do the same kicking thing you did, Tayt."

"You idiot," Tayt seethed. She walked straight up to the renegade hunter and shoved his chest. Despite being a full foot shorter than the man, her spirit seemed just as strong. "You're going to ruin everything."

"Uh, Tayt," Sindri whispered. "Wilden. Maybe you should quiet down before—"

"Before what?" Wilden snapped.

"Hey!"

Sindri, Tayt, and Wilden spun at the voice. There, standing at the corner of the wagon, was one of the burly half-ogre slavers. It stuck out a ham-sized fist and pointed a stubby finger at the trio. "Intruders!" he bellowed. "They're trying to free the slaves!"

As shouts rose from behind the wagons, Sindri turned back to the startled Wilden and Tayt.

"Before," Sindri said with a shrug, "*that.*"

CHAPTER

11   EMANCIPATION

The sounds of dozens of men hollering at the tops of their lungs and unsheathing deadly weapons shattered the peacefulness of the clearing. All Sindri could do was stand there as the sounds of boots pounding against compact soil filled the air like rolling thunder, sending unseen animals rustling through the underbrush.

"What is this?" Wilden demanded, unfazed.

Tayt didn't answer him. Jaw clenched, she fumbled through her pack with shaking hands and pulled out the renegade hunter's scythes.

His mouth halfway open to answer Wilden, Sindri found himself interrupted by the burly men rounding the wagon. One of the half-ogres snorted and tossed a battle-axe between his hands.

The slavers came to a halt when a man in the lead raised a hand. This man was just as tall and broad as the rest of the slavers, but his brown beard was cropped short and his dark eyes flashed with an intelligence the others lacked. With his sword pointed at Tayt and Wilden, he stepped forward. Both hunter and spellfilch stood completely still.

"You two," he growled. "What are you doing back here? What did you do to Abram?"

Certain he'd been overlooked because of his height, Sindri walked up to the man and tugged at his shirt. "Excuse me," he said.

The lead slaver started then looked down at the kender with an irritated expression on his scarred face. "What?"

Sindri stepped back and shrugged, ignoring the predatory glances of the other slavers. "Well, first, I just wanted to point out that there are three of us," he said. "It's only polite to threaten everyone, not just humans."

The lead slaver's brow furrowed. "You're a kender," he said.

"Indeed I am," Sindri said.

From behind him, Tayt hissed, "What are you doing?"

Sindri ignored her. "Second, I have a question," he said. "Who's Abram? It'd be easier to tell you what became of him if we knew who he was."

The slaver's sword lowered a bit. Turning, he looked at the men behind him with his jaw slack, as though asking what they thought. One of the half-ogres snickered as the others whispered among themselves.

"Well?" Sindri asked. He dared a glance back at Wilden and Tayt near the trees. They hadn't moved from their spot. He wanted to tell them to get ready to move, but he couldn't take any chances.

Scratching at his matted hair, the lead slaver turned back around to face Sindri. "See that man there?" he said, gesturing toward the guard who still lay snoring beneath the wagon. "That's Abram."

"Oh." Sindri shrugged. "Sleeping spell. Oldest trick in the

book, I heard, but if some dolt still insists on letting only one man guard their wagon, they probably deserve to get robbed. Or so I've been told."

Sneering, the lead slaver once again raised his sword. He brushed past Sindri, his animal-skin cloak fluttering behind him. "Which one of you is a wizard!" he shouted at Tayt and Wilden. "Tell me now, or your deaths will be a lot slower and painful than they need to be."

"He is," Tayt said, pointing accusingly at Wilden. At the same time, Wilden tilted his head toward Tayt. "She's a spellfilch," he said.

With a snarl, the man leaped toward the two of them as though intending to attack. Standing in the shade of the wagon filled with captive gully dwarves, his men caterwauled with approval.

"Hey!" Sindri called. The lead slaver stopped but didn't turn around. Sindri stomped his foot. "Hey!" he called again.

Slowly, the sneering slaver looked over his shoulder. "Something to add, kender? Perhaps *you* want to explain? Do it and I'll let you go and only punish these two."

All eyes on him, again Sindri shrugged. "I don't want to explain. I just wanted to add that they're not the only wizards. I am too."

For a moment, everyone stood in complete silence. The only sounds Sindri could hear were the rustling of the trees swaying in the breeze and the distant snorts of the horses tied behind the wagons.

Then the lead slaver turned all the way around. He shook and his face was red, as though he were overcome with rage. But then, with a gasp, he let out a peal of laughter.

"A kender," he gasped between laughs, "a kender *wizard?*"

Finally getting it, all of his men near the wagon let loose. They hollered their laughter to the sky, some doubling over and clutching at their stomachs, others wiping tears from their eyes. One of the half-ogres leaned against the side of the wagon and pounded his fists against the wall as he laughed in boisterous guffaws.

With a shrug and a knowing smirk, Sindri spread both hands out at his sides. As Tayt and Wilden looked on in confusion, and as the slavers continued to slap their knees with laughter, Sindri recited a spell.

"Tak'kelihatan edar, pesona semua dalam."

There was a quick flash then a sparkling circle of light whooshed from Sindri's outstretched hands. It slammed into the chests of the laughing slavers, knocking them to the ground. As they fell to the dirt, their guffawing ceased and their faces calmed into a relaxed, dreamlike state. The sparkling light from the magic circle lingered around their eyes, and they watched the pinpricks of light in awe.

The last to be hit was the lead slaver. Startled, he raised his sword as though somehow it would protect him. Instead, the circle punched him in the gut, and he fell on his back at Wilden's and Tayt's feet. He, too, stared into the blue sky. Chuckling, he reached up with one glove-covered hand and tried to snatch at something none of them could see as sparkles danced in front of his eyes.

His spell cast, Sindri let out a great big breath and fell to his knees. His heart was pounding, and he felt blood and magical energy coursing through his body.

Now that their potential attackers lay out of commission, Tayt shoved the scythes back into her pack and leaped over the fallen slaver at her feet. Wilden made chase, running awkwardly because of his hands clasped behind his back.

"What was *that?*" Tayt asked as she came to Sindri's side. Her eyes were wide with surprise. "Good idea, catching them off guard, but you shouldn't be able to do something that powerful!"

Clenching his eyes closed to block out the sunlight that now seemed much too bright, Sindri shook his head. "It's nothing," he said. "Just something I read in a book I found under Maddoc's bed."

Sindri opened his eyes to see Wilden shaking his head. "And you wonder why the conclave wants you two so bad," he said. "What were you doing?"

"Freeing the slaves," Sindri muttered. Stumbling slightly, he got back to his feet. The spell had been a rush, but it had also been a bit bigger than what he was used to casting. He wasn't sure he'd be able to do anything bigger than a simple cantrip for a little while at least.

"Slaves?" Wilden asked.

Tayt gasped then spun around to look back at the wagon surrounded by the dazzled slavers. The door with the eye symbol was open slightly, and Sindri could see a grubby face peering through.

"Yes, slaves," Tayt snapped at Wilden. Without looking back, Tayt stomped toward the door. "Your shouting earlier almost got us killed for trying to free slaves."

"Slaves," Wilden whispered. His eyes clearly unsettled, the renegade hunter lowered his head. Strands of his blond hair fell to cover his face. "This isn't allowed."

Patting himself all over to make sure he hadn't dropped anything, Sindri looked around at the victims of his spell. One of the first ones hit, a dark-skinned man with eyebrows like black caterpillars, had started to blink, his face scrunched with confusion.

"Hey, Tayt," Sindri called, not taking his eyes off the fallen slavers. When the girl didn't respond, he turned to face her. "Tayt!"

Lips pursed, Tayt ignored him. The door to the wagon was open wide and she had her arm around the waist of a tiny gully dwarf, helping him or her down the short steps.

"Tayt," Sindri said again, "they're waking up. We should run."

"Never," she and Wilden said at the same time. Surprised, Sindri spun around to face him as Tayt stopped midstep down the stairs to stare at him.

The renegade hunter stood straight, his black cloak and hair flowing in the breeze and his strong jaw clenched in resolve. "Never," he repeated, "will I let something like this happen when I can stop it. Let me help."

Grunting in disgust, Tayt turned from him to lift the little gully dwarf and set him or her—Sindri still couldn't tell—on the ground. "Not on my life," she said.

Near Sindri's feet, one of the half-ogre slavers stirred as well. His legs dug into the dirt, as though he were trying to run while lying down. Behind him a man with a face that was more beard than anything else, flailed wildly with his right hand, trying to grab the wagon and pull himself up.

With a shake of his head, Wilden looked down at Sindri. "Come on," he said. "Let me help."

Those who at first appear enemies will help you.

The words from the map came to Sindri in a flash. Biting his lip, he looked from Tayt, who was guiding two more gully dwarves to freedom, to Wilden, who waited for his response with a reassuring and friendly smile.

Decision made, Sindri reached into his cloak, feeling through his pockets. All kender tended to find unexpected treasures in their many pockets, though rarely did they ever remember putting them there. But Sindri was the only one he knew who always seemed to find the exact right *magical* item in his pockets when he needed it.

Sure enough, his nimble fingers found themselves grasping the silver ring that they'd used to lock Wilden's cuffs. Pulling it from his brown robes, he held it up for Wilden to see. The renegade hunter grinned.

"What are you doing?" Tayt shouted, noticing the ring glinting in the daylight. "When did you take that?" Turning away from the sickly gully dwarves, she ran toward Sindri with her hand outstretched, her pack slapping and jangling at her back.

"I didn't take anything!" Sindri said. "I must have conjured it."

"You didn't conjure anything, Sindri. You *handled* it like any kender. But don't free him, he'll—"

Before she could get close, and before Sindri could unlock Wilden's cuffs, they were both stopped by a feminine howl from atop the wagon.

A shadow loomed over them, like that of a hawk swooping in for a kill, and to their surprise they saw the woman who had been turning the spit. Dressed in leather rags, her long red hair hung in a tangled coil down her back, and her face contorted into a feral snarl. In either hand she held two long, curved scimitars, their edges tainted with stained blood.

The woman tilted back her head and let out another howling, bloodthirsty scream. Then she leaped.

Tayt shouted in surprise as the woman fell toward her. She

JEFF SAMPSON

leaped out of the way just in time. The feral woman's swords sunk deep into the ground like the claws of a terrifying beast. Landing in a crouch, she tilted her head toward Tayt and growled.

Shaking her head, Tayt clutched her pack to her chest. "And to think I felt sorry for you."

Leaving the swords in the ground, the woman pounced. Tayt swung her pack, hitting the woman square in the face and knocking her down near the slavers, who were still trying to rise. Tayt ran toward Sindri and Wilden, but the woman's hand shot out and grabbed her ankles. Tayt fell chest-first into the ground, sending her pack sliding across the grass toward them.

"Sindri!" Wilden bellowed. "Hurry!"

Not wasting a second more, Sindri pulled up his robes and ran to Wilden. The renegade hunter waited impatiently as Sindri tried to find the indent where the ring fit. Meanwhile, some of the slavers managed to get to their feet, rubbing their foreheads in a daze.

"Come on, come on," Wilden muttered, bouncing on his toes.

"Hey, stop moving," Sindri said. "*I'm* supposed to be the impatient one."

Finally, he saw the indent. Sticking the flattened, knotted end of the ring in place, he twisted the lock. The clawed ends unclasped with a click, and the cuffs fell free.

Tayt cried out in anger. Sindri gasped when he saw her kicking and punching at the animalistic red-haired woman, who dragged Tayt by her ankles toward the two swords. Beyond them, the gully dwarves that had managed to get out of the wagon huddled in the shadows behind the wagon wheels and between the trees.

Not wasting a minute, Wilden leaped toward Tayt's fallen pack. The scythes were in his hands in a flash. He muttered a phrase, a shadow flowed over him, and he was gone.

"Tayt!" Sindri cried. Following Wilden's path, he ran toward his new friend. The animalistic woman dropped Tayt's legs as they reached the two scimitars jutting up from the dirt. Keeping one bare foot pressed firmly on Tayt's chest to keep her from scrambling away, the woman grabbed the hilts of both scimitars and wrenched them from the dirt.

"Tayt!" Sindri cried. He tried to run faster, but he stumbled over his long robes, falling to the grass and dirt with an *oof!*

"No!" Tayt shouted as the woman raised both swords over her chest. "No! *Tida*—no, no—*keaw*—no, what are the words!"

The wind knocked out of him, all Sindri could do was watch as the feral woman smiled wide, revealing crooked yellow teeth, and plunged the swords toward Tayt's unprotected chest and neck.

A living shadow appeared right behind the red-haired woman. His blue eyes blazing with fury, Wilden gripped the woman by her knotted hair and pulled back hard. The woman let out a guttural cry as her head snapped back, and both scimitars missed their mark. Tayt, eyes clenched closed, flinched as the swords bit into the ground, sending dirt flying.

With a screech of fury, the woman spun on Wilden, jerking her head so fast that a clump of her knotted red hair remained clenched in his fist. Holding her blood-stained scimitars high, she leaped to bring the swords down upon Wilden.

Wilden's lips moved as though he were trying to cast a spell, but the woman moved too fast. The renegade hunter ducked her blows and swung one of his scythes into her gut.

With a gasp, the woman doubled over. All Sindri could see was her back, so at first he wasn't sure what had happened. The scimitars slipped from the woman's hands, and she stumbled backward, turning as she did. Her hands clutched at her chest and stomach as sticky blood gushed between her fingers.

The woman howled, long and mournful. As Sindri watched from where he still lay splayed on the ground, the woman's eyes rolled back into her head. Her howling catching in her throat, she crumpled to the ground, dead.

Tayt still lay on the ground as well. The two of them stared at Wilden, who stood completely still, his eyes closed. In his right hand, one of the scythes dripped with fresh blood.

"No!"

Sindri's head shot around to look toward the trees. The lead slaver stood there, hands clenched into fists, his nostrils flared wide. "No!" he roared again. Pointing his sword toward the three intruders, he bellowed, "Get them!"

By then the other slavers had all mostly snapped out of Sindri's spell. One of the half-ogres tilted back his head and let out a ferocious war cry. The other slavers bellowed in response, their axes and maces and swords unsheathed and ready for battle.

Tayt scrambled to her feet, sending dirt flying. She raced to Sindri, picking up her pack as she ran past where it lay in the grass. Sindri shoved himself up to stand, ready to defend himself.

The slavers surrounded them. One leaped forward and swung down with a clawed club, barely missing Sindri's head. Others circled them, holding their weapons at the ready. The mostly bearded man sneered and grabbed at Tayt's arms as the slaver with the caterpillar brow tried to punch Sindri's face in. Sindri ducked the blow as Tayt shot out with her booted feet, hitting her attacker square in the knee. There was a loud crack, and the man let out a shriek of pain.

"You wench!" the bearded man howled. Hopping backward

on his good leg, he rammed into one of his companions, sending them both sprawling backward.

"Come here, you blasted kender," Sindri's attacker said as Sindri once again ducked the man's blows. He tried to call to mind a spell—any spell—that could stall his attacker or the other slavers.

As Sindri ducked another punch and darted beneath a half-ogre's legs, he saw Wilden. The renegade hunter had leaped atop the wagon and stood in an attack position, facing off with the lead slaver.

The slaver swung his sword. Wilden dodged, rolled across the roof, and spun in one fluid move. He called out a phrase Sindri couldn't hear over the shouting of the attacking slavers, and a bolt of black lightning shot from the hunter's fingertips. The edge of the second wagon's red roof exploded into flame. Beneath the wagon, the freed gully dwarves huddled together in fear.

The lead slaver dodged the flying shrapnel. Crying out, he leaped forward again, his sword aimed directly at Wilden's neck.

A pair of legs appeared in front of Sindri, blocking his view before he could see what happened next. Before Sindri could react, a boot shot out, hitting him square in the chest. He flew backward onto the ground, sliding between the half-ogre's legs he'd crawled between only moments before.

"Hey!" Sindri cried, but his voice was lost under the taunts and angry shouts of the slavers. Beside him, Tayt, too, had been knocked to the ground. Another half-ogre, this one with his hair tied back in an intricate braid, raised a spiky mace. As the throng of slavers loomed above them, Tayt let out a defiant, furious shout.

As though echoing her anger, something else screamed . . . something big.

Immediately, the slavers stopped shouting, stopped attacking. Everyone turned to look at the southern edge of the forest, where Sindri and Tayt had sneaked earlier. One of the men barked out, "What in the Abyss is that thing doing *here?*"

The throng parted, and that was when Sindri saw it. The creature hovered above the trees, its cloudy black body swirling with magic fury. Beneath it the trees swayed, caught in its tornadolike wake. A misty black aura seeped from its body to darken the sky as dozens of shimmering, spiderlike eyes darted across its body.

The dark beast had returned.

CHAPTER

12 RETURN OF THE DARK

The dark beast shuddered then shrank inward, as though taking a breath. When it expanded once more, the air exploded with a hideous shrieking. A wave of powerful wind met Sindri, whipping his long black hair straight back.

Fallen leaves, twigs, and dirt swirled through the slaver camp, getting into their eyes, scratching at their skin, filling their mouths with gritty dust. The slavers backed away, their confused and frightened shouting lost beneath the roaring of the beast's wind.

Squinting his eyes to keep dust out, Sindri crawled toward Tayt, who lay sputtering in the grass. She tried to shout something at him, but he couldn't hear anything she was saying.

The wagons shook and Wilden, who was still on top of the one holding the slaves, stumbled from side to side. The lead slaver, his trimmed beard quivering on his chin, stood defiantly at the wagon's edge, screaming at his men to maintain their ground. But everyone was too overcome by the furious wind to do anything.

"No!" the lead slaver howled, shaking his sword toward the dark beast. "She promised it wouldn't come here! She promised!"

The dark beast attacked.

Striking out like a snake, a serpentine black tentacle shot from the hovering beast's billowy body, straight at the lead slaver. The tendril wrapped around his midsection and, quick as a whip, pulled the screaming man through the air. The teeth Sindri had seen before appeared, endless, sharp, shredding teeth that came out of nowhere on the creature's cloudy body. As a strange, mechanical whirring joined the wretched screech of the wind, the beast tossed the screaming slaver into its gaping, jagged mouth. Tayt looked away, but Sindri couldn't help but watch in disgusted amazement.

Panic coursed through the remaining slavers as they watched their leader die. They turned to run, shoving each other aside and stumbling from the force of the wind at their backs. Another tentacle shot out from the beast, gripping a nearby pine and pulling it from the ground in an explosion of soil. The tree whooshed right above Sindri's and Tayt's ducked heads. It crashed next to the wagon, crushing several of the fleeing slavers.

The wagon shuddered from the impact and began to tip over. Sindri watched through squinted eyes as Wilden made a desperate leap. The wagon crashed to the ground behind him as he landed in a roll in the dark, waving grass. The exposed gully dwarves shrieked in fear and ran into the trees, their tiny bulk barely enough to keep the swirling wind from picking them up and carrying them away.

"Run!" Wilden bellowed as he raced toward Sindri and Tayt. Blond hair whipped at his cheeks as his leather cloak tugged backward, choking him.

Tayt and Sindri stumbled to their feet as the dark beast let out another tremendous screech. "The gully dwarves!" Tayt shouted.

"Tayt, we—" Wilden started to say.

Like a bolt of black lightning, another tentacle shot out from the dark beast's body, straight toward them. Heedless of his own safety, Wilden shoved Sindri and Tayt behind him and held up a hand. A soft blue glow emanated from his palm, and instead of striking them, the tentacle curled back on itself, as though hitting a wall.

"Run!" Wilden bellowed again.

Sindri and Tayt didn't argue. Holding up the hem of his robes, Sindri raced toward the southern edge of the clearing. He heard Tayt behind him, and farther back the whinnying of frightened horses that had been abandoned by their masters.

As he reached the edge of the darkened forest, Sindri glanced back over his shoulder. Teeth clenched, Wilden still stood tall, hand upraised. With his other hand, he pulled free one of his scythes and swiped, sending the tip of the tentacle flying. It melted into smoky nothingness as it hit the grass. The rest of the tentacle pulled back into the beast's body.

Not wasting his chance, Wilden ran after Sindri and Tayt. Above the trees, the beast again screamed.

Tayt at his heels, Sindri led the way south through the trees. He didn't know exactly where he was going, but he did know that the sky above them was still dark with the monster's presence and the trees still shook from the lashing winds. Birds squawked and took wing as more trees were uprooted behind them. The trees crashed into the dirt with thunderous booms.

Ducking beneath tree branches and slapping aside leaves, the forest seemed a blur of black and green as Sindri ran. Though he was curious to know more about this beast, he wasn't so curious he'd risk a much-too-soon death to find out.

Out of the corner of his eye, Sindri saw something small and brown darting parallel to him through the bushes.

"Kender man," a familiar voice rasped as they ran side by side. "Kender man, use map. Map show way." The speaker darted under a bush and disappeared.

It was the furry lizard creature. Of course! Wherever it went, so went the dark beast.

"Oh," Sindri said in sudden realization. "The map!"

Skidding to a stop in the underbrush, Sindri reached into his pocket and pulled out the map. Gulping for air, Tayt stopped at his side. Catching up, Wilden leaned on his knees and tried to regain his breath.

"Why . . . " Tayt said between gasps for air, "are . . . you stopping?"

"The map," Sindri said, not taking his eyes off the parchment as he unfolded it. "It'll show where I'm supposed to go, remember? We can hide there or—"

Soil exploded, hitting Sindri square in the face. A few paces to their right, a tree flew into the air. In the sky the dark beast loomed.

"Go!" Wilden shouted.

They ran, not caring about the branches smacking them in their faces or the vines scratching at their arms. Sindri kept the map unfurled, following its directions while trying not to trip over his robes. He could see himself as the smaller glowing dot. Straight ahead was the larger glowing dot that represented his destination—the place that the map had promised would be the start of Sindri's journey.

Soil, leaves, and branches hit their backs as they ran, the roaring wind still whipping about their clothes and hair. More trees thumped to the ground behind them, and Sindri could hear the endless whirring of the creature's gnashing teeth.

"It's getting closer!" Tayt yelled over the noise of the beast.

"Keep going!" Wilden shouted back. "Just keep going!"

Sindri didn't have time to respond. His heart pounded with excitement as the two glowing dots on the map grew closer and closer. Shoving the map into his pocket, Sindri ran even faster, not caring about the burning sensation in his limbs and the aching of his lungs. He was almost there!

There was a sudden incline in the woods, so abrupt that Sindri and Tayt both fell. Pulling himself into a ball, Sindri went with it, letting himself roll down the steep hill, bouncing between trees and bursting through bushes. Behind him, Tayt yelped in surprise as she slid down the hill on her backside, grabbing at branches to slow her descent.

Sindri reached the bottom of the hill first, landing in a dirty heap. Twigs stuck in his hair and mud caked his robes, but he didn't care. He glanced back to see Tayt almost to the bottom of the hill. Wilden was a little farther up, running awkwardly while clutching at tree trunks to keep upright.

In the sky, still following and still watching with its blank black eyes, was the dark beast. Tentacles shot from its flowing body, piercing the ground only a few paces behind Wilden and sending underbrush flying.

Taking a deep breath to fill his aching lungs, Sindri turned. He was there, he had to be. This was the destination the golden dot had shown him.

At first he didn't see anything. It seemed like nothing more than endless forest, hanging with vines and overgrown with unusual orange flowers with wide, flat petals. As Tayt skidded to a stop at his side, however, he noticed strange, rocky pillars jutting from the earth. They were caked with dirt and overgrown with ivy, but they were definitely not natural formations.

"Go, go, go!" Wilden cried behind them as he raced to the bottom of the hill. The dark beast was almost upon him now, its tornado winds swirling leaves around them, its screeching ripping at their ears. Another tentacle shot down, ripping up a nearby birch and almost slamming it against Wilden's side. He ducked the tree's roots and raced past Sindri and Tayt.

Sindri didn't wait a second longer. With Tayt at his side, he ran toward the stone pillars. This was it, this had to be the spot. As he got closer, he saw that the overgrown forest floor was not soil after all, but cracked, broken tile. Trees burst through the tile, but at one point a building had stood here. Sindri raced over the floor, trying to study the pillars around him, noticing crumbling walls and arches so covered in ivy they seemed to be nothing more than unusual trees.

"Where is the place you were talking about, Sindri?" Tayt yelled over the screaming of the beast.

"Here!" Sindri shouted back.

"What?"

Sindri didn't listen. Instead, he focused on following Wilden. The renegade hunter paid no mind to the mystery of the crumbling ruins, instead darting between broken walls, trying to find a place to hide.

"Sindri," Tayt said, "we—whoa!"

Ancient stone burst from the ground at Tayt's feet, right where another of the beast's tentacles had hit. She slammed into Sindri, and both of them sprawled forward. They landed at the base of a wall.

The beast was all they could see.

Wind tugging at his black hair and making his eyes sting, Sindri stared up at the thing in defiance. The sky behind it, once as blue as a sparkling gem, was almost pitch black. The trees and the crumbling ruins were shrouded in darkness, and the roaring of the beast was all they could hear.

Tayt seemed unable to move, her firsts clenched so tight, Sindri was certain her fingernails were cutting into her palms. The beast lowered itself closer, its writhing, wispy body flowing between the trees and the vine-shrouded pillars. Its darting black eyes pooled together to stare directly at Sindri as a gash of a mouth tore open, revealing its deadly teeth.

Sill Sindri did not move. He hadn't come this far just to die. He had to think of a way to get out of this. He just had to.

Something felt warm near his chest. Instinctively he felt his pocket. It was the golden scale.

A tentacle surged forward, rushing toward Sindri like a blast of water. Struggling to find the magic words to stop it, Sindri clung to the ivy hanging down the wall behind him and pulled himself up.

But as the tentacle grew near, something happened. Its speed slowed dramatically, as though the creature were hesitating. The wind lessened, and the endless screeching dissipated. The tip of the black tentacle hovered near Sindri, darting over his body as though it were a dog sniffing at a new discovery. It spent quite a bit of time studying Sindri's chest.

Then, to Sindri's astonishment, the tentacle pulled back.

As Tayt clutched at her side, Sindri tilted his head back and watched the dark beast hover. It did not move from its spot, nor did it resume its tantrum of wind and screams. Its eyes swam across its surface, studying Sindri, studying Tayt, studying the ruins.

Slowly, carefully, Sindri reached into his pocket. His fingers found the warm, ridged scale, and he pulled it free.

As he did, everything changed.

It was as though the world had just awoken from a dream. With a whooshing sound like someone letting out a deep breath, the ruins transformed.

It wasn't noticeable at first. Sindri could only *feel* the change, a comforting, magical feeling that warmed him from the tips of his toes all the way to the ends of his shaggy hair.

But then the vines fell free from the walls and the pillars, disappearing into the soil beneath the faded, cracked tile. Trees leaned away from the walls and the pillars, as though pushed aside by unseen giants. The walls, the arches, and the pillars all seemed to double in size as ancient, leaflike carvings unfurled like flowers opening wide to catch the sun.

Most startling and most wonderful of all was when everything began to glow. A shimmering, golden sheen spread over the ruins, starting from where Sindri stood and flowing over the tiles to reach the walls and pillars like a river of sunlight. Ancient carvings were highlighted on the walls in the new light, the tiled floor revealing an intricate scene of ancient magic-users.

Above them, the dark beast shuddered. Tentacles sprouted on its sides, making it seem like some giant, floating jellyfish. But instead of striking out, the beast rose higher into the sky. Its eyes darted back and forth, the shining black orbs reflecting the golden light. Letting out one last roaring wail, the beast turned back to the forest. It tore into the distance, taking with it the blackness that had shrouded the lovely spring sky.

Sindri sat there, watching the beast go, still clutching the golden scale. He could scarcely breathe for what he'd just witnessed. This is it, he thought. At last, he could get some answers.

"Wow," Tayt whispered beside him. She ran a trembling hand through her closely cropped hair. "I don't know what you did, Sindri, but I'm glad you did it."

"I didn't do anything," Sindri said. "It's this place. We're here. We made it." Smiling so broadly he thought his face might actually split in two, Sindri clapped his hands. "We made it!"

Sindri heard footsteps not far away, and Wilden raced around the wall. Skidding to a stop, he grinned in what seemed like actual relief at the sight of the two of them. "You're all right," he said.

"Yes," Tayt said, clutching protectively at her pack. Pressing one hand against the wall to support herself, she scooted her way up to stand. "You're not taking us back," she said.

Wilden sighed and spread his hands out, defeated. "Look, I have a duty, I . . . "

Sindri ignored their bickering, bored by the same old arguments. Mouth agape, he wandered through the ruins. Reverently, he ran his fingers over the shimmering golden walls and the ancient writing that he could see etched into the stone. Something about this place tugged at him. He was a part of the flowering pillars, the intricately carved arches. He belonged here.

"You found!" a voice rasped. "I knew you would. I knew!"

Sindri spun around. There, sitting on a pillar that had fallen in half, was the furry lizard creature. It sat on its hind legs, balancing itself with its thick tail. It tilted its triangular head to the side and blinked its slit amber eyes.

"You!" Sindri said. He stepped closer then held up his hands to calm the thing when it started back as though it would leap away. "You brought me here. Why?"

"Black eyes after you," the creature said, shaking its head. "Chasing, hunting. Bad. You needed to know, kender man. I make you know, before beast gets you. I make you know."

With that, the creature did turn to dart away. Fed up with chasing and questions, Sindri pointed a finger at it and said, *"Capik."*

The creature was midway into a leap when it froze, paralyzed. Before it could fall to the hard tiled floor, Sindri shot out his hand and grabbed it by its thick tail.

Holding it upside down in front of his face so they were eye to eye, Sindri smiled. "Not so fast," he said. *"You* have got some explaining to do."

CHAPTER

13   Temple of Revelation

Holding the paralyzed lizard thing by its tail, Sindri strolled back over the tiled floor to where Tayt glared up at Wilden with her hands propped firmly on her hips.

"You want to know something?" she said, her tone sharp. "You know those slavers? They were taking those gully dwarves to a wizard. A wizard who was going to use them for dark magic. But I bet your Conclave doesn't care one bit about that, does it?"

Wilden crossed his arms and smirked. "No need to be so angry," he said, shaking his head. "If you're right about what you say, then the Conclave won't punish you. But you *were* using magic and stealing from people, and right now that's all we care about."

Tayt snorted. "That's worse than taking slaves and torturing them?"

Sindri cleared his throat, and both humans turned to stare down at him. Unable to move anything else, the lizard creature's eyes darted back and forth, studying them and the shimmering gold temple.

"You know," Sindri said as he walked to stand between the

two, "my old uncle Barty Suncatcher once had a run-in with a pretty snooty Knight of Solamnia. Back then that was pretty rare, since no one liked the knights till the war and all, so Barty was fascinated with the man. But of course, all the knight did was accuse Barty of stealing his things—daggers, steel, the usual. Barty did no such thing, but since he didn't want the knight to be mad at him and not invite him on any more quests, Barty always handed over the daggers and steel from his own pockets, so as to stay friends. After a while, Barty got pretty tired of this and told the knight that no way, no how would he give the knight any more of his own things, and if the knight couldn't learn to keep track of his belongings and stop accusing people of stealing, then he could go jump in the Blood Sea for all he cared."

With Tayt and Wilden both watching him with raised eyebrows, Sindri walked past them. A petal-shaped protrusion from one of the shimmering gold walls was low enough to work as a little chair, and Sindri sat down. He set the rigid, paralyzed lizard creature on his lap and leaned back against the glowing wall.

"Of course," Sindri went on, "the knight was none too pleased about this. See, both Barty and the knight just *knew* they were right, and neither would ever just admit that maybe the other one might have a point. So despite no longer adventuring together as friends, the knight still followed Barty around, and Barty followed the knight around, and whenever they ran into each other accidentally-on-purpose, they did everything they could to make the other's life miserable. Barty would put a bucket of tar above the knight's door when they both stayed at an inn so that the bucket would drop on the knight's head when he left his room. The knight would rip holes in all of Barty's packs so that his belongings would fall as he traveled. And that was just the beginning. It got worse and worse every year. All the kender in the family used to take bets on how far each one would go. They figured Barty was having too much fun with the pranks and that the knight would never admit defeat, so it really could have gone on forever."

"What happened?" Tayt asked.

Sindri shrugged. "One day they argued their way into a cave. They were so busy bickering that they didn't notice that the cave belonged to a manticore. It ate them both and tossed the bits of them it didn't like to the buzzards."

Wilden laughed. "What a heartwarming story."

Tayt scrunched her eyebrows. "What does that have to do with us? That doesn't help anything."

Again Sindri shrugged. "Nothing, but it got you two to stop fighting for a moment, didn't it?"

Tayt sighed and shot a look at Wilden, who was hiding his laughter behind his hands.

"That it did, Sindri," Wilden said.

"Look around!" Sindri said, gesturing toward the beauty of the shimmering walls and arches set against the backdrop of a peaceful spring forest. "We just helped free some slaves, escaped a creature that is intent on killing us, and stumbled into a magical temple, and you two are still worried about your duties or your anger. Wilden, I think if you really wanted to drag us back to the Conclave right this very moment, you're more than capable of using magic and weapons to do so, right?"

Wilden raised a thick, blond eyebrow. "Right."

"And Tayt," Sindri said, "if you weren't curious about what was going on, you'd have run away by now to go find a city to disappear into, right?"

Tayt bit her lip and said nothing. Wilden and Sindri both stared at her expectantly. "All right, all right," she said. "Yes, I'm curious. Someone sent a monster after you, Sindri, and those slavers heading toward . . . Well, I think we should find out what's going on before anything worse happens."

Sindri smiled. "Exactly!"

In his lap, the furry lizard mumbled something, but Sindri couldn't make it out between the creature's frozen lips.

"Just hold on," Sindri said, petting the creature's sleek fur. "You'll be able to talk soon enough."

Calmed down, both Wilden and Tayt studied the ruins. They seemed to be near the exact center. The wall Sindri sat upon crumbled into the forest on one end and ended in a pillar on the other. Jutting from the pillar was half an arch, as though at one point there'd been a doorway there.

Wilden walked close to the wall next to Sindri and traced the etched writing with his fingers. "Hmm," he said, studying it with eyes that sparked with inquisitiveness. "This is old writing, from hundreds of years before the Common language we have now. But I can make some of it out. Something about a dead power . . . no, an old power. From within, not without, it says. A power that was lost that is meant to return." Brushing his windswept blond hair out of his face, Wilden turned his head to look at Sindri. "This is interesting, definitely. What you've managed to do as a kender, it's not supposed to be possible. It's like you have the magic of the dragons."

Sindri's thoughts flashed back to a few years earlier. He, Catriona, and Nearra had been trapped in the lower, long-closed-off area of a tor, an old volcano. There, enclosed in a cavernous room, was the long-dead spirit of a tortured dragon. The spirit blew a circle of mystical smoke around Sindri when Sindri freed him. A gift, the dragon spirit had said.

He'd always been a wizard, hadn't he? But it was true that before the dragon's gift, he hadn't been able to do any of the type of spells he now did with ease. Curious.

"Here," Wilden said, pointing toward another set of the etched writing. "This one talks about another place like this one. South and east, and a dead land? A barren land? Probably a desert. Maybe it means Khur. It says more can be found there."

"Khur," Sindri whispered to himself, remembering the name. He'd been there before, when he and Catriona had traveled with Elidor. They'd found a city created by the evil undead king known as the Defiler.

Near the southern edge of the glimmering ruins, Tayt crouched next to a stream that bubbled through the cracks of the ancient tile floor. Cupping her hands, she took a sip of the water then wiped her mouth with the back of her sleeve.

"There's a lot written over here too," she said, studying the walls. "I don't see anything valuable, but maybe what these say . . . People could study them."

"*I* could study them," Sindri corrected.

"Yes, of course," she said, not looking at him. Crawling toward a nearby wall, she, too, traced the etchings with her fingers. "I have an idea."

Opening her pack, she pulled out a tightly rolled sheaf of parchment and a small cloth pouch. Untying the parchment, she revealed it to be stacks of unused paper. From the pouch she produced two sticks of charcoal.

"See, look," she said. Standing up, she went to the nearest wall and laid the parchment over it. Rubbing the side of the charcoal over the paper, she revealed a perfect copy of the ancient text.

Wilden smiled. "Smart." He walked over to her, grabbed a piece of the parchment and another stick of charcoal, and went to another wall. "Say, where did you get these? These must have been expensive."

Tayt looked away. "Yeah, they were."

Wilden shook his head. "Spellfilches," he muttered.

The lizard creature stirred in Sindri's lap, regaining the use of his limbs. Prepared, Sindri gripped the thing gently beneath its two front arms and held it up at eye level.

"Can you speak now?" Sindri asked.

The creature squirmed, lashing its tail. "Yes," it wheezed. "Yes, I speak. Don't hurt."

"Don't worry," Sindri said with a reassuring nod. "I would never hurt you. I just want to know everything you know."

The creature trembled, its eyes darting into the quiet forest as though expecting someone to be watching. "I no tell," it said. "I can't. They will know."

"Well, let's start with something easy," Sindri said. "Do you have a name?"

The creature's tiny chest heaved, revealing sharp ribs that stuck out beneath its skin. "Rizzek," it said, ducking its head. "Black eyes said I am Rizzek."

"Rizzek?" Sindri repeated. "Is that your name?"

The creature nodded its furry, triangular head.

"Well," Sindri said, "that's a start. What are you? What is that cloud thing that's chasing you? Where did you get the map and the dragon scale, and how did you know to give them to me? How do you even know about me?"

Clenching its tiny claws, Rizzek whimpered. "Too fast," it said. "Too fast."

Sindri sighed. He had so many questions. Peering over his shoulder, he looked back to see Tayt and Wilden working side by side at the walls, making impressions of the etchings. Beyond them and the glowing ruins was more forest. If he looked hard enough, he could almost swear that he could see the dark towers of Cairngorn Keep, waiting for him to come home.

"Well, let's go slow, then," Sindri said, turning back to Rizzek. "What do you know?"

Rizzek started to breathe harder, clearly frightened. "You must go to desert. Temple there, you go there."

"The desert, like it says on the wall?"

Rizzek nodded its tiny head and flicked its tail. "You go there, you find, I know you find. You in trouble, kender man. Things after you. Black eyes sent dark beast. Black eyes send more things."

"Who is 'black eyes'?" Sindri asked.

Rizzek whispered. "Can't say! I say . . . I say no more. But no trust dark wizard, kender man. Dark wizard lies."

"Who?" Sindri asked. "Who is the dark wizard? Is it . . . is it Maddoc?"

Shivering, Rizzek's eyes darted left and right. With a snap of its head, it nipped at Sindri's hand—not enough to hurt him, but enough to startle him. Instinctively letting go, Sindri let Rizzek drop to the tiled floor, where the creature landed expertly on all fours. But instead of running away into the woods, the creature leaped onto Sindri's brown robes. Climbing the cloth, it made its way to Sindri's shoulders, curled around his neck, and buried its head.

"I go with," it mumbled from beneath the cloth. "Tell later."

"All right," Sindri said, patting at Rizzek's back. "You can come with us. I bet you're just as tired of being chased around as I am, huh?"

The creature made a strange noise in its throat in response, somewhere between a purr and a click.

"I think we've got as much as we need," Wilden called from behind Sindri, studying one last piece of charcoaled parchment. "Or, at least, as much as we can take." Rolling it up, he handed it to Tayt. The shorter girl nodded and put it in her pack.

"Now," Wilden said, his look resigned, "the best thing to do is take these to the Conclave. They'll—"

"What?" Tayt snapped. Leaping to her feet, she stomped to stand in front of him. "We already told you we're not going back there. I won't let you. *We* won't let you."

Wilden sighed. He sounded as weary as Sindri felt. "I already told you, I have a duty. I have to report to the Conclave. I have to give you to them as ordered. I don't want to have to hurt you."

Tayt snorted. "You should have thought of that before you decided to become a bounty hunter."

"*Renegade* hunter," Wilden said. "There's no bounty."

Tayt ignored him. Gesturing wildly toward the uprooted trees lining the hill they had just descended, she stomped her foot. "You saw what one of your 'sanctioned' wizards was doing with those gully dwarves. You can't seriously still believe everything the Conclave's told you. The wizard I stole magic from? She has slaves and has done worse things than you can ever imagine. You have no idea the things I've seen."

Wilden shook his head. "Doesn't matter. I have my weapons and my magic again. And trust me, I'm a lot more powerful than you can ever hope to be using stolen magic. Do you really want to face me in a fair fight?"

Tayt sneered. "I took you down once. I can do it again."

"That was a cheap shot," Wilden said. "Did you hear the part about a *fair* fight?"

"What world were you raised in?" Tayt protested. "I've had to live in this one, and one thing I've learned is life never sets up a fair fight. You play dirty, you do what you need to do, or you die. I figured someone like you who attacked people from the shadows would know a thing or two about *that*."

Sindri watched them argue, his head bobbing back and forth between the two as though he were watching a game of toss. He was interested to see what would happen were they to actually fight, but what he was more interested in was getting back to Cairngorn Keep, reuniting with Maddoc, and finding out what exactly all these warnings and etchings meant about him and his powers, especially the part about his powers not being what they seemed.

So as the tall, broad-shouldered renegade hunter and the short, feisty spellfilch continued their useless arguing, Sindri walked calmly to stand before them, raised his hands, and cast a spell.

He didn't use any spells he'd studied, nor did he use any spell components or specific hand motions. What he did was remember the feeling of the swirling power in his gut and thought hard about the two of them being very far apart.

Each cut off midword. It was as though invisible men had seized both Wilden and Tayt by their arms. Shouting in protest, both humans were pulled backward, their feet dragging on the tile, until Tayt slammed against one of the glowing pillars and Wilden stumbled and landed in a patch of the wide-petaled orange flowers.

Standing where they'd been only a moment before, Sindri looked at Tayt then at Wilden. Rizzek purr-clicked from his shoulder.

"I think we've had enough bickering for now," he said to a stunned Wilden. "And I think you'd be best to tell the Wizard's Conclave that, as much as I appreciate their offer to come visit their establishments, I don't really like the way they went about getting me there, and so for now I will have to pass."

Turning to Tayt, he shook his head. "I like you, Tayt. I think you'd fit right in with my friends. But if all you're really looking out for is yourself, then I don't really trust your reasons for saving those gully dwarves, and I don't think you'd really want me or Maddoc helping you. You're welcome to come with me to Cairngorn Keep, but only if you promise you're not going to try anything funny."

Both humans stared at Sindri, completely slack jawed. Sindri, however, felt for the first time a bit of pride about standing up to them. Too often he was accused of taking people at what they told him and not what he saw, but everyone always assumed all kender were stupid, short people who never did anything but run across Krynn like overgrown puppies, stealing anything they could get their hands on.

Well, he'd show them. If he really was special, if he really was something that wasn't supposed to exist, that meant that he could be one of the first kender to show all the people of Krynn that he and his people weren't what everyone made them out to be.

Wilden was the first to recover from Sindri's spell. Brushing himself off, he stood and walked slowly toward Sindri.

"Sindri," he said, "you've surprised me more than I ever thought possible. But the fact still stands that you're a kender wizard and you could cause a lot of trouble. For that reason, you—"

"By the gods, hunter, do shut up."

Sindri stiffened at the voice. It wasn't Tayt, it wasn't him, and it certainly wasn't Rizzek.

Sindri spun around, excitement racing through his bones. Standing there, surrounded by guards and a strange little man Sindri recognized as the Goblin Man, was the one person Sindri knew, just *knew,* was the only one who truly understood him.

Maddoc had found him.

CHAPTER

14   REUNITED

Sindri's trail through the forest had been easier to follow than Maddoc would have imagined.

It started with the wagon in the woods and the destruction of the forest behind it. The farther they went, the closer they got, the more Maddoc felt not only Sindri's pure, untested power shimmering through the underbrush, but also a vast and unknown dark power that crackled through the air in the wake of an unseen force.

He, Arvin, and his guards had stumbled upon the destroyed slaver camp before too long, attracted by the screaming of some creature in the distance. When they'd arrived, they saw trees flattened, burly men lying dead, and dozens of gaunt, grubby gully dwarves climbing out of a fallen wagon into another that still stood, eating whatever food they found there.

Knowing Sindri had to be close, Maddoc stormed away from the destroyed camp, shoving through branches, rounding giant holes in the ground where trees had once grown, not caring that his fine black robes and his neat gray hair became splattered with dirt. Arvin waddled along behind, the guards clomping along in their irritatingly slow fashion. The spindly tracker was nowhere to be found. Maddoc had rid himself of the irksome man.

Then, finally, after several days of worry and anger since the renegade hunter had first shown up at Cairngorn Keep, Maddoc found Sindri.

The kender stood in the middle of what appeared to be the overgrown, crumbling ruins of some long-destroyed temple. A furry creature hung around his neck, and he was scolding two young people Maddoc had never before seen—a short, angry, dark-skinned girl wearing the dirty clothes of a common thief, and a tall, blond-haired man wearing once-fine traveling clothes fitting only of the upper class.

It wasn't until the blond man rose from the patch of orange flowers he'd fallen into, telling Sindri that they needed to go to the Conclave, that Maddoc realized who the man was.

"By the gods, hunter, do shut up," he said, interrupting the renegade hunter's irritating knightlike speech of duty. As he did, Arvin scrambled to his side, the guards stumbling down the hill behind them.

Sindri spun around, his violet eyes wide with surprise. Jumping in glee, the kender lifted up his robes and ran toward him. "Maddoc! You're here!"

Maddoc was surprised to find himself relieved at the sight of his kender apprentice, still alive and well and wandering through long-dead ruins. Smiling as much as he ever allowed himself, he nodded as the kender approached.

"Of course I am," Maddoc said. "You think I would let the Conclave kidnap my apprentice without a fight?"

As Sindri grew near, Maddoc felt the mysterious power that

emanated from him. It was stronger than ever before and so intoxicatingly ancient and mysterious that Maddoc clenched his hands to keep his lust for knowledge at bay. The bones of his dead right hand creaked in protest.

"Oh, Maddoc," Sindri said, bouncing. "So much has happened! At first I thought it was just the Conclave that wanted me, but this giant cloudy jellyfish monster has been ripping apart the forest chasing Rizzek." He paused to point at the sleek, reptilian, fur-covered creature wrapped around his neck. "Then Rizzek gave me a map to this place, and it had all sorts of warnings about someone else who was after me too, someone who knows about me and I guess wants me dead, 'cause then the dark beast came after me. That's how me and Tayt and Wilden ended up here, and when I touched the golden dragon scale, the temple sort of *unfurled* and started to glow and there was writing everywhere and—oh, good, you got your hand back!"

Maddoc stood still, waiting for Sindri's typically rambling story to end. Caught off guard by Sindri's observation, he lifted his hand to stare at it. He hadn't removed the glove since he'd put it on to cover the monstrosity. A scent of decay wafted from beneath the black leather, and still he could feel no sensation in his fingertips.

"Yes," Maddoc muttered, not taking his eyes off his hand. "I suppose I did."

Arvin snorted. Beady eyes open wide, the stocky man leaned down so he was nose to nose with Sindri. "We worked all night to get it back on. Well, Maddoc did. I only observed, since I lack the power he has."

Sindri tilted his head, sending his long black hair rustling over the lizard creature draped over his shoulders. "You're the

Goblin Man," the kender stated. "I remember you. How have you been?"

Arvin leaned back and shrugged. "Same old, same old. Living in a cave, trying to cast magic with disastrous results, pieces and bits of myself turn into goblin parts upon occasion. You?"

Sindri grinned. "Lots. It'd take a whole book to tell you!"

"Maddoc!"

Snapped back to attention, Maddoc held his hands behind his back and turned to face the crumbling, gray temple. The renegade hunter stood at its entrance, seemingly unperturbed. His hands hovered near his sides, where his two scythes hung. Seeing them glimmer in the midday light, Maddoc felt a surge of anger.

"You," he said with a sneer, pushing past Sindri and Arvin to stride forward. "You have much to answer for. I will not stand for a trespasser, kidnapper, and vandal such as yourself to go unpunished."

Still the renegade hunter did not move, nor did he reveal any expression. Behind him, the dark-skinned girl slunk backward into the shadows between the vine-shrouded walls.

"Maddoc," the renegade hunter said again, his voice practiced and professional. "As I was explaining to Sindri, I am bound by my duty to bring him back to the Conclave, especially now that he has discovered this temple. We've taken rubbings of the etchings you see on the walls here. The wizards at the Conclave have vast resources and can quickly get to the bottom of Sindri's powers and what all this means."

Furrowing his brow, Maddoc studied the ruins. If he hadn't had a practiced eye, he wouldn't have noticed them at all, so overgrown were they with underbrush, vines, and trees. The crumbling gray stone beneath the climbing ivy had clearly at one point been pillars and walls, and there seemed to be tile beneath the overgrown grass, but he saw no sign of any etchings.

Shaking his head, he peered back over his shoulder. Arvin and Sindri waited, Arvin with a hideous smile of yellow teeth, Sindri with wide, curious eyes. Behind them, standing in a clump between the trees that rose up the hill, the guards waited, swords drawn.

With a bit of a smile at the edge of his lips, Maddoc turned back around and raised an eyebrow. A breeze flowed at him from the ruins, rustling his black robes.

"Hunter," he said, "do you honestly think that I care what the Conclave has to say, after you nearly burnt down my great hall and destroyed my hand? There is nothing you can do now. You no longer have the element of surprise, and you are clearly outmatched by at least three to one when it comes to magic—four, if my suspicions about that girl hiding in the shadows behind you are correct."

His fingers tensing near the handles of the scythes, the renegade hunter shook his head. "You shouldn't do this, Maddoc," he said. "You'll regret it, I guarantee."

Maddoc raised his other eyebrow. "I don't believe that I will."

Snapping back his left arm, he held his hand high in signal. The guards rose to attention at once. Armor clanging, they shoved past Arvin and Sindri and came to Maddoc's side.

One of them—the fat one with the crooked nose, as Maddoc knew him—pointed at the renegade hunter with his sword. "Is that him?" he asked, his voice nasally. "Is that the one who attacked us?"

"That's him," Maddoc responded. "Have fun."

Narrowing his squinty eyes, the fleshy guard raised his sword high and let out a nasal whine that Maddoc supposed was his battle cry. The other half dozen guards joined in, racing as one toward the hunter.

The blond man didn't hesitate. The silver, cresent-shaped scythes were in his hands in an instant. He watched with passive blue eyes as the guards ran to surround him.

Mumbling a phrase, the renegade hunter stretched his hands out. A shimmering bubble of white burst from his body on all sides, hitting the guards and bouncing them backward.

The guards at the rear managed to maintain their balance and avoid their fallen comrades. The renegade hunter reared back into an attack position. The first guard to reach him let out a strangled cry and slashed wildly with his sword. Steel met steel with a clang as the hunter blocked the blow, trapped the blade between his two scythes, and slammed the hilt into the guard's chest. Gasping, the guard stumbled backward, slipping on the grass and falling on his backside.

Maddoc watched with rapidly dwindling calm as the renegade hunter continued to expertly block his guards' attacks. Two of them brought their swords down at once, but the hunter disappeared in a burst of shadow. The two guards' blades met the tiled floor with jarring clangs, sending up sparks. Almost instantaneously, the renegade hunter appeared behind them, grabbed them both by their hair, and slammed their heads together with a crack that echoed through the trees.

As the remaining guards continued their worthless attacks, and as the renegade hunter continued to flip and spin and evade every last blow, Maddoc couldn't help but clench his fists in anger.

It figured he'd have to do it himself.

His left hand arched like a bird's talons, Maddoc strode toward the oblivious renegade hunter fighting between the crumbling pillars. His lips twisted as words of dark magic tumbled through, the sound and shape of the words leaving his mind as he spoke them, as they were apt to do.

Before Maddoc could get two steps, however, he was stopped by a tugging at his black robes. His spell interrupted, he sneered and looked down. "Let go!"

Startled, Sindri did as he was told, his innocent face clearly clouded with hurt.

As the sounds of fighting continued ahead of him, Maddoc let out a sigh. As calmly as he could, he asked, "What is it?"

Sindri bobbed his head. "Maddoc, don't hurt Wilden. He's not all bad, just a little bit too loyal, maybe. There's got to be another way."

Maddoc couldn't help but snort. "There is no other way, Sindri. This man was trained as a child to do nothing but use magic, fight, and follow the Conclave's every word without question. He will not stop chasing you until he's completely incapacitated."

"But, Maddoc, I—"

Arvin appeared behind Sindri and clutched at the kender's arms with hands that had shriveled into red claws. "Never question your master," the jowly man hissed in Sindri's ear. "He knows best."

Done coddling the kender, Maddoc turned, raised his hand high, and began muttering a different spell. By then only two of the guards remained conscious, but seeing as how the renegade hunter was swinging around a pillar in the center of the ruins and lashing out with expert kicks, Maddoc was certain that wouldn't last long.

Power flared over Maddoc's outstretched hand, a glowing mist of deadly magic that pulsed red and black, as he wound his way past his fallen guards. He muttered the last few phrases of the murderous spell as he reached the point where the grassy forest floor met the cracked tile of the long-destroyed temple. He'd rid himself of the renegade hunter once and for all.

Something hard and invisible slammed into Maddoc's face. With a cry of surprise, he stepped back and dropped his hand, his new spell ruined as well.

Clutching at his nose, he looked straight ahead into the over-grown ruins. The renegade hunter was still distracted with the two guards, so he couldn't have cast a spell. Reaching out tenta-tively, Maddoc tried to pass his hand over the border between forest and temple.

His hand met something solid, tingling with magic. As his fingers passed over this invisible barrier, he saw the scene of the temple's ruins flicker between the overgrown pillars he'd seen only moments before and a different set of ruins, one that shimmered golden in the sunlight. But the flickering image of the other temple lasted only a moment, and Maddoc lowered his hand.

First one, then the other guard flew past Maddoc on either side, landing in unconscious heaps next to their companions. The renegade hunter stood before Maddoc in the temple's ruins, his chest heaving with effort and his blond hair wild about his young face. Despite this, his features revealed no sign of strain. Maddoc clenched his jaw, barely containing his anger.

"What was it you were saying about not regretting this?" the renegade hunter said, his lips curled into a gleeful grin.

Maddoc did not give the annoying renegade hunter the benefit of a response. Instead, he watched as the girl who had sneaked up behind him swung a thick branch. The makeshift club met the young man's skull with a crack, and he crumpled to the ground.

The girl—the short, dark-skinned one Maddoc had seen hiding earlier—dropped the club on the fallen hunter's back with a look of disdain. "For all his skills," she said, "he never thinks to look behind him."

A blur of brown robes and shaggy black hair raced by Maddoc—Sindri. The kender leaped to the renegade hunter's side, apparently not affected by whatever barrier that kept Maddoc from entering the temple or seeing what Sindri, the girl, and the renegade hunter had seen. Crouching next to him, Sindri poked gently at the cut on the hunter's head.

Behind him, Maddoc heard groans as the guards awakened. Almost silently, Arvin sidled next to Maddoc to join in watching Sindri tend to the man who had kidnapped him.

"I don't suppose," Maddoc said in a low voice, "that you see a glowing, golden temple here, do you?"

Arvin looked left and right. "Where?" he asked.

"Didn't think so."

Apparently satisfied that the renegade hunter was fine, Sindri stood and looked over at Maddoc. "Please don't kill him," he pleaded. "Tayt knocked him out for you. Can't we just put him in the dungeons until this all blows over?"

Maddoc clenched his right hand. As always, the bones creaked, as though they were the hinges of an unoiled gate. He wanted to lash out at the kender, chide him for befriending someone so dangerous to their cause. He wanted to leap through the invisible barrier and rip out the heart of the cocky man who'd disfigured him.

But he was a refined wizard. Lately, he'd let his anger get the best of him on more than one occasion. It was not fitting of a man of his age or status. What was important was making sure Sindri did not lose his trust in him, did not abandon him before Maddoc knew what power the kender possessed.

After a long moment, Maddoc nodded. "As you wish, Sindri," he said. "We will keep him alive."

"Oh good!" Suddenly remembering the girl, Sindri turned to tug at her arm. The girl clutched her pack to her chest and held back, seeming unwilling to get any closer to either Maddoc or Arvin.

"This is Tayt," Sindri said. "She's a spellfilch that Wilden captured too. I was going to help her hide for a few days so that her awful master wouldn't be able to find her."

Gray eyes stern and wary, the girl nodded in greeting.

Maddoc tried not to sigh. Sindri had a knack for finding new friends wherever he went. Though Maddoc had quite enjoyed seeing the girl knock the renegade hunter upside the head, if she was anything like Sindri's previous companions, she'd likely prove bothersome. But he supposed she couldn't cause too much trouble in a few days.

"That's fine," Maddoc said, returning her nod. "I am Sindri's master and mentor, Maddoc. This is a friend of ours, Arvin Derry."

Arvin stepped forward. His ears rose into ragged, batlike flaps as he leered at the girl. "Pleasure to make your acquaintance," he said, then let out a high-pitched giggle.

The girl stared at him with bewilderment. "Thank you," she mumbled.

"Where's that blasted hunter?" The fleshy guard popped up at Maddoc's side, eyes wide and hands clenched with fury. The others came to his side, rubbing at their heads.

"There," Maddoc said, waving a dismissive hand at the fallen form of the renegade hunter. "We're keeping him alive for now. Make sure he is securely tied up, and confiscate his weapons."

The guard nodded and led his companions to do as instructed.

As Sindri whispered to Tayt in the crumbling temple, all the while stroking the fur of the lizard creature that still sat with its head burrowed beneath Sindri's robes, Maddoc turned to Arvin.

The Goblin Man flashed his yellow teeth. "That went well," he said. "Due not at all to my help, as usual. Where to next?"

Maddoc looked south, beyond the crumbled temple riddled with secrets, over the thick forest, to where he knew Cairngorn Keep lay—to where his experiments could once again resume.

A slight smile tugged at Maddoc's lips. "Home."

CHAPTER

15   UNANSWERED QUESTIONS

They set out immediately from the ruined temple, hiking late into the night until they finally neared Cairngorn Keep. Remembering that Nearra used to live around the area north of the keep, Sindri kept an eye out for a woodsman's hut that might belong to her family, but Maddoc insisted on avoiding as many people as possible.

As soon as they reached the keep, the guards dragged the awake but tied and gagged Wilden deep into the underground dungeons. Sindri had never really ventured there, for the dank, dark cells usually contained absolutely nothing of interest.

Maddoc called for his servants and had the grouchy dwarf Nitty usher Tayt upstairs to one of the guest rooms. Sindri, not feeling tired in the least despite the late hour, bounced excitedly next to Maddoc, begging to discuss the previous few days' events. But Maddoc sent him off to bed, promising a full discussion the next day.

Finally back in his cozy, comfortable room, Sindri first set up a little pillow in the corner near his wardrobe and lay Rizzek there to curl up and sleep. Then, resigned that his aching curiosity would have to wait until morning, Sindri curled beneath his covers.

Hazy light washed over him after what seemed like only a few moments. He didn't even remember falling asleep. Breakfast was already waiting, so he ate, washed his face at the basin filled with steaming water, and pulled on a fresh robe. Stuffing the magic map and the golden dragon scale into one of his new pockets, he leaned next to the wardrobe and tried to wake Rizzek. The lizard thing only curled itself up into a ball and clenched its eyes tighter. Not exactly sure what it ate, he left an apple and some leftover eggs on a plate on the table.

Then, finally, the morning routine was done. Lifting up the hem of his robe, Sindri burst through his bedroom door, almost knocking over a young servant girl who usually attended at dinner.

"Sorry!" he shouted over shoulder.

Sindri found Maddoc in his study, located in the top room of the keep's southern tower. Not bothering to knock, he burst through the heavy wooden doors and skidded to a stop on the ornate rug that covered the black stone floor.

"With all your enthusiasm last night, I expected you sooner."

Maddoc sat in a large, padded leather armchair in front of a fireplace. Flames roared in the hearth. Not turning to look at Sindri, the wizard's hands traced absentmindedly over the carvings that decorated the armchair's wooden limbs. Next to him, on a side table, sat a decanter of brown liquid and a small crystal cup.

"I guess I was more tired than I thought." Regretful at having disturbed his master's silence, Sindri crept farther into the study, closing the door behind himself. The room was rather small, as the keep's rooms went, but the warm fire and the decor made the room seem cozy rather than cramped. Curved bookshelves lined the walls, and smaller versions of Maddoc's large chair were set on the other side of the room for reading. In the back corner, near a window that showed the pine forests that surrounded the keep, Sindri noticed what looked like a birdcage covered with a black cloth, hanging from a hook.

Maddoc uncapped the crystal decanter and poured some of the liquid into his cup. Lifting the cup—with a hand covered in a black leather glove, though the wizard had never worn it before—Maddoc swirled the drink while staring at a tapestry that hung above the fireplace.

Sindri followed his gaze. The tapestry depicted a woman dressed in an ancient, royal green gown. Jet black hair hung long down her back, and her pale face, while lovely and regal, was taut with a fierce determination. A golden amulet hung from her neck and at her feet lay a slender sword with emerald flecks embedded in its blade.

He'd seen the tapestry many times. But only now, seeing the deadly gaze of her violet eyes, did he realize he knew the woman the tapestry depicted.

"That's Asvoria!" Sindri scrambled in front of Maddoc to get a closer look. There was a dark stain in the tapestry's lower corner. Surely Maddoc could have gotten it cleaned at some point. Sindri wondered why he hadn't.

"Yes," Maddoc said. Sindri turned to look at the wizard's lined face. Somehow, his hair and neatly trimmed beard seemed peppered with even more gray than before.

"You have no idea, Sindri," Maddoc went on. He paused to take a sip of his drink, his eyes never leaving the tapestry. Sindri waited as patiently as possible, feeling the heat of the fire at his back as the burning logs crackled and popped.

Maddoc lowered his glass and took a breath. "Years I spent

working on my Asvoria project," he said. "As soon as I read about her, I knew she had secrets that could change the world if discovered. As soon as I entered this room for the first time, as soon as I saw this tapestry, I was consumed . . . possessed with the idea that I needed to know what she knew."

Sindri nodded. He understood that feeling quite a bit. "Davyn, Cat, Nearra, Elidor, and me, we kind of ruined it for you, didn't we?"

Amused, Maddoc smiled. He set his drink to the side, his gloved right hand still absentmindedly tracing the carvings on his chair. "Yes, you and your companions did cause quite a bit of trouble. But in the end, Asvoria was the one who did me in. She even claimed that she controlled me from her tapestry, arranging for her release."

"Wow," Sindri said. Sitting down cross-legged on the plush carpet, he stared up at Maddoc reverently. "Do you believe that?"

Maddoc furrowed his brow. "I'm an old man, Sindri," he said. "I spent thirty-five years studying Asvoria. I can't believe that everything I did was because I was bewitched, or else my life was wasted. But I've moved on." Maddoc lowered his gaze from the tapestry, his blue eyes boring directly into Sindri's own.

"I've moved on," he said, "to studying you and your powers."

It was almost as though Maddoc had read the question from Sindri's mind. All through the journey home to Cairngorn Keep the day before, his mind had raced to understand all the new revelations. He was different, that was what the map and the temple said. It was what *everyone* said. His powers were something unique to anyone on Krynn. And yet Maddoc had never told him about it. Maddoc was his friend, he knew, but he couldn't help but remember Rizzek's vague warning: *Dark wizard lies to you.*

"You knew, then?" Sindri asked with a tilt of his head. "That I was different?"

Maddoc nodded. "I knew the moment you entered my keep and started casting spells. It wasn't possible, and yet there you were, conjuring and casting without use of any artifact. I came to like you, Sindri, so I wanted to help you develop your power . . . and perhaps learn a bit more about it myself. The one thing I sensed about it right away was that it was ancient, an old power. That interested me quite a bit."

"You knew this whole time and never said something?" Sindri jumped to his feet and ran a hand through his long hair. "How was I supposed to ever develop my magic if you never told me that I wasn't a normal wizard? Was I just an experiment . . . like *her?*" He flung a hand back at the tapestry of Asvoria, the long-dead sorceress watching over them with unseeing amethyst eyes.

Sighing, Maddoc lowered his bearded chin to his chest and steepled his fingers in front of his stomach, as though thinking carefully about what to say. Sindri bounced in place, wanting anxiously to hear his response but unsure if he actually wanted to know the truth if it were what he suspected.

"You were never 'just an experiment,' Sindri," Maddoc said finally. "All these goings-on about your powers—where they came from, what they are—I am still a long way from understanding them. I planned to tell you once I actually had something to tell. I knew nothing of the ruined temple you stumbled upon, or we would have traveled there long ago."

Smiling in relief, Sindri ran to the side of Maddoc's chair. "I knew it," he said. "I knew you were planning on telling me. Cat was wrong about you."

Maddoc raised one of his bushy eyebrows. "Oh?"

"Oh," Sindri said with a shrug, "it's nothing. She just didn't want to send me here by myself. Even after everything we all went through together, she still thought we couldn't trust you. But I told her she was just being overly cautious. You know Cat."

The wizard nodded and looked into the fire. The flames reflected in his eyes, casting them in red. "Yes, I do know Cat."

"Well," Sindri said, "now that we've got all that settled, we have to leave at once! I found out a whole lot on this trip, so at least it wasn't wasted. I think we're supposed to head to Khur, that there's another temple there. It'll probably tell me even more about what's going on, and that would help in your studies. Let's see, maybe the map says something."

Sindri pulled out the map to unfold it when Maddoc's right hand shot out and grabbed the kender's arm. Sindri was startled by the man's grip through the leather. Something didn't feel quite right about the fingers clasped around his wrist, as though the flesh were too soft and the bones were sticking through. He also noticed a strange smell, kind of a sickeningly sweet scent that was rotten at the same time.

Maddoc shook his head, sending gray hair swaying. "We shouldn't rush into anything, Sindri. We're still unsure what's going on. Someone is clearly after you. For all we know, they sent that lizard creature—"

"Rizzek," Sindri interrupted.

"Yes, Rizzek," Maddoc said. "For all we know, they sent Rizzek to you with that map and the dragon scale as a trap, to lure you toward that dark monster and kill you. We don't yet know if we can trust any of the writings you found in that temple, let alone know whether we can trust that we should follow their directions. We don't want to run off into a wasteland like Khur if it's all someone's dark plan to capture you. Don't you agree?"

Shrugging, Sindri tried not to show his disappointment. "I suppose you're right," he said. "There are lots of little things that happened too, that I should probably tell you before we make plans."

"Exactly." Letting go of Sindri's wrist, the old wizard leaned around to pour himself another glass of his drink. "Why don't you leave the map and the dragon scale with me for this morning, Sindri?" he said. "I will study them and determine their authenticity. Later today, perhaps we can go over the rubbings you took and see if we can't decipher them and also discuss your journey a bit more. Does that sound all right?"

It didn't sound all right, but Sindri didn't want to disobey his master and mentor, especially since he knew how much effort the wizard had been putting into finding out more about Sindri's powers, all just to help him.

Without saying anything, Sindri nodded his consent. Maddoc held out his hand expectantly. Sindri folded the map and placed it in the wizard's gloved hand, then pulled the golden dragon scale from his pocket and set it on top.

"Good," Maddoc said, a smile on his lips. "You should go find your friend. What was her name?"

"Tayt."

"Yes, Tayt. Go find Tayt and see about getting those rubbings. She had them in her pack, correct?"

Sindri nodded.

"Good. We will meet again here after lunch, once I have had time to perform a few warding spells on these"—he held up the map and the scale—"just to be safe. Until then?"

Sindri forced a smile. "Until then."

Leaving Maddoc to his thoughts and his drink, Sindri stepped through the door and shut it quietly behind himself. Though the hallway was carpeted and lit torches lined the black stone walls, it suddenly felt much colder in the keep.

Taking it slow is fine, Sindri thought. Maddoc knows best, after all. Once he says we're ready, I'll get to go to Khur. It's not like I'll never get to find out everything, right?

Not convinced, Sindri raced down the hallway to the spiraling steps that led down into the main floors of the keep to find Tayt.

Maddoc did not move until he was certain Sindri was no longer outside the door. Clenching the map and the glimmering, golden dragon scale in his dead right hand, he lifted his snifter of brandy with the left and took a sip. Once again he found his eyes studying the familiar image of Asvoria, the woman's gaze a deadly reminder of his past failures.

Finishing off the drink, he set the cup down and rose from the padded leather chair. The fire at his back, he walked purposefully toward the birdcage that had once held his beloved falcon familiar, Shaera.

Pulling free the black cloth that covered the cage, he revealed the undead creature he'd brought into existence only a few days before. The skeletal falcon opened its hard, pale beak and squawked. Watching Maddoc with glowing red eyes, it flapped its wings of bone and wire as though attempting to fly.

"*Tanda burun*," Maddoc intoned, waving his left hand in front of the cage. "*Sestana det belit*."

A pinprick of black pulsed within the undead bird's rib cage. It beat like a heartbeat, once, twice, then began to swell. Black mist seeped between the falcon's bones, surrounding the skeleton with mystical feathers. In moments the skeleton became a wispy bird of shadow.

Unlatching the cage's door, Maddoc opened it wide then turned the cage so it faced the nearby window.

"Take wing," he whispered to the bird. "You are my new Shaera. I need you to be my eyes where I cannot see."

The undead falcon screeched and bobbed its misty, glowing head. It cocked its head and met Maddoc's gaze with one of its fiery red eyes. Then, with another predatory screech, the bird flapped its misty wings and flew out the window, circling up into the gray sky.

The spell done, Maddoc turned back toward the fireplace. Striding past the reading chairs and shelves of books, he walked around his armchair to stand directly in front of the flames. Unemotional, he watched the logs crumble to ash.

With a flick of his wrist, he tossed both the folded map and the golden dragon scale into the fire. He stood there, arms crossed, watching the edges of the parchment blacken and curl, the golden scale char and bubble from the heat.

With a knowing smile, the wizard turned from the flames and left the study, certain at last that his plans were back on track.

CHAPTER

16   RUNNING FROM THE PAST

Hey there, watch where you're going!"

Sindri bounded around a corner, almost running directly into Nitty, who was busy dusting a set of ancient black armor that was on display in the hallway. The dwarf leaped back, her gray bun pulling her stern features tight. She brandished her feather duster like a sword and shook it at Sindri.

"Blasted kender," she said, "never looking where you're going."

"Sorry, Nitty!" Sindri said as he skidded to a stop. "Have you seen Tayt?"

The dwarf put her hands on her considerable hips. "Who?"

"The girl from yesterday. She came back with us. Remember?"

"Oh, her." The dwarf turned back to the armor, dusting its plate-mail chest. Apparently ticklish, the armor shuddered and let out a grunt.

"Shut up, you," Nitty said with a smack to the armor's side. Resuming her dusting, she glared over at Sindri. "She's up in one of the guest rooms. I put her in the one across from your room."

"Thanks, Nitty!" Sindri bounded down the wide hallway,

racing past more sets of armor and the display of ancient weapons Maddoc had arranged decoratively on the black stone walls. Behind him he heard Nitty hit the side of the armor again with a loud clang, muttering something about hare-brained kender and irritating magical armor.

Sindri was breathless by the time he reached the top of the spiraling staircase that led up to the hallway where his room was. Thumping over the carpeted floor, he made his way to the room across from his own. Murmuring voices slipped through the slightly ajar door. Curious, he pushed the door open as quietly as he could.

At first all he saw was the bed and the wardrobe—the room was laid out similarly to Sindri's own. As he opened the door further, he caught sight of one of the black-haired serving girls, probably the one he'd almost run into earlier that morning. For the first time that Sindri could remember, the thin-faced girl was smiling as she laughed at some joke that Sindri hadn't heard.

Stepping all the way into the room, Sindri saw that the servant girl was in fact helping Tayt button up a dress—an old yet attractive violet gown that must have come from Asvoria's old collection. Fingers playing with the multicolored gem that hung from the silver chain around her neck, Tayt watched herself in the mirror as the servant girl buttoned the last pearl button up her back.

"Wow, you sure look different."

"Sindri!" Tayt spun abruptly away from the servant girl. The servant girl stepped backward and bowed her head, her smile completely gone.

"Uh, thank you, Rienne," Tayt said with a gentle touch to the girl's arm. Nodding swiftly and sending stringy black hair bouncing over her shoulders, the drably dressed servant girl brushed past Sindri and out into the dark hallway.

"Her name is Rienne?" Sindri asked. He walked to Tayt's unmade bed and leaped to sit upon it. Bouncing on the bed's edge, he tilted his head. Curious that he'd never found out the serving girl's name before. Usually that would have been the first thing he'd have done. All his time studying with Maddoc sure had changed him, he realized. He wasn't sure if that was a good thing.

Seemingly embarrassed by her new clothes, Tayt self-consciously tugged at the bodice hugging her sides. With her freshly scrubbed face and brushed short hair, she seemed like some exotic noble.

"Yes," Tayt said, her hand once again rubbing the gem at her throat. "They took my traveling clothes to wash them and insisted I wear this. I asked for one of the servant's dresses, but that dwarf woman seemed cross at the thought."

"You look really pretty," Sindri said with a smile. "Looking like that, I bet you could go run off and marry some prince and no one would question whether you were royalty or not."

Tayt laughed and shook her head. "I doubt it," she said. "I don't think I'm suited for royal, married life. And this dress is too long anyway. Rienne promised to bring back my normal clothes soon."

Lifting up the flowing hem, Tayt walked to the bed and sat down next to Sindri. "I suppose you talked to your master about everything that happened?"

Sindri nodded. "He wants to study all the stuff we found before we go running off anywhere. I guess it makes sense, but I was really hoping to go to Khur."

Tayt shook her head violently. "No, you really don't. I used to live near there. It's definitely not a place you'll want to travel."

Crawling backward onto the plush bedsheets, Sindri crossed his legs and tilted his head to the other side. "You know, for someone who tries to hide her past, you sure keep accidentally mentioning it a lot. Can't you tell me where you're from and why you're on the run?"

Tayt leaned back and met Sindri's look with conflicted gray eyes. For a moment, she didn't say anything. Beyond her a pale white curtain fluttered in the midmorning breeze.

Finally, Tayt let out a sigh. "What have you guessed so far?"

"Well," Sindri said, scratching at his black hair in thought. "I noticed that necklace of yours, and the way you carry yourself. You seem awful practiced at noble life, and right at home in a place like this keep. So my guess is that you were a princess somewhere distant and exotic, and you lived in a palace and were sheltered and you hated every minute of it. Your parents tried to make you marry a half-ogre or something, so you ran away, met an awful wizard, stole some of her stuff, and now you're here. Am I right?"

Tayt laughed. "Not quite," she said. "I'm certainly no noble, and trust me, if I were some sort of princess, I would never have run away."

"What, then?" Sindri asked.

Tayt shrugged and bit her lip. "I . . . I was a slave. A servant, I mean, like Rienne. I don't really know where I'm from. All I know is that I was young and traveling with my parents here in Solamnia when . . . well, bandits attacked us."

"Oh no," Sindri said. Leaning forward on his knees, he gave her a concerned look. "Did they get hurt?"

Tayt swallowed and looked down. "Yes," she said. "They did. The bandits, they took me with them and they sold me. To *her*."

"The wizard you talked about?" Sindri said. "The one with the slavers?"

Tayt nodded. "I grew up in her keep. It was all right at first, but the wizard, she started to go a bit . . . insane. I was curious about magic, so I started to read her books. I found this necklace and when I put it on, it helped me cast spells. I used to pretend sometimes, when I was in my room, that maybe I *was* a princess. Like a wizard princess who lived on her own and didn't do dark magic. Things were fine for a while, but then . . . she found out."

Sindri nodded knowingly. If Maddoc was any example, wizards hated people going through their things and discovering their secrets. When Sindri had first come to live at Cairngorn Keep, Maddoc was always scolding him for going into rooms he wasn't supposed to go into, and he was Maddoc's apprentice. Imagine if one of the servants had been so bold!

Jumping down from the bed, Tayt walked across the plush carpet to stand once more in front of the full-length mirror. "I ran away," she said. "I had to. It was hard being on my own in the towns and cities at first, but I used to have to fight with some of the other servants over meals, so I knew how to handle myself when the street thugs tried to attack. Once I started using magic to . . . to steal, I managed to get by pretty easy. I never stayed in one place too long, just to be safe." She sighed. "But she found me anyway."

Sindri bounced once, then twice, then right off the bed. Scrambling to Tayt's side, he looked up at her. "That sounds exciting," he said. "Traveling from place to place, getting to use magic without anyone trying to tell you what you can and can't do."

Brow furrowed, Tayt gave Sindri a look. "I lived on the streets with rats," she said. "Not exactly a life of luxury."

Sindri shrugged. "Better than being a slave."

"I suppose." Tayt shook her head. "I just wish I knew what exactly was going on. I expected her to try and have me captured, but to then stumble upon slavers she'd hired? I have to wonder if maybe you and me being taken at the same time wasn't just a coincidence."

"Rizzek knows," a raspy voice said from behind them. "Black eyes sent beast. Black eyes wanted kender man alive. She wanted thief girl dead."

Sindri and Tayt spun around to find Rizzek peeking around the bottom corner of the door. It blinked its wide amber eyes, its slit pupils narrowing in the daylight that shone through the windows.

"Rizzek!" Sindri said. He dropped to his knees so as to be more at the tiny creature's level. "Did you get to eat? I wasn't sure what you liked, so I left a little bit of everything."

Nodding its head vigorously, Rizzek opened its triangular jaw in a jagged-toothed smile. "I got," it said. "I thank you."

Grasping at the carpet with its black claws, the lizard creature crept into the room. Its fur-covered tail lashed out behind it as it warily studied the corners.

"You know something more than what you told Sindri at the ruins?" Tayt asked. She crossed her arms and gave Rizzek a hard look. "Are you going to tell us more than riddles now?"

With a sudden leap, the creature jumped to Sindri's shoulder. Startled, Sindri jumped to his feet.

"Yes," Rizzek rasped from its perch on Sindri's shoulder. "Yes, I tell. Safe here."

Near the wardrobe was a low table, just as in Sindri's room. Sitting in one of the chairs, Sindri gently lifted Rizzek from his shoulders and set the creature on the table. "All right," he said. "Start at the beginning. What did, er, 'black eyes' do?"

Bobbing its head nervously, the creature scratched at its sleek brown fur. "Black eyes, she wanted test. She wanted to capture kender man and kill thief girl with beast. She wanted to make sure beast work first. The man, he made map and scale for her. Scale like kender man, he said. Someone with scale would no be hurt by beast if spells worked, so beast no hurt kender man."

"A test?" Sindri asked.

Tayt clenched her jaw. "The gully dwarves, Sindri. If that scale was supposed to mimic you, they probably planned to give one to a dwarf and let it and the others run free. If the dark beast killed the rest and left the one with the scale alive, then they'd know the dark beast could do the job right."

Rizzek's head bobbed up and down in agreement. "Thief girl right," it said. "Black eyes, she want kender man taken by beast and thief girl to be there too. She went to wizards and send them to get kender man and thief girl."

So their suspicions had been correct. Something big was going on, something bigger than the Conclave. Whoever 'black eyes' was, she wanted Sindri and was willing to unleash a hideous monster to kill everything in its path to get him.

"Why me?" Sindri asked. "How did this wizard know about me?"

Rizzek shrugged its bony shoulders. "Don't know. Man who made map and scale, he told me secrets. He said kender man need saving from black eyes. He told me scale and map were not for black eyes, but for kender man, and to take them and run. I did what man say. I steal and run to find kender man. But beast, it come after me."

Tayt nodded and met Rizzek's eyes. "So she set it up to have both me and Sindri taken at the same time. She was going to test the beast using the gully dwarves, but you took the map and the dragon scale before she could, and then it chased you instead. That's when we saw you in the woods the first time."

"The man," Sindri said. "Do you know his name? Who he was or how *he* knew about me?"

Rizzek shook its furry head. "Don't know name. He told me what warnings to say to you. He said message on map, power of scale, and temple would only be for you. Then man go away."

Sindri shoved away the chair and jumped to his feet. Leaning on the table, he stared Rizzek straight in its catlike eyes. "That can't be it," he said. "Didn't the man say anything else? What he wanted me to do now that I found the temple?"

Shrinking back at Sindri's sudden move, the lizard creature let out a low rumbling in its chest. "Sorry," it said. "Sorry. I not mean to make mad. Don't hurt."

Sighing, Sindri leaned back. "No, I'm sorry," he said, reaching forward to pet the creature's sleek fur. "I didn't mean to scare you. It's just, the more answers I find, the more questions I have. But can you remember? Did the man say anything else?"

Rizzek closed its eyes and purr-clicked as Sindri scratched behind its shoulder. "He say you need follow instructions at place you find," it rasped. "You find new place, you find more."

"Khur!" Sindri turned to Tayt and grinned. "That's it, then. This 'black eyes' must have found out about me and wanted to exploit my powers, and somehow that man found out and decided to help. I bet if we translate those etchings, we can get directions to the next temple in Khur."

Tayt swallowed. "Anica," she said. At Sindri's questioning look, she said, "That's her name, the wizard Rizzek's talking about. The servants, we used to call her 'black eyes' when we talked about her. Her eyes . . . they're not normal."

"Ooh," Sindri said. "That sounds interesting. I'd like to see what she looks like."

"Trust me," Tayt said, "you really don't. And you don't want to go to Khur, either. Temple or no, that place is dangerous. And that's where Anica lives."

Distracted, Sindri wasn't ready when Rizzek leaped to land upon his shoulder. Stumbling backward, Sindri thumped against the bed.

"I sorry." Rizzek's voice was muffled, its head once again hidden under Sindri's robes.

"It's all right," Sindri said, patting reassuringly at the creature that sat on his shoulders. "So all that's happened to us the past few days was because of one wizard. She arranged to have us kidnapped so that she could use that beast to capture me and kill you. That still doesn't explain why these people care about me at all, or what the temple meant about me having an old and ancient power, like the dragons."

Tayt shrugged and turned to stare out the window. "Anica has always done strange experiments, creating creatures in her laboratories, but nothing like that thing that attacked us and chased us through the woods. You've studied magic as long as me, Sindri. You know creating something like that involves intense dark magic. I don't think Anica was working alone. Maybe someone else is behind all this. All I know is it seems everyone wants only one thing, and that's to be the one controlling *you*. Your powers must be pretty special for everyone to go through so much trouble."

Leaping to Tayt's side, Sindri stuck his hands on his hips. "Then let's go, then! No point in waiting around to see who comes after me next. Let's find that next temple, face Anica, and get to the bottom of all this."

Raising her hands, Tayt backed away. "Hey, this is about you, not me," she said. "All Anica wanted to do was kill me for stealing from her and making her look like a fool. I'm not going back there and making it easy for her."

"But, Tayt—" Sindri started.

Shaking her head, the girl turned away.

Tugging at her gown, Sindri stomped his foot. "Tayt, you can't just run forever, can you? Anica went to a lot of trouble not just to get me, but to get you too. She won't give up, not from what you've said. We wouldn't just be stopping her from getting me, we'd be stopping her from getting you *and* stopping her from taking more slaves and torturing them. Like those gully dwarves, remember?"

Tayt stiffened at the mention of the dwarf slaves, her gray eyes clouding with anger. For a moment she continued to look through the wispy curtains at the gray sky beyond.

"Maybe," she said after a moment. "Maybe . . . I just don't know, Sindri. I've been running for so long."

Sindri shrugged. "I just think it might be nice not to have to run away for the rest of your life. Don't you think?"

Tayt smiled, though her eyes seemed sad. "Yes," she said. "That might be nice."

Spinning around with sudden energy, Tayt studied the comfortable room they stood in. Apparently finding what she was looking for, she ran to a corner near the door. There, hanging from a hook, was her pack.

Tayt took a deep breath. "All right," she said as she pulled the pack down from the wall. "Now I'm not making any promises, Sindri, but for now I guess I can at least help you figure out where to go. And if you're serious about going to face Anica herself, I can tell you how to get to her and explain what the inside of her keep looks like so you don't get lost. Does that sound all right?"

Clapping his hands, Sindri couldn't help but jump in glee. Finally they were getting somewhere. "It sounds great!"

Tayt stifled a laugh and shook her head. "You know, Sindri, sometimes you seem positively *normal.* But other times you're clearly a kender, through and through."

Thrusting his brown robes behind him extravagantly, he bowed low. "Why, thank you. Being normal all the time would be a bore."

"You're very welcome. Now here." Strolling back across the room, she held out the rolled pieces of parchment that were covered with the black charcoal rubbings. "I guess you'll want to show those to your master."

"Of course!" Sindri said as he took the pages from her. "Maddoc said he'd do anything to help me. With what we know now, we can probably set out for Khur first thing tomorrow." Reaching up to pet Rizzek, Sindri followed Tayt's gaze as she once again looked out the window. "What are you looking at?" he asked.

Tayt's eyes darted toward Sindri. "Just looking," she said with a shrug. At Sindri's insistent, inquisitive stare, she let out a sigh and elaborated. "Maybe it's stupid, but . . . I keep expecting to see that dark beast hovering over the forest again. I thought I saw something black and misty fly by earlier, but it was probably just a bird."

Sindri tilted his head. "Do you think it'll try to come attack us here?"

"Maybe." She scratched at her cropped black hair. "Maybe not. I don't know. All I know is that you were right before, Sindri. Anica is relentless, and being able to create the dark beast means she's more powerful than ever."

Light brown features taut with concern, Tayt once again clutched at the multicolored gem around her neck. "I have a feeling that soon she's going to come at you, at *us*, with everything she can send."

She turned to meet Sindri's curious gaze. "And I don't know if next time we'll be able to escape."

CHAPTER

17 Truths and Lies

With Rizzek cuddled comfortably on his shoulders and Tayt strolling behind him with the hem of her violet gown rustling against the carpeted hallways, Sindri led the way toward the dining room. Though they were supposed to meet in Maddoc's study after lunch, it was still early enough that Sindri figured the wizard would just be settling into his meal. But when they pushed open the double doors, he found the vast dining room to be completely empty. The long vallenwood table was clear of any sort of table settings, the candles in the center unlit.

"Wow," Tayt muttered. She adjusted the pack over her shoulder as she eyed the dozens of chairs around the table. "Your master didn't seem like someone who'd invite people over for dinner, but this . . ."

Sindri shrugged. "He's not. I think it's Asvoria's old table, actually. She probably needed all the room for her crazy followers."

"Who's Asvoria?"

Sindri almost laughed. Gesturing across the room toward the doors that led to the kitchens, he walked around the head of the table. "Oh, no one important," he said. "But I'll tell you, it's been a long time since I've ever heard anyone say that!"

Pushing the double doors open, Sindri poked his head inside the kitchen. Rizzek pulled its head from Sindri's brown robes and did the same. The creature adjusted its position on Sindri's shoulder, its claws pulling at his black hair.

"Ow," Sindri whispered.

"I sorry," Rizzek said. Pushing off with its back legs, it leaped to the black stone floor and peered up at Sindri with a cocked head. "Food here."

"See anyone?" Tayt asked from behind him.

Sindri looked around. The fires beneath the cauldrons were unlit, and all the pantries were shut and latched. Cast-iron pans lay atop a wooden counter, freshly washed and drying. Straining his ears, Sindri heard the sounds of murmured voices coming from around a corner.

Waving her forward, Sindri walked all the way into the kitchen. He in his formal apprentice robes and she dressed in Asvoria's much-too-fancy gown, they seemed completely out of place. Looking excited, Rizzek left the two of them behind and scrambled around the corner.

Flickering firelight met them as Sindri and Tayt followed Rizzek. A small room connected off the side of the kitchen, and standing in it were Nitty, the two black-haired serving girls, and a fat man Sindri recognized as one of the cooks. All four of them watched slack jawed as a man in black wizard's robes hunched over their small oak table. Slobbering slurps echoed through the low rafters.

"Maddoc?" Sindri started to race forward to grab the wizard's shoulder, but the man turned around at the sound of Sindri's voice.

It was Arvin. The man's jowly face had pulled back taut, his skin a dark shade of red. Nose squashed flat and ears pointed, the Goblin Man chewed on what appeared to be a raw piece of chicken.

Swallowing, the man let out a string of harsh, guttural Goblin words, sending spittle flying into Sindri's face. Tossing the raw chicken on the table with a wet plop, Arvin stalked toward Sindri as though intending to throttle him.

"All right!" a gruff voice cried out. "Enough of this!"

Brandishing a pan almost as big as Sindri, Nitty waddled right up behind the slobbering, salivating Goblin Man. The pan whacked the back of the wizard's head with a clang.

Startled, Arvin reached back to rub the back of his head. As he did, the red rushed from his face and his skin loosened back into its usual wrinkly, jowly appearance.

"Ow," he said, then let out a high-pitched chuckle.

"All of you!" Nitty shouted. "Out of my kitchen!"

"Sorry, Nitty, we—" Sindri started to say.

Raising the pan high, Nitty glared right back at Sindri. "Out!"

Not wanting to upset her, Sindri only smiled and backed away. Behind her, Rizzek had leaped upon the table and, holding the chicken between its front limbs, tugged at the raw meat with its triangular jaw. Nitty noticed straight away and the lizard creature had to duck a swing of the pan to escape.

As Sindri, Tayt, Arvin, and Rizzek stumbled out of the kitchen and back into the dining room, he heard the cook moan about not having any chicken ready for the next meal.

"Well, go outside and chop off another one's head!"

"But that's so far to walk!"

All Sindri heard after that was the sound of a metal pan hitting

someone else's head, and the giggling of the two servant girls.

"Looking for Maddoc, eh?" Arvin said as the kitchen doors swung shut. Pulling out a chair, he squatted to sit down.

"Yes," Sindri said. "Have you seen him? It's important."

Arvin shrugged. "Not recently, no. He was supposed to meet me here for lunch, but he never showed up. Not that I can blame him. I hardly ever have anything interesting to say." Letting out a giggle, the man's beady eyes flickered to Tayt. "My, my," he said with a lick of his lips. "Don't you look . . . delectable."

Glaring at the squat, strange man, Tayt crossed her arms over her chest and said nothing.

"You saw him earlier, though?" Sindri asked. "Did he say anything about me or going to Khur?"

Arvin scratched at his thinning gray hair and gave Sindri a confused look. Then, taking in a breath as though realizing something, he flashed his jagged yellow teeth in a smile that was clearly fake, even to Sindri.

"Ah, yes," the Goblin Man said. "Oh, he's very busy with your discoveries, very busy. I bet he's poring over that map you gave him right now, even. Probably a lot more interesting than dining with me, I can imagine."

"He's in his study, then?" Sindri asked.

Drumming his fingers together, Arvin chuckled yet again. "Most definitely. Casting spells, doing research, making plans, all to help you, you, *you*."

"That's nice of him," Tayt muttered. "Thank you." Grabbing Sindri's shoulder, she dragged him toward the double doors and into the hallway. Rizzek leaped between them, dodging their feet and the flapping of their clothes.

"That man is disgusting," Tayt said as the dining room doors shut behind them. "Who would do that to themselves? And did you *see* how he was looking at me?" Again she tugged self-consciously at the form-fitting dress. "Just awful. Black Robes . . . "

"Hey," Sindri said with a scowl. "Don't start that again."

Tayt gave him a look but said nothing.

"Come," Rizzek rasped. The creature had darted farther into the stone hall. It raced back and forth between the black walls, agitated. "Come, we need go to other place. Black eyes, she find."

Sindri led the way to Maddoc's study, leading Tayt and Rizzek down hallways and up staircases until finally they were in the southern tower. The hallway leading to the study was shadowy and dim, the torches having been snuffed out. Gray light streamed in from a window at the end of the hall, barely enough to see by.

Unlike some of the hallways, this one had not been carpeted and fitted with lamps to make it more modern. Sindri and Tayt's footsteps and the clacking of Rizzek's claws against stone echoed in the rafters as they walked cautiously toward the study door.

Sindri raised a fist and rapped three times on the wooden door. "Hello?" he called out. "Maddoc? Are you in there? It's me, Sindri."

There was no answer.

"Should we go back downstairs?" Tayt whispered. "Maybe he went to lunch after all."

Sindri shrugged. "This is strange," he said. "Usually if he wants me to find him, he's very clear where he'll be. Maybe we should just wait inside."

"You can't just go in there," Tayt whispered, tugging at Sindri's brown robes. "If he found out . . . "

Looking up at her curiously, Sindri tilted his head. "I'm telling you, Tayt, Maddoc isn't like this Anica woman. He wouldn't mind. He lets me in here all the time."

Scratching at the wooden door, Rizzek peered up at the two of them. "Inside," it rasped. "Hurry."

Lifting the handle, Sindri pushed the door open. At first he poked only his head in, looking around. The fire had gone out, and the empty birdcage was uncovered. On the table next to Maddoc's chair, where once the snifter and bottle had been, was a stack of books bound in wrinkled leather.

No one was there.

"He's probably just working on something in another room and lost track of time, is all," Sindri said. Opening the door wide, he walked confidently inside the study. Rizzek darted past him, leaping at the shelves lining the walls and climbing to hide on the dusty top. Tayt tepidly came as well, shutting the door behind herself.

Sindri plopped into Maddoc's armchair. The leather was soft and worn from years of use. Sinking into the plush chair, Sindri imagined for a moment that he was finally a full-fledged wizard. He'd taken the Test, and he had his own keep and his own apprentice and his own giant chair in front of a fireplace. Everyone in the world would know of him and not a single one would ever be able to think the words, "Kender can't do magic."

"Should we do something?" Clutching her pack to her chest, Tayt hovered near the door. Her gray eyes darted around the dimly lit room.

"Sure!" Sindri said. Leaping from the chair, he landed on the plush carpet and walked toward the fireplace. "I'll clear some of the ash and start a fire so we have something to see by." Jabbing at the remnants of the previous fire with a curve-tipped poker, he glanced back over his shoulder at Tayt. "You can sit down, you know. I promise it's all right."

She nodded then sat in the chair nearest the door. Pack held between her legs, she dug through its contents to pull free the rubbings. "Maybe there are some books in here that will help us translate these," she said as she unrolled one of the pieces of parchment and looked at it, tilting her head.

"Probably," Sindri said, turning back to the fireplace. "Maddoc's got lots of books on—"

There was a soft clink as Sindri's poker hit something hard. Something metallic, from the sound of it, so it was not the stone of the fireplace and definitely not ash. He poked again in the same spot, and the sound was distinct. There was something in there.

"Oh, I hope Maddoc didn't lose something in the fire," Sindri muttered as he reached in. "He'd be awful upset."

He dug through the soft, flaky ash, his fingers turning black as they fumbled for the object his poker had hit. Finally he felt it, something small and hard and cool to the touch. Pulling it free, Sindri brushed at the soot covering his find.

As soot fell, gold glinted in the daylight from the back window. Lifting up the hem of his brown robes, he cleaned off the item as best he could, leaving behind black stains that would surely earn him a shout or two from Nitty. Cleaned, he could see the item clearly.

Sindri's eyes narrowed when he noticed the item was just big enough to fit in the palm of his hand, and that it was triangular in shape. Though its surface had bubbled up into a thin, charred layer, it looked awfully familiar.

It looked like a dragon scale.

Digging into the scale with his fingernails, he flicked off pieces of the charred, bubbled surface. Flakes of burned gold drifted into a little pile at his feet, revealing unmarred gold beneath. The grooved scale was strangely warm to the touch, as though coming alive in his hand.

It wasn't just *a* dragon scale, Sindri realized. It was *his* dragon scale.

Behind him came the sounds of Tayt digging through the shelves. "Lots of books on necromancy," she said, seemingly more at ease in the room. "Nothing on languages, though. Do you know if there's any sort of organization to these?"

Sindri didn't answer. He couldn't move, let alone speak. His scale, the one he'd given Maddoc, the one Maddoc said he'd take care of—it had been thrown into the fire.

No. No! It couldn't be. Maybe Maddoc accidentally dropped it in. But, no, that wasn't right. Maddoc never accidentally did *anything*, let alone drop something as rare and magical as the scale into a fire.

Trembling with unfamiliar feelings of confusion and hurt, Sindri's eyes darted back to the hearth, scanning the debris for anything else. Most of what was left of the fire was black ash that crumbled at his touch. But there, hanging just a little out of the side of the hearth, was the mostly burned remains of a piece of parchment. He'd noticed it when he first crouched down, but gave it no mind since it had been blank. But, with the dragon scale in his hand, dark lines appeared.

Sindri's hand shot out to grab the parchment. It was stiff and pieces flaked at his touch, but he didn't care. Lifting it up to his face, he narrowed his eyes and read what words he could see.

" 'Those you think of as your friends,' " Sindri read, " 'are not.' "

"Sindri?"

Sindri turned to find Tayt standing behind the large armchair, her hands resting on the carved wooden armrest. She looked down at him in concern.

"Is something wrong?" she asked. "What did you find?"

The room became blurry as tears welled in Sindri's eyes. Tears! Wiping furiously at his eyes with the back of his sleeve, Sindri stood up. He wasn't sure why Maddoc had done it, but the wizard had. Maybe it was to keep him from running off on some quest and getting hurt. Or maybe everything Maddoc had ever said to him had been a lie, like everyone had always told him.

"Sindri?" Tayt said again.

Shoving the golden scale into one of his pockets, Sindri looked up and met her eyes. "I think you're right," he said. "We probably shouldn't be in here. We'd better get back downstairs."

Though her look was confused, Tayt turned to get her pack. Sindri looked up to where Rizzek peered over the ledge of a dusty shelf with a cocked head. "You too, Rizzek," Sindri said. "It's time to go."

Getting down on his knees in front of the hearth, Sindri brushed away as much ash and gold flakes as possible, trying to hide that he had ever been there. That done, he stood up and clapped his hands together, his eyes drifting above the mantel to the tapestry of Asvoria. The woman's lifeless, woven eyes seemed to stare back at him.

Asvoria. She had been a terrible woman, but a woman who had been an unwitting subject of Maddoc's experiments, as Nearra was when Maddoc had put Asvoria's soul into her body, as Elidor was when Maddoc placed the crown of the Defiler upon the elf's brow.

As Sindri was.

"I'm ready," Tayt said. She stood near the door, pack over her shoulder. One hand lifted the hem of her too-long dress so she could move quickly, while the other hovered over the door's handle. Rizzek was on all fours at her side, its whole body tensed to run.

With one last glance around the room to make sure it was exactly as they had found it, Sindri walked toward the door. For a moment he thought he saw something misty, black, and bird-sized outside the window by the birdcage, but it was gone in a blink of his eye. Probably just his mind playing tricks.

They slipped out the door as quietly as possible, Tayt pulling it closed.

"Sindri," she whispered as she made sure the door was firmly shut. "What did you find? What happened?"

"I—"

Down the dark hallway, from the stairwell, echoed the sounds of two pairs of feet climbing up into the tower. Voices sounded, what they said garbled murmurs even to Sindri's powerful ears.

"Sindri?" Tayt asked, not yet hearing.

"Someone comes!" Rizzek rasped, its body tensed once more. "They find! They hurt!"

"Shh," Sindri said. Clutching at Tayt's arm, he turned to run toward the window. There were no other doors in the hallway, no other stairs leading down. He couldn't run into Maddoc, not now.

"What are you doing?" Tayt whispered, her arm trembling as they ran faster and faster toward the window. When Sindri didn't slow down, she struggled to pull free. "Sindri, what are you doing!"

"Just trust me," he said.

They reached the window at full speed, Sindri's fingers gripping Tayt's wrist iron tight. Rizzek didn't seem to be following them, but Sindri didn't pay it any mind; he was sure the creature could hide anywhere.

Then, before he had a chance to reconsider, Sindri jumped onto the window ledge and leaped out, dragging Tayt along with him.

Tayt didn't scream or shout, which was good because at that same moment, Sindri heard Maddoc and Arvin reach the top of the stairs. But as far as Sindri could tell, it was because she was far too busy gasping for air to even think of letting out a cry for help.

As the wind blew back his robes and long black hair, and as the red brick courtyard rushed up at him, Sindri held his arms out wide, wiggled his fingers, and cried out, *"Pfeatherfall!"*

It was as though they'd jumped from the window into a giant, fluffy pillow. They were still descending, but an unseen cloud of air had pooled beneath his and Tayt's feet, lowering them to the ground as gently as a leaf falls to the grass.

"Oh wow," Tayt said between gasps for air. She clutched at her bodice, her chest straining to breathe through the tight fabric. "You've got to warn someone when you're going to do that, Sindri."

Sindri shrugged. "I didn't want Maddoc to hear us."

Their feet finally reached the ruddy brick courtyard, and the spell dissipated. Sindri gestured forward, leading Tayt into the shadowy entrance to the keep where he'd met Maddoc for his test only a few days before.

"All right," Tayt said, crossing her still-trembling arms and leaning back against the black stone wall. "Now you've got to explain. I know kender aren't afraid of anything, but I'm starting to think I don't particularly enjoy falling from great heights."

"We're leaving," Sindri said, keeping his voice low. He peered down the dark hallway and outside, making sure no one could hear.

"What?" Tayt asked. "Why? Sindri, just a little bit ago you were all about waiting to hear what Maddoc has to say, now you're just going to leave?"

Looking down, Sindri kicked at the stone. The last thing he wanted to do was admit that maybe he had been wrong about Maddoc. He still didn't know the whole story, and he wasn't one to not trust his friends. But he needed to find out more about his magic. He just had to. For some reason Maddoc didn't want him to go, but if he set out when Maddoc wasn't looking, surely the wizard would understand. In the same position Sindri was, Maddoc would do the same thing.

"I don't think Maddoc's going to be ready to leave for a while," Sindri finally said. "And I think I'd rather know now. I need you to take me to Khur. And we should bring Wilden with us."

"I already told you—no." Shaking her head, Tayt leaned away from the wall and crouched down next to Sindri. "I don't know what you found, Sindri, but I can't take you there. Especially not with the renegade hunter. Why do you want him to come anyway? We're all better off with him in a dungeon."

"Because Anica is a much bigger threat to the Conclave than either of us will ever be," Sindri said, meeting her look. "He's powerful, and he can fight like no one I've ever seen. If I'm going to face an evil wizard, I want him to be there."

Shoving past her, Sindri began to walk down the hall. "You

don't have to come with me, Tayt," he called over his shoulder. "But I'd sure like you to. You don't even have to take me all the way there if you don't want to."

Turning to look back into the darkness of the arched hallway, Sindri walked on. For the first time in a long while, he felt . . . uneasy. He wasn't used to being sad or angry all the time, like some humans he knew. It just wasn't his way. He didn't like the feelings one bit.

"Hey," Tayt called. Holding up her dress and pack thumping at her back, she raced to Sindri's side and matched his purposeful stride. "All right, fine. I'll come. But only part way, you got it? By then that hunter will probably have translated the rest of the rubbings and you can get there yourself."

Clenching his jaw tight, Sindri nodded. "Good," he said. "Now come on, we need to get changed and get out of here."

As they walked, Sindri noticed something lift out of the shadows, something wispy that moved with the breeze—smoke, he guessed.

"We just have to make sure we sneak out before Maddoc notices," he went on. "So be quick."

Unnoticed by Sindri, the smoky thing flapped wings that creaked with bone and wire. It hovered for a moment, watching with glowing red eyes as Sindri and Tayt disappeared into the keep. Then it turned and flapped off into the sky, off to find its master.

CHAPTER

18   CHANGES

Sindri studied himself in his mirror.

He usually wasn't one to do so. Most of the time he was traveling without any mirrors nearby, so he just wasn't used to seeing himself and didn't bother paying much attention to his appearance. There was always something vastly more interesting to look at.

But he felt he needed to see himself. He'd shed the soot-stained robes as soon as he'd rushed into his bedroom, dropping them into a brown heap in the corner. Digging through his wardrobe, he found his old traveling clothes, the ones he'd worn for years before giving up adventuring to study magic.

Before, on the days Sindri glanced at himself in his mirror, he would see himself in his brown robes embroidered with magical symbols and felt an overwhelming sense of pride. He'd always thought of himself as a wizard, but being in the keep, having a master, having the robes—it was everything he'd ever wanted. Unlike the magic school he'd briefly attended in Palanthas, he felt right at home in Maddoc's keep. Maddoc had accepted him for who and what he was.

Sindri once again wore his old ensemble of black trousers, a blue shirt, and a belt with pouches clipped to every place possible. Hanging from his shoulders was the purple cloak he'd purchased after he lost his first one, its inside sewn with dozens of pockets handy for storing mystical items. And in his hand he carried his trusty hoopak staff—a magical wizard's staff, fighting staff, and traveling staff all rolled into one.

He saw the old Sindri reflected in the mirror. Only, looking at himself, he wasn't sure if looking like the old him felt any more right than wearing brown robes had.

Someone knocked at the door, and Tayt poked her head in. Sindri waved her in silently, and the girl stepped all the way through. Her pack was flung over her shoulder, and she, too, was dressed in her traveling clothes, her pants and tunic washed but still just as drab in color. Something was different about Tayt's face in those clothes. The gown had made her features seem almost delicate. Her traveling clothes made her seem hard.

"Are you ready?" Tayt asked.

Sindri looked back at his room. The giant bed had been made by one of the servants and was littered with mounds of pillows. The curtains fluttered quietly in the windows, the light that flowed through them letting Sindri get one last good look at the wizard portraits Maddoc had hung on his walls for inspiration. It was going to be a while before he'd get to wake up there again.

"I'm ready," Sindri said, puffing out his chest and holding his head high. "Let's go."

Gathering his own pack, which he'd filled with rations he'd found hiding in the pockets of his old robes, and without another glance behind, he led Tayt out into the hallway.

Keeping to the shadows and creeping along in practiced silence,

Sindri and Tayt made their way down to the first level of the keep. They passed servants as they went, though none seemed to notice them. Tayt especially seemed to blend in with the walls.

The great hall of the keep still showed fire damage from Wilden's attack, but mostly it had been repaired. Guards were stationed there, but they were too busy sitting around a table playing a card game Sindri recognized as Knights and Dragons to notice the two of them creeping into the room. Sindri and Tayt managed to dash from pillar to pillar, unseen, until they reached a locked side door hidden in the shadows of the pillars and arches. Not wanting to say any magic words and catch the guards' attention, Sindri let Tayt work the lock with her picks until the door opened with a soft click.

The door opened into darkness. The triangle of light that shone in from the open door revealed a flight of narrow steps leading down beneath the keep. Sindri walked toward the steps, a musty, wet smell meeting his nose.

Tayt slipped past the door after Sindri, shutting the door behind herself and plunging them into pure blackness. Holding his staff high, Sindri whispered, "*Shirak.*"

Atop his hoopak staff was a woven sling that the kender used to throw rocks or other hard objects at attackers. On most of Krynn, hoopaks were little more than decorative, oversized slingshots, but as Sindri spoke the word of his spell, the woven end of the hoopack glowed with yellow light that burned away the gloom.

Beside Sindri, Tayt looked down into the darkness and shook her head. "I never thought I'd willingly go down into a dungeon," she whispered. "And I never once thought I'd go out of my way to help someone free a man who wants to take me prisoner."

JEFF SAMPSON

"That's what makes life fun," Sindri said. "It's always what you don't think will happen that does!"

Staff held high to light the way, Sindri led Tayt down the steps. At first the steps seemed like the rest of the keep, made of perfectly square, black stone blocks. As they descended, though, Sindri noticed that the steps seemed to be carved from the earth itself. The walls changed too, their color still black but their surfaces rippled and smoothed. Water dripped in some places, leaving behind white stains and clinging mold.

The steps spiraled, the curve so slight that at first Sindri didn't notice. But as they neared the bottom, he was certain they had made a complete half circle as they descended. The dungeons were right beneath the great hall.

Sindri waved his hand, quenching the staff's light as he and Tayt reached the bottom step. There was another wooden door there. Orange firelight flickered through the crack where the door met the floor.

Placing his pointed ear against the door, Sindri listened for the sounds of guards—drunken murmurs, pacing footsteps, laughter at their hapless prisoner. He heard nothing but the labored breathing of a single man—Wilden.

Certain they were safe, Sindri pointed his fingers at the locked doorknob. *"Perubahan."*

There was a flare of orange light around the doorknob, then a clicking sound. The door swung open with a screech of little-used hinges.

"After you," Tayt whispered. She stood back on the steps, her hand playing with the gem once again hidden beneath her shirt.

Pushing the door open, Sindri peeked inside. Due to the absolute dullness of an empty dungeon, Sindri had only ever sneaked down there once or twice, but he knew the layout pretty well. Directly in front of him were a table and a stool, where a guard was supposed to sit at all times when a prisoner was there. Torches lit the area with bright orange light. Sindri's brow furrowed as he noticed strange spiky devices littering the table, as though someone had been recently tortured.

To his left were the rows of cells, lining both sides of the dungeon. No light was lit there, and the farthest cells back were almost completely dark. Dirty, dusty hay was flung in the corners of some cells as makeshift beds, while others were nothing but cold stone floor surrounded by bars.

Straining his eyes, Sindri finally saw Wilden locked in the darkness of the farthest cell back. The renegade hunter was only a shadow, but it looked like he was standing up with his arms held high over his head.

"It's all clear," Sindri whispered back over his shoulder. "Come on!"

With Tayt's soft, padding footsteps sounding behind him, Sindri crept forward between the cells. There was a strange smell down there, like sewers strewn with copper. Sindri wasn't sure what the scent was, but it reminded him of something he couldn't quite think of.

As they approached, Sindri saw that Wilden wasn't standing up at all. The man's arms were clasped above his head in chains. His head hung limp, unkempt blond hair falling to cover his face.

"*Shirak*," Sindri said, and once again his hoopak glowed with yellow light.

Chains clanked as Wilden's head shot up. Teeth bared like a dog, he seemed ready to fight. Tayt jumped back, startled.

Wilden blinked in recognition when he finally saw that it was

Sindri standing in front of him. "Oh, it's you," he said, nodding socially. "Hello."

"Hello," Sindri said with a pleasant nod back.

With his staff lit, Sindri saw that Wilden had been stripped of everything but his muddy trousers. His bare chest was taut with muscles from years of battle training, his flesh decorated with curving tattoos that started at his navel, traveled up to his shoulders, and ended at his wrists. The symbols seemed familiar to Sindri, like the written form of some warding spell he saw in one of Maddoc's spell books.

It wasn't just the renegade hunter's hands that had been clasped above his head, his feet had been chained to the floor as well. He hung from the chains, limp, his skin pale and dripping with sweat. Red lacerations could be seen on his shoulder. But despite this, he still flashed Tayt a grin as he noticed her standing behind Sindri.

"Ah, Tayt," he said, his usual jovial tone wheezing with the strain of speaking through a parched throat. "You came to visit too? I don't suppose the two of you realized I was right and are here to offer yourselves up to the Conclave, are you?"

Tayt's glare was the only response.

"Hmm, well, guess that did seem a bit far fetched."

Leaning his staff against the cell's bars, Sindri knelt to the stone floor to study the lock. "We're here," he said as he poked at the keyhole, "because I need your help."

Wilden cocked a thick eyebrow. "Oh?"

Sindri nodded. "You remember those slavers, right?"

"I do."

"Well," Sindri went on as he searched his pouches for a spell component, "we know who was behind capturing those gully dwarves. It's the same person who was behind sending that dark beast after us. She even manipulated the Conclave into sending you to capture me and Tayt. She wants me for something really evil, she tortures hundreds of people and creatures, and she creates giant beasts to mindlessly kill everyone it meets. You think that's something the Conclave might want to look in to?"

From where he dangled from his chains, Wilden shook his head. "It isn't possible," he wheezed. "We would have heard about it and put a stop to it. Kidnapping and torture are not taken lightly."

"Ha," Tayt muttered.

"Hey now," Wilden said, peering at her through his sweaty, straggly hair. "I resent the implication that I do either of those things. At least, not on the scale of whoever this woman is."

Tayt stomped to Sindri's side. Sticking her face up to the bars, she spat the name. "Anica."

Wilden tilted his head. "Sorry?"

"Anica," Tayt said again. "The woman's name is Anica. She's the one who you're taking me back to, remember? She's doing some dark, dangerous magic to kill me and take Sindri. You saw the writing in the temple, same as we did. Sindri's powers are special. If someone like her gets her hands on him . . . "

Wilden let out a sigh. "Look," he said, his voice so strained it seemed he'd soon lose it. "We can look in to it, all right? How're you doing there, Sindri?"

While Tayt and Wilden spoke, Sindri worked to undo the lock. His usual unlocking spell hadn't worked, and something told him Tayt's thin lock picks weren't going to cut it.

"I'll get it open," he said, peering directly into the dark keyhole.

"Well, if you could hurry, that'd be grand," Wilden said, his voice like two rocks scraping against one another. "My shoulders are in much pain. And if you do, I promise after I take you to the Conclave we—"

"*After?*" Forgetting about the lock, Sindri leaped to his feet. "There is no after! Something is after me. Don't you understand? Everyone has been lying to me, tugging me back and forth to confuse me, and all this time it turns out I have some sort of power that no one's ever seen before. I have to know more! There won't be any after. If I let you out, we're going straight to Khur, we're going to see Anica, and we *are* going to find that next temple. Got it?"

The dungeon's main door slammed.

Sindri and Tayt both jumped and spun toward the door. Grabbing his hoopak, Sindri brandished it with both hands, ready to defend himself.

There, standing near the table and stool, were several guards and the hunched, black-robed form of Arvin. Standing in front of them, arms crossed and an unreadable expression on his face, was Maddoc.

"Sindri," he said. Though deep and calm, his voice reverberated through the room, and Sindri felt he could hear the echoes of it deep in his bones.

"Maddoc," Sindri said. Lowering his hoopak, he tried not to let his feelings of anger and betrayal rush back.

Gesturing with one of his black-gloved hands for his guards and Arvin to stay back, Maddoc walked down the narrow passage between the cells. Hands clasped behind his back and black robe flowing behind him, Maddoc once again seemed more a regal king than an aging wizard.

As Tayt stepped warily back and Wilden sighed and lowered

his head, Sindri walked forward. Apprentice and wizard met in the middle, their eyes locked on each other.

"Sindri," Maddoc said again, his voice a low whisper. "Why are you down here?"

Sindri tensed, unsure what to say. He'd never once in his life thought of lying to someone, but it seemed like the thing to do. But even as he opened his lips to make up some excuse, he realized he just couldn't.

"I came down here to free Wilden," Sindri said. "Me and him and Tayt, we're leaving. I'm going to Khur."

Closing his eyes, Maddoc took a weary breath. "Why?" he asked. Something about his tone made Sindri wonder if the wizard already knew.

Feeling tears well up again, Sindri reached into his purple cloak. "Because we were in your study earlier," he said, his voice wavering. "Waiting for you so we could talk about my journey, like you said when I gave you the magic map and the dragon scale. I was making a fire and I found *this*."

Pulling his hand free from his cloak, he held up the dragon scale. Golden light reflected off it in the glow from Sindri's staff.

For a moment, Maddoc only stared at the dragon scale glittering in Sindri's hand, his expression completely unreadable. Nobody moved or spoke. Tayt and Wilden, Arvin and the guards, all watched in anticipatory silence.

Finally, Maddoc looked away, shaking his head. Gray hair tumbled about his face.

"You were going to leave this keep?" the old wizard said. "You were going to abandon our studies without first speaking with me?"

Wiping away the wetness from his eyes, Sindri stomped his foot. "Of course I am," he said. "Why shouldn't I? Catriona was right; you're nothing but a liar. And Tayt was right too. All Black Robes *are* evil. All that stuff you told me about only using dark magic for good because it was more powerful, I bet that was all just to make me come with you so you could make me your latest project!"

Maddoc seemed taken aback. Stony face twitching into something resembling hurt, the wizard shook his head. "Never," he said. "I did not lie to you, Sindri. Everything I did was for your own good, for *our* own good. I knew that you had been in my study and that you planned to run away. I know that you figured out who is chasing you and that you want to run off and face her. I didn't approach you about this because I thought you'd trust me enough to tell me yourself. After all I've done for you, this is how I'm thanked?"

"He's lying," Tayt hissed from behind Sindri. "Don't listen to him, Sindri. He's lying!"

Sneering, Maddoc pointed a gloved finger at the girl. "Quiet. Your opinion is neither needed nor wanted."

Sindri ignored them both. Head down, he backed away from Maddoc. He didn't know what to think about any of it. Maddoc *had* been there for him when no one else was. He'd given him a home, been his mentor. Why would he lie? But then, why did he destroy the only clues Sindri had found to learn more about his magic?

With a start, Sindri thought of something.

"Wait," he said, looking up into Maddoc's blue eyes. "How did you know what we'd found out? Have you been watching—"

The ground shook as the sound of a loud explosion of stone

came above their heads. Dust rained down from the high ceiling as they heard the frightened shouts of guards running for their lives. A high-pitched roar reverberated through the stone walls.

"What was that?" one of the guards shouted, clutching at the table, strewn with torture devices, to maintain his balance. Next to him Arvin grinned a sharp-toothed grin and let out one of his insane chuckles.

"It's back," Tayt said, stumbling backward. "We have to run! We have to—"

The ceiling exploded before anyone could move. Black stone flew through the air, the force of the blast throwing everyone to the floor. Wilden, bound by his chains, screamed as the strain pulled at his joints. A furious wind blew down at the huddling wizards and guards, snuffing out the torches as easily as someone blowing out a candle.

His black hair whipping around his head, Sindri shielded his face from falling dust and tried to stand. All around him, people shouted in surprise and fear.

A swirling, inky black tentacle shot down from the destroyed ceiling. It grabbed one of the screaming guards and pulled him up and out. A familiar whirring sound mixed with the screams of the wind, and the guard's shouts fell silent.

The world turned to shadow as the creature's black aura enveloped the keep and sky in darkness. No longer blinded by dust, Sindri lowered his arm and looked up to the destroyed great hall above, already knowing what he'd see.

CHAPTER

19   UNDER SIEGE

R*un!*" Panicked, one of the guards—the fleshy one Sindri had seen so often—turned to race back through the door. With a roar, the dark beast shot down another living tentacle, grabbing the guard by his fat ankles. The man fell, cracking his head against the stone. Then he, too, was pulled up to the creature's gnashing mouth.

That was when everyone else finally recovered from the shock.

As three of the five remaining guards dashed toward the door, Arvin leaped over the fallen debris to Maddoc's side.

"Come on, get up, get up!" the little man howled as the terrifying winds tugged at his robes.

"Help," Wilden rasped. Sindri turned to him as, louder, the hunter cried, "Sindri, I can protect us, but I need to be unshackled!" Shaking his chains, he struggled to get free.

No longer worrying about Maddoc's truths and lies, Sindri raced to Wilden's cage. Behind him he heard one of the guards howl in triumph as he successfully batted a flailing tentacle away **197** with a sword in one hand and a spiked whip in another.

Trembling, Tayt lay where she'd fallen, staring at the monster floating above them with a clenched jaw. Sindri leaped past her to the iron bars that held Wilden. He shook them furiously, testing for weaknesses, as the usual calm and collected renegade hunter panted in pain.

"Maddoc!" Wilden cried, his voice so dry it hurt Sindri to hear it. "Let me out of here! You can't leave me to die! The Conclave won't hear of it!"

Sindri spun to look at Maddoc. The old man had stood with his hands tensed and raised as he watched the dark beast's tentacles lash out. The creature managed to grab another one of the guards, wrenching him into the sky with an audible snap of his back.

"Maddoc!" Sindri screamed over the beast's roar. "We have to free Wilden!"

Peering back over his shoulder, Maddoc's face was stern. Arvin huddled behind him and clutched at Maddoc's robes with hands that had transformed into wretched red claws.

"Free him?" Maddoc snarled. "After what he—"

"Maddoc, look out!" Wilden shouted.

The older wizard turned just in time. A tentacle snaked toward him, intent on grasping him by his middle. With a shout of magic words, a flare of red blazed over Maddoc's hands, forming a shimmering ruby shield. The beast's wiry limb struck the shield, sending up a flare of mystical sparks. Maddoc cringed from the blow and stumbled backward, sending Arvin falling on his backside.

"This is it," Tayt said, her voice flat. "We're going to die."

"No we're not!" Sindri said. Stomping his foot, he shouted at Maddoc, "Let him out now!"

"Arvin!" Maddoc called as another tentacle lashed at his dwindling magic shield. "Go free the hunter. We're trapped down here, and he could be of some help."

"Of course, of course," Arvin said, bowing his head. "Gods know *I'm* not helpful in a situation like this."

"*Go!*" Maddoc roared, wincing at another blow. Wind rushed into the wizard's face, making him squint as it blew back his gray hair.

Scrambling over the stone, Arvin shoved Sindri aside and stood in front of the door. Pulling a key from a pocket of his decaying robes, he unlocked the door with a twist to the left, a twist to the right, and two more twists to the left. The iron-barred door clicked open, and the Goblin Man hobbled inside, muttering a few spell words as he came to Wilden's side.

With a clattering of chains, Wilden fell to the floor in a heap. Gasping for air, he struggled to stand as the winds fought against him, pushing at his bare chest and whipping his blond hair in his eyes.

"Aargh!"

There was a cracking sound, like a leather whip snapping in the air, and Maddoc flew backward. Through the hole in the ceiling, the dark beast watched them with its dozens of black opal eyes and let out a screeching roar.

"Watch out," Wilden said, clutching at Arvin's shoulder to pull himself up. "Sindri, get out of the way. Snap Tayt out of it." Meeting Sindri's eye, Wilden gave him a curiously sad look. "Get ready to run."

Before Sindri could say anything, Wilden took a deep breath and leaped out of the cell. His bare feet crunching over the stony debris, the renegade hunter raced toward the door. As Sindri watched with intense worry for his sort-of-friend, the dark beast's gash of a mouth opened wide to reveal its bloodstained teeth. All of its eyes seemed to be on Wilden as he ran.

A tentacle shot out.

"Wilden!" Sindri screamed.

The living black whip was seconds away from grabbing the renegade hunter and pulling him up to his death when Wilden spread his arms wide. A shadow enveloped his body, and he was gone. The tentacle crashed instead into the rusted iron bars of one of the empty cells. The beast cried out, shaking the floor beneath Sindri's feet.

In another swirl of shadow, Wilden reappeared by the open door. All the guards were gone, having raced up the stairs. His tattooed chest heaved for air as Wilden fought the force of the winds to stand near the table with the torture weapons. The beast's eyes didn't notice his new position. Instead, they rotated to set their sights on Sindri, Tayt, Maddoc, and Arvin.

"Hey!" Wilden called. In two swift moves, he grabbed a barbed mace and a razor-edged flail. He threw them hard, and the weapons landed against the creature's side, very near its eyes.

The dark beast reacted immediately. Three new tentacles swirled down through the air, ready to tear Wilden apart. Raising his hands, Wilden mumbled words Sindri couldn't hear over the roaring of the beast. Blue light glowed from his palms, just as they had back at the slaver camp. Only this time, the spell was stronger. The light spread out into an impenetrable wall of white magic.

Sindri grabbed Tayt's shoulder and shook her hard. "Come on," he said. "We have to go!"

Nodding numbly, Tayt climbed to her feet. Behind them, Arvin helped a groaning Maddoc stand. Without a word, all four of them leaped over the fallen stone blocks toward Wilden and the door.

"Hurry!" Teeth clenched, sweat poured down Wilden's forehead. His biceps trembled from the strain of holding the spell aloft as the dark beast punched at it with enough force to crush him if it got through.

With Sindri in the lead, the older wizards and Tayt bounded through the door and into the carved stone stairwell. Sindri heard Wilden grunt with effort, then the sound of the door slamming shut as he, too, bounded through. There was a loud thump as something struck the door. Then there was another thump and the creaking sound of splintering wood.

"It's trying to come after us!" Wilden called as he leaped up the stairs two at a time. "Run!"

His hoopak lighting the way, Sindri leaped over the slick steps, his purple cloak a streamer behind him. Ahead of him he heard the murmuring of frightened voices, though they were nowhere near the top of the steps. Skidding to a stop, he saw that the three remaining guards were huddled on the steps, shaking with fear.

"What are you doing?" Tayt cried as she stopped at Sindri's side. "Go!"

The guards shook their heads furiously. One, a youngish guard with a goatee, pointed up the stairs. "These lead right to the great hall, remember? The great hall where that thing is sitting, waiting to pick us off?"

Sindri looked back. Maddoc stood still as Arvin leaned on his knees, gasping for air. Farther down the steps, Wilden clutched at the moldy stone wall, his face pained and his skin much too pale. There was another thump at the lower door as the dark beast tried to break it apart with its tentacles.

"What do we do?" Arvin gasped between pants for breath.

Sindri met Maddoc's eye. Despite the attack, he still felt a mixture of hurt feelings.

"We can't hide forever," Sindri said. "Any second now that thing's going to get mad that it lost us and start tearing the keep apart. If we don't get outside and away, we'll be crushed. And as interesting as that sounds, I think it's probably something most of us would like to avoid."

Another guard, one with a full red beard, began to tremble. "Crushed?" he stammered. "I knew working for a wizard might be dangerous, but I never thought I'd end up crushed!"

A screeching bellow echoed above them, so loud that the walls shook. Everyone looked up as the sound of falling stone blocks booming against the ground met their ears. Dust from the impact of the destruction above rained down on their heads.

All eyes turned to Maddoc and Sindri.

Maddoc raised an eyebrow. "You heard Sindri," he said in his low, deep voice. "The only way out is up."

The young, goateed guard stood on wobbly legs. "But, Master Maddoc, that monster—"

Wood splintered and flew into the air as below them the door to the dungeons burst inward. A tentacle snaked up the steps, grasping onto Wilden's ankle before he could react. It tugged, pulling him down hard. The renegade hunter caught himself with his hands, but not before his chin met the stone ledge and left a deep cut.

"*Anak!*"

A red, magical dart burst from Maddoc's gloved fingertip and exploded against the tentacle's tip. It loosened its grip for just a moment, enough time for Wilden to pull his leg free and scramble back up the steps.

Turning back toward the guards, Maddoc roared, "Go!"

No one wasted a moment. With the tentacle smacking back and forth between the slick walls, grasping spastically at the air, the guards and the wizards trampled up the steps like a stampeding herd of cattle.

Huddling around the top step, no one dared be the first to open the door. Beyond it they heard the creature let out a furious bellow. Wind howled between the pillars, and distantly Sindri could hear the servants screaming from other hallways as they ran to hide.

Sindri looked around. His eyes rimmed with dark circles and his face pale, Wilden seemed on the verge of collapsing. Tayt's eyes were determined, but her shivering limbs betrayed the fear she fought to hide. Arvin hid behind Maddoc, his nose quivering with nervousness. Maddoc himself suddenly seemed much older than usual, his face drawn and weary.

Knowing that the cowardly guards would be of no help, Sindri decided that it was up to him.

"All right," he said, standing up straight. "*I'll* go first." Pushing through the four cowering guards, he grabbed the door handle and looked back. "I think if we sneak around the pillars, we can make it outside. I'll lead the way."

No one argued.

Shrugging, Sindri pushed the door open and peeked through. Black mist seeped around the door's edge as he did, darkening the air in the stairwell. No longer blocked by the walls and the door, the creature's tornadolike winds met Sindri head on.

Tiptoeing forward, Sindri left the door partially open, knowing everyone was watching him and probably expecting his certain death. But Sindri couldn't pay any mind to them.

The creature was so vast that it took up the entire center of the once cathedral-sized great hall. Pillars lay broken in half, and the fine tapestries that had hung from the ceiling fluttered in the wind, tattered to shreds. The beast's body inflated and deflated, as though breathing, and its strange black eyes darted over the entire surface of its cloudy flesh, searching for its escaped targets. A lone tentacle waved lazily above the creature's body, occasionally snatching at a half-fallen arch.

Sindri looked to his left. The entire row of pillars on that side of the room seemed mostly intact, but the front of the great hall was a pile of black rubble. The creature had apparently torn through the front of the keep without any trouble—even the ancient, magical stone walls of the place couldn't keep it at bay. Sindri felt unsettled when he saw the bodies of some of the guards, who had been playing Knights and Dragons earlier, crushed beneath fallen debris.

Brushing his hair out of his eyes, Sindri peered back at the others huddled in the stairwell and waved them forward. He pointed to his left. If they kept quiet and hidden behind the pillars, they could climb over the rubble and get outside.

With tepid steps and fearful eyes, the others followed. First a few of the guards, then Tayt, Maddoc, Arvin, and a rather ill-looking Wilden trailed after Sindri. No one's eyes left the thrashing beast, whose tentacles still struck down into the dark dungeons, reaching for prey that was no longer there.

Sindri led them forward, past fallen tapestries and over a collapsed pillar. The dark mist swirled around them, the endless winds blew dust in their faces. But no one made a sound.

Except for Arvin.

It started deep in the stubby man's throat as a low growl. Stiffening, everyone turned to stare at him as red spread over his hands and his face. His skin shriveling and his ears growing into ragged points, Arvin was rapidly becoming more goblin than man, and with his transformation, the growling grew louder.

His head took on the hideous visage of a goblin. Arvin leaned back, opened his sharp-toothed mouth, and let out a guttural yapping call. With a leap, he bounded past the pillars into the main hall, pounding at his chest while crying his goblin war call.

The dark beast's eyes darted. Tentacles burrowed from beneath its shifting flesh, lashing out toward Arvin. The Goblin Man ducked as one flew by, but wasn't quick enough to dodge another. The heavy black tentacle met him in his chest, sending the old man flying through the room. He landed in a heap, his face returning to normal.

"That really isn't the most convenient of afflictions, is it?" Sindri said.

No one paid attention. All eyes were on the dark beast, watching as the creature's empty eyes swirled in their direction.

"Run!" one of the guards shouted. Arms flailing, he raced toward the fallen wall that led outside, his companions behind him. In a flurry of black dust, the dark beast wrenched free a pillar and threw it at them. The guards skidded to a stop as the pillar slammed into a wall, sending stone falling to block their path.

The hideous, giant creature let out a roar that made the entire keep quake.

"What do we do now?" Tayt shouted.

"To the other side of the hall!" Maddoc called, his voice deep and commanding. "We will escape through the servants' halls."

"But—"

Another roar and another pillar exploded above their heads. Ducking, no one wasted another moment. The only escape was to run forward, right past the beast itself.

Sindri ran as fast as he could, his pack thumping against his shoulder blades as he clenched his hoopak tight. Tentacles flew and he dodged, ducking some, smacking others away with his staff. All he could see was black mist and flailing limbs. It was almost like some incredible game.

Almost. Behind him he heard Tayt's steady footsteps, Maddoc's swishing robes, and Wilden's pained wheezes. Distantly he heard one of the guards shriek as he flew through the air toward the creature's mouth, his screams ending abruptly.

Rolling beneath a tentacle, Sindri saw the servant door on the other side of the hall, the one he'd tried to escape through when Wilden had attacked him and Maddoc. The table where the guards had sat earlier was crushed in front of it, a heap of splintered wood. One of the guards lay unconscious near it, blood oozing from a gash on his head.

"I see it!" Sindri shouted over the screaming of the wind. "We're almost there! Keep running!"

No one responded, too focused on fleeing the beast. Sindri was so close to its cloudy, writhing body that he could reach out and touch it, but he managed to resist the urge.

The door was close. Five steps away. Four. He leaped over the fallen man and the crushed table. Three steps. Two.

"Sindri!" Tayt yelled behind him. "Heeelaaaaaah!"

Skidding to a stop, Sindri spun on his feet. Smacking at his black hair to keep it from whipping into his face, at first he saw only Maddoc and Wilden racing past him to reach the door, unable to hear Tayt's screams over the wind with their human ears.

Tayt clung to the craggy edge of a broken, fallen pillar. One of the tentacles was wrapped around her waist, squeezing her so tightly that her eyes bulged. Behind her, the beast loomed, its mouth opened wide and ready to devour her.

"Sindri!" Tayt gasped, unable to hold in her fear. "Sindri!"

Before Sindri could move, the beast wrenched Tayt from the pillar. As Sindri watched in terror, the girl flew into the air, straight toward the monster's shredding teeth.

CHAPTER

20   A Thrillingly Dangerous Plan

For a moment all Sindri could do was stand amidst the rubble of the great hall with his hair and clothes whipping in the monstrous winds. His heart pounded with fear for his friend as Tayt flew backward through the air, her features caught in fearful resignation.

No. She couldn't die. Not at Anica's command, not when she came so far to escape life as a slave.

"No!" Sindri cried. "*No!*" Pointing his fingers toward the tentacle that whipped Tayt toward the beast's mouth, Sindri cried, "*Capik!*"

The tentacle froze mere feet from the beast's mouth. Blood-stained teeth churned within its gaping maw, waiting to tear Tayt apart. But though the creature's serpentine limb quaked, Sindri's spell held.

For the moment.

"Tayt!" Sindri shouted as the dark beast roared again. "Tayt, catch!"

Squeezed within the tentacle's grip, Tayt had closed her eyes, her whole body shaking. At the sound of Sindri's voice, she looked down.

Reaching into his pocket, Sindri pulled out the dragon scale. The gold scale was warm in his hand, pulsing with magic like a beating heart. Hoping his idea would work, he aimed toward Tayt and threw.

The golden scale spun through the air. At first it seemed Sindri's aim was true, that it would reach Tayt and save her. But in a gust of wind, the scale flew to the side, caught in the creature's tornadolike wake.

"No!" Sindri cried again. His fingers aimed toward the scale and his forehead crinkled in concentration, Sindri magically forced the flying scale to fight against the wind. Sweat beaded on his forehead as he guided the scale through the thrashing winds toward Tayt's outstretched hands.

Another immense roar shook the ground beneath Sindri's feet. The tentacle holding Tayt moved, inching closer to the beast's waiting mouth.

"Sindri!" Tayt shouted.

"Hold on, hold on," he said as he strained to keep magically guiding the scale. "Just be patient!"

"Be *patient?*"

The tentacle lurched and Tayt let out a surprised yell. With a gasp of effort, Sindri pushed the scale into her hand—just as the paralyze spell fell free and the dark beast came alive once more.

"Ahh!"

The tentacle dangled Tayt over the beast's mouth, about to throw her to her death as simply as a party guest might toss an appetizer into his mouth. The tip of the tentacle loosened.

The tentacle stopped. The beast ceased its screaming, and the wind lessened. Dozens of black eyes swam over the creature's body to stare directly at Tayt. She clutched the scale so tightly that Sindri saw a line of blood dripping down her forearm.

The dark beast held Tayt up, peering at her curiously. As it did, Sindri looked to the left and the right, trying to find someone to help him cast spells and keep it from killing anyone else. All he saw were more fallen tapestries and piles of stone blocks. The guards and the Goblin Man had fled outside.

"Sindri," Tayt called down, her voice wavering despite herself. "What do I do?"

The dark beast tilted her to the other side, making a strange grumbling sound deep within its cloudy bulk as it studied her curiously.

"The scale!" Sindri called, cupping his hands around his mouth to make sure she heard him. "The magic of the scale keeps the beast away somehow. Use it!"

Glancing between the dark beast and the scale clutched in her palm, Tayt seemed to come to a decision. Holding the scale like a knife, she stabbed down, deep into the inky flesh of the dark beast.

Golden light, much like sunlight, flared. The beast roared, lashing out with more tentacles and knocking down more of the arches. Apparently harmed, the tentacle let go of Tayt, and she fell to the hard ground.

"Tayt!" Sindri cried in relief. As the furious winds once again began to build, he raced to the fallen girl's side. Grabbing her hand, Sindri pulled the girl up and, without wasting another moment, they raced toward the servant door.

They bounded up the steps two at a time as behind them, black stone blocks disappeared, torn away by the vicious creature trying to make chase. One thing was clear: It wanted Sindri, bad. It wouldn't let a little thing like an ancient fortress get in its way.

Skidding into a hallway, kender and girl veered to the right, leaving the sounds of the destructive dark beast behind them. Sindri heard frightened voices up ahead and saw light beneath the back door leading into the kitchens. Tugging at Tayt's arm, he led her forward and the two burst through the door.

The kitchen was in chaos. The two thin, dark-haired servant girls were there, as was the chef from earlier in the day and several other workers Sindri was ashamed to realize he didn't recognize. Maddoc and Wilden were nowhere in sight.

"Calm down, you lot!" Nitty shouted from the center of the kitchen. She hefted a cast-iron pan and clanged it against the side of a cauldron to get everyone's attention. "You act like getting attacked by murderous magic creatures is something rare!"

"But I saw it eat the guards!" an older human woman wailed. She clutched at a wooden counter for support, her legs wobbling beneath her dress. "We can't go downstairs to escape or it'll devour us!"

Hands on her hips, Nitty stomped over to the wailing woman. The stout dwarf, her gray hair unraveling from her bun, looked up at the woman and wagged her finger. "And if we stay here, we'll get crushed when the tower collapses. You must have heard the rumors about the caves below the keep. Well, I tell you, missy, as I am a living, breathing dwarf, those aren't rumors. This place was bound to have a cave-in someday. That thing out there is tearing the place apart. It won't be long before the whole keep comes crashing down on top of us."

Sindri tilted his head back and met Tayt's dauntless eyes. Behind him, he could hear the pounding of the dark beast's destruction even louder than before. If what Nitty said was true—and he figured it must be, since dwarves seemed to know their stuff when it came to buildings—a lot of people would die if they didn't find a way to get everyone out before all of Cairngorn Keep collapsed.

"Nitty," Sindri called, slipping into the room through the back servant door. "Did you see Maddoc come through here with a blond man?"

Startled, Nitty turned to glare at Sindri. The other servants murmured among themselves nervously, calmed by Nitty's common sense but not so calm they could figure out what to do on their own.

"Maddoc?" Nitty grunted. "And that boy with no shirt? Yes, they ran through here, went to go take that boy to get his clothes and weapons, from what I heard. By Reorx's beard, what are you wearing that garish cloak for?"

Sindri looked down at his purple traveling cloak. "What's wrong with it?"

With a disgruntled sigh, Nitty shook her head. "Dingbat kender," she muttered. Turning back to the other servants, she put her hands on her hips once more. "All right, here's what we're doing . . . "

"Sindri," Tayt whispered, tugging at his cloak. Kneeling down, she put her mouth near his ear. "I can hear it coming. We have to run before everyone else blocks the way."

Sindri peered up at her curiously. "Tayt?" he said. "You want to just leave them behind for it to eat?"

"I . . . " Tayt started to say. Her eyes darted up, catching the gaze of the dark-haired servant girl Sindri now knew was named Rienne. Kneading at her cropped black hair, Tayt seemed

JEFF SAMPSON

conflicted. "I don't know, Sindri. I almost died. I just want to get away."

Sindri looked around the kitchen at all the servants huddled in fear, too afraid to flee out the doors below. Distantly he heard the beast still pounding away at the walls, burrowing its way through. The creature was relentless, and it was going to destroy everyone and everything in its path.

All to get *him*.

The golden dragon scale still glimmered in Tayt's cut hand. It had harmed the beast, he was sure of it. The magic of the thing was enough to cut its flesh and make it hurt. According to what Rizzek had told them, Sindri shared that same power.

Rizzek! Sindri had almost forgotten about the little lizard creature. He shook his head. No time to worry about it now, or even Maddoc or Wilden for that matter. No, he had to focus on doing something thrillingly dangerous, something that Tayt would have to help him with, though he was positive she wouldn't find it near as thrilling as he would.

Gesturing toward the doors to the dining room, Sindri led Tayt away from the planning servants. Once through the double doors, he leaned back against the table and told Tayt his plan.

"We're going to *what?*" Tayt asked. Raising her hands, she stepped back. "I'd rather make a break for it with the servants."

Sindri banged his hoopak against the stone floor. "It's the only way!" he said. "It'd save everyone, and maybe even the keep, Tayt."

Once again gripping at her short hair, Tayt closed her eyes. "Sindri, you know you're insane, right?" she said, then shook her head. "Fine. All right. We can do this."

Sindri grinned. "Let's go tell Nitty. Once she's ready, we do it."

"All right," Tayt said, turning the dragon scale over in her hands as though preparing herself. "All right."

The two of them burst back into the kitchens. All eyes turned to them, fearful, as they came back into the room. Sindri strained his ears for sounds of the dark beast down below, but he didn't hear anything. Perhaps it was taking a break. Maybe this wouldn't be so tough after all.

"Nitty," Sindri said, "we need everyone to run back through the dining room and head left down the hall when I say. All right?"

Scowling, the old dwarf stomped her foot. "We have our plans already, *Master* Sindri," she grunted. "I do not need your help."

"Look," Tayt said, putting her hands on her hips, mimicking the dwarf. "We don't have time to argue. If you all want to live, you'll—"

The floor exploded.

Pots and cauldrons clattered against the walls as the servants flew backward. One of the chefs landed hard against a wooden counter, crushing it beneath his bulk. Sindri shielded his eyes as stony shrapnel flew through the room.

Hacking, Nitty tried to get to her feet. A giant hole had appeared in the ground where she'd been standing, dark mist seeping through. Wind rushed up through the hole, sending loose spices flying through the air and unraveling Nitty's bun.

"What in the Abyss—" Nitty started to say.

A black tentacle shot up through the hole, grabbed the dwarf around her middle, and wrenched her into the darkness below. She didn't even get a chance to scream before Sindri heard the whirring of the dark beast's teeth.

"Run!" Sindri yelled to the cowering, crying servants. "Through the dining room—go!"

Screaming and crying, the servants stumbled over fallen cauldrons as they raced to reach the door. Behind them several tentacles lashed up through the hole, feeling around like giant black fingers.

Sindri and Tayt shoved through the kitchen doors and into the dining room as the servants pushed against one another to get through and escape. The floor rumbled, sending paintings tilting on the walls and candelabras clattering atop the long vallenwood table. The screams grew louder as the floor to the kitchen began to give way.

"Osburn!" a woman screamed, shoving back through the fleeing servants. *"Osburn!"*

"Come on!" Tayt cried, grabbing at Sindri's wrist and tugging him away from watching the panicked humans.

Tayt in the lead, they leaped onto one of the high-backed chairs and then onto the table, racing through the center of the room. The dozen surviving servants ran on either side of the table, two rivers of fear and flailing arms.

A furious booming sounded behind them as Sindri and Tayt neared the end of the table. Dust from the kitchen collapsing into the halls below billowed into the room, blown farther in by the dark beast's furious winds.

Tayt was the first to reach the edge of the table, and she jumped, landing hard against the door. She shoved through just as the servants reached her, forcing the girl forward into the hall.

"To the left!" Sindri shouted over the screaming of the winds. He stood at the edge of the table, gesturing wildly to the fleeing servants as dust blasted into his face. "To the left!"

Beyond the kitchen doors, which hung loose from their hinges, darkness seeped into the air like a deadly fog. From its depths, several of the vinelike tentacles lashed forward, grasping for the air as the unseen beast let loose another screaming roar from the floors below.

"Sindri, come on!" Tayt shouted. He spun around, purple cloak whipping about his shoulders, to find the girl leaning back against the wall. She gestured wildly toward the right hallway as the last of the crying servants raced past her.

A shadow fell over Sindri. Looking behind his shoulder he saw that the slim, vinelike tentacles had twisted together to form a dragon tail–like rope of dark magic. The tree-sized tentacle slammed down, crashing into the table. Splinters flew as the table split in two.

Sindri leaped, landing in a roll at Tayt's feet. With her clinging to his cloak, Sindri raced forward—up another flight of steps that would lead them onto the great hall's balconies.

"I can't believe we're doing this," Tayt muttered as they struggled to keep standing while the floor quaked.

Sindri dodged a falling beam and rounded a corner to another flight of steps. "Just make sure you don't let go of that scale, and you'll be fine."

"Don't worry. I have no intention of letting this thing out of my sight."

Ahead was a mahogany door, freshly polished. Though the wind had died down as they raced away from the dining room and the kitchens, the sound of the dark beast could still be heard. The creature's black aura seeped beneath the doorframe.

Sindri tilted his head back and gave Tayt a look. "Ready?" he asked.

She took a deep breath. "Ready."

Bracing himself for the onslaught of wind, Sindri opened the door.

They were on a stone balcony, a story above the shattered floor of the great hall. In front of them fluttered one of the few tapestries that hadn't fallen from the ceiling, its tattered edge flapping in the dark beast's wind.

The dark beast itself was directly beneath them—or, at least, its backside was. It had burrowed through the walls in its desperate chase to get them in the kitchens, and at that moment floated over the rubble and shattered furniture of the lower floors.

"We have to get its attention," Sindri shouted up to Tayt, "and get down to the main floor!"

"I learned a trick once when I was robbing a second-story shop and I had to get out in a hurry!" Tayt shouted back.

"Oh?"

Tayt narrowed her eyes and turned to face the tapestry. "Yes. The only way out was through a window. And the only thing to grab onto was a banner they'd hung outside."

Reaching down into her boots, Tayt pulled free two ornate daggers—daggers that used to hang from Maddoc's weapons display. She tossed one back to Sindri, and he caught it with his free hand. Then, with a deep breath, she turned, stepped atop the balcony's low wall, and leaped forward.

Sindri scarcely believed his eyes as Tayt stabbed the dagger into the tapestry, the hilt clutched in both hands. The knife sliced through the fabric, slowing her fall as she descended toward the unbroken ground below.

"Neat," Sindri whispered. Making sure his pack was sturdy on his back and clenching his hoopak tightly, he, too, ran forward. Leaping from the balcony, he flew threw the air, arm outstretched and ready to impale the tapestry.

He slammed against the heavy fabric, the knife slicing through the image of a red dragon blasting flame. He clung to the knife's hilt with one hand as his own weight pulled him down to the floor, just as Tayt had done.

Sindri reached the bottom and landed on the ground next to Tayt. Above them the shredded tapestry twisted in the winds as Sindri peered at the daggers.

"Did you steal these from Maddoc?"

Tayt shrugged. "Well, yes."

Sindri mimicked her shrug. "Oh well." Then, spinning on his heels, he flung the heavy iron knife through the air. It spun so fast it seemed a blur of silver. Its pointed edge met the dark beast's cloudy body, bouncing off its apparently tough exterior.

"Huh," Sindri said. "I thought it would just fly through. Must be solid."

The roaring stopped, the winds died down. For a moment, nothing happened. Their eyes on the dark beast, Sindri gripped his hoopak as Tayt slipped her stolen knife back into her boot.

A single, shining black eye darted over the dark beast's body. It spun as it looked at the kender and the girl standing there, their images reflected in its glossy surface.

The dark beast screeched and roared, shaking the entire building. Cracked arches fell from the ceiling in a cloud of dust as a wall near the destroyed entrance crumbled into a heap.

"*Let's go!*" Sindri shouted over the beast's screams.

Packs thudding against their backs, Sindri and Tayt ran through a wide, arched hall that led to the back of the keep and out to the courtyard, away from the beast.

The plan was working perfectly. The beast seemed to want

only him and was only killing and destroying because the building and the people in it were in its way. With Tayt—who the creature specifically wanted to kill—at his side, Sindri was certain they could lead it away from the keep and face it outside, where it was safe.

Only his idea seemed to be working a bit too perfectly. Sindri fled as fast as he could possibly go. He didn't have to look back to know the beast was closing in. Its wind blasted at them from behind, billowing Sindri's purple cloak in front of him and flinging his long hair in his eyes. Its misty aura joined the shadows of the already black hallway, darkening it into night. Its roars shook the ground as its tentacles grazed his back.

Ahead, they saw an arch of gray light and red brick—the courtyard.

"We're almost there!" Sindri yelled at Tayt over the screaming wind. "Keep running!"

Tayt nodded her head but didn't speak.

Then they were outside. Fresh air met them in a wave, bringing with it the scent of rain and pine trees. Far above, black birds screamed in fear as they fled the tower crenellations.

Sindri and Tayt ran to the middle of the brick courtyard, tripping over the places where bricks lay in disheveled piles. Skidding to a stop, Sindri turned back to face the dark beast.

The creature billowed in the archway, its body crunching the stone blocks above it. Cracks spread along the keep's side as the beast's tentacles lashed out against the stone walls and pulled itself free from the tight hallway. Its dozens of eyes were focused on only Sindri as the black mist seeped from behind it to overtake the gray sky.

"Hold on to that scale until the last moment, all right?" Sindri said. "And don't forget to send it to me when I need it."

Jaw firm, Tayt nodded. "I won't, Sindri."

Slamming the bottom of his hoopak hard against the brick, Sindri stood tall, free hand on his hip. Chin high and stern, his cape billowed around him as he stared down the dark beast.

"Go hide," Sindri said to Tayt as the dark beast swelled out from the half-destroyed main tower and started to flow toward him. He smiled. "Leave this up to me."

CHAPTER

21 SHOWDOWN AT CAIRNGORN KEEP

It wasn't until Maddoc and Wilden were in the kitchens and the hunter had called out behind him that Maddoc realized Sindri and his friend weren't there.

"Maddoc," Wilden wheezed, shoving past the trembling servants who had congregated by the ovens. Sweat dripped down his neck and tattoo-covered chest as he grabbed onto a counter to support himself. "I need . . . my clothes . . . my weapons."

"Master Maddoc," an old woman muttered, bowing her head as she came forward to clutch his robes. "Master Maddoc, I saw something downstairs. What is it? What is happening?"

Maddoc ignored her, eyes scanning the room for his kender apprentice. The ground shook as distantly the dark beast slammed its flailing appendages against the walls, destroying more of Maddoc's home. His fingers clenched.

"Maddoc—" Wilden gasped.

"Master Maddoc—" a dwarf servant grumbled.

"Quiet!" Maddoc roared. "All of you! Run or hide. That thing will kill you if you stay. You"—he pointed his dead right finger at Wilden—"come with me."

A ripple of panic flowed through the room, an electric charge of fear that Maddoc brushed aside as he shoved past his servants and into the dining room. Wilden followed as he shoved into the hall, turned left, and ran through the corridors and up stairs to the southern tower.

"Here," Maddoc said as they reached the top step of the long, black, stone hallway, at the end of which was his study. "I had your belongings brought up here so I could examine them. You can have them back, so long as you help fight that creature."

Wilden took long strides to match Maddoc's pace as they sped through the plain hall, past doors that led to other, little-used rooms. The renegade hunter's feet slapped against the stone, the footsteps echoing.

"Thank you," Wilden said, "for this and for saving me earlier. I know you couldn't have wanted to, what with your hand."

Maddoc didn't answer. He shoved through his door, waving the renegade hunter to follow him onto the plush rug.

In the study, distant from the destruction of the great hall, it almost seemed like a normal day. Sindri was down in the bowels of the keep fighting the creature, but Maddoc knew the kender would be all right. Kender had a knack for escaping the deadliest of situations completely intact, and from what he'd overheard as the undead Shaera had flown outside the girl's room earlier that day, the dark beast was out to capture Sindri, not kill him.

Maddoc pulled the renegade hunter's belongings free from a hidden cabinet and turned to let the young man peel off his dirty trousers and put on fresh clothes without an audience. The wizard studied the room, dimly lit from the gray sky beyond the back window. He'd spent decades of his life in this room. His most prized books were here; magical artifacts were hidden behind

JEFF SAMPSON

the walls. Asvoria on her tapestry hung above the fireplace. She had been an unspeaking companion who had captivated him, destroyed him, and ultimately led him to the doorstep of a completely new power.

This room, this keep, were where he'd come up with his greatest of plans and magical inventions. It was to be destroyed, though, as swiftly and unexpectedly as his right hand.

Peering over his shoulder, Maddoc saw the renegade hunter. His back was to Maddoc as he laced his boots and tugged on his shirt. It would be so simple to destroy him, to incapacitate him and leave him here to die when the keep crumbled. He was the one who took Maddoc's hand. He was the one who started the whole chain of events that led to that creature of dark magic tearing apart the walls of his home, far below.

He gripped the glove covering his right hand and tugged, pulling it free from his dead flesh for the first time. The leather gave, one finger at a time, freeing a stench that almost made Maddoc gag. With a cold stare, he studied the green-tinged loose flesh and the bits of white bone that had worn through the skin of his knuckles.

Right hand raised and aimed toward the renegade hunter's back, Maddoc brought to mind a spell—a spell of pain, of suffering— enough to break the man and make him unconscious.

Then the roars echoed outside and Maddoc saw the dark beast's black aura floating in front of the window, turning the gray sky into one of night.

That was when he sensed Sindri's unusual, ancient power coming from the direction of the courtyard.

"Sindri," Maddoc muttered. "He lured it outside of the tower. Good boy."

Wilden cocked his head as he strapped his silver scythes to his belt. "The creature," he said, raising a bushy blond eyebrow, "it's out of the keep. We can escape."

"Yes." Maddoc pulled his glove back on his decaying right hand. With one last glance at his beloved study, he turned and headed toward the door.

"But Sindri!" Wilden called, chasing after Maddoc as he walked purposefully to the window at the end of the hall that overlooked the courtyard. "We need to find him. Why are you heading this way?"

Maddoc ignored the younger man. Arms behind his back, he stood at his window and looked down.

Sindri was there, as he'd suspected, racing around the dark beast on quick, tiny legs like a fly buzzing around a much larger animal. The billowing, unnatural creature lashed out with its swirling tentacles, slamming into the brick courtyard and sending the stone flying into the air in an explosion of red dust and soil.

Hoopak held high, Sindri dodged flailing tentacles. With a magic cry, he shot a blaze of fire from the tips of his fingers into the creature's vast underside. It let out an anguished roar. Battering ram–sized tentacles slammed backward against the keep, quaking the floor and sending Maddoc and Wilden sprawling to the ground.

There was a rumbling, distant at first and then close, very close. Cracks snaked along the ceiling, sending down broken pieces of stone. The world swayed as a roaring that was neither the beast nor its furious winds filled Maddoc's ears.

"What's going on out there?" the renegade hunter asked as he struggled to stand on weary feet. "Did I see Sindri? Is he all right?"

JEFF SAMPSON

Maddoc was surprised to hear genuine concern in the renegade hunter's tone. Maddoc could use that.

"He is," Maddoc said, grabbing at the wall with his hand to steady himself against the crumbling floor. "But he could certainly use your help."

Quickly Maddoc relayed his plan. Grim faced, but showing no fear, the renegade hunter nodded in agreement. Spinning around, Maddoc cast his spell. Then he ran, letting the renegade hunter do his work.

As Maddoc fled past the open door of his study, he saw chairs lying on their sides and ancient books tumbling to splay open on the ornate rug. Shaking his head, he ignored the destruction of his life's work. He ran as fast as his aging legs would take him, out of the collapsing hall and down the stairs.

"Sindri, look out!"

Sindri ducked as yet another tentacle smashed into the courtyard behind him, sending bricks flying. Out of the corner of his eye, he saw Tayt, crouched behind the walls of an empty stall in the nearby stable. Behind her, horses whinnied in fear, slamming their hooves against the wooden walls.

"Sindri!" the girl called out again, pointing a finger up at the beast.

Jutting his hoopak into a patch of soil in the broken courtyard, Sindri leaped up, using the hoopak to support his weight and propel himself higher. A thick, tail-like tentacle flew beneath his feet. He landed in a crouch and spun around.

"*Cermin saya,*" Sindri called out, pointing his fingers toward the other end of the creature. "*Keajukan saya ayun!*"

A flash of white light pulsed from Sindri's fingers and coursed over the courtyard beneath the dark beast. The creature's eyes, reflecting the white light, all darted to follow the spell. The ball of light stopped, hovered in the air for just a moment, then widened. A figure appeared in its blazing center, just a shadow at first. As the light died away, the figure was revealed—it was Sindri himself. Or, at least, an illusion of him. Though the image stood there motionless, like a grinning painting of Sindri, the creature roared and attacked the fake kender.

Using the brief distraction, Sindri raced beneath the creature's cloudy bulk, across the courtyard, to the stables. "Tayt!" he cried as the winds whipped his cloak beneath his feet, threatening to make him stumble. "Give me the scale! My spells aren't working to bring it down. I'm going to find a way up!"

Tayt nodded and pulled the scale from her pocket. She threw it through the air, and Sindri caught it.

Spinning to face the creature, Sindri saw its eyes darting over its billowy body. The mirror image of Sindri was gone.

"Hey!" Sindri called. He pointed his fingers, shooting out a thin, snaking bolt of lightning that sparked against one of the beast's eyes. "Over here!"

The beast shrieked, making the trees beyond the keep's walls tremble, and its eyes found Sindri as he raced straight toward it. He was going to have to let the creature grab him. He'd avoided doing so at first, intending to use magic to make it fall so he could climb its side. But he figured it was the only way now.

That was, until he saw the gray-haired figure standing in the window of the south tower, watching him with intense blue eyes.

"Maddoc," Sindri whispered, brushing the flailing hair from his face.

The south tower appeared to have taken a heavy blow from the beast's tentacles. Stone crumbled from its side as cracks split the wall in half. Still Maddoc stood, watching him with his hands raised, muttering a spell.

The ground beneath Sindri's feet jumped.

Ducking another swing of the dark beast's tentacle, Sindri leaped back. As with his test, the brick bounced up and down like bubbles in a boiling cauldron. The blocks leaped into the air to pile atop one another, forming Sindri's old foe, the block man.

From the window came the sound of a warrior's call. Dressed all in black and with his blond hair flowing behind him, Wilden leaped from the window. He tumbled through the air toward the dark beast's back, his eyes fierce as he held both of his scythes forward.

The scythes met the creature, digging into what was apparently actual living flesh and not just the cloudy mass it appeared to be. Hanging onto the scythes with his feet firmly planted in the creature's back, Wilden looked down at Sindri.

"Sindri!" he yelled. "When you get up here, grab my hand!"

"Huh?" Sindri said, not sure he'd heard the renegade hunter right over the noise of the monster and the wind.

What felt like two strong hands gripped Sindri under his arms. Glancing over his shoulder, he saw the block man. With one giant heave, it flung Sindri into the sky. As Sindri's feet left the ground, the block man crumbled into a pile of bricks.

Air rushed past Sindri's face as he flew up past the dark beast. Tentacles lashed out, whooshing by his feet and grazing his face, but none of them struck.

Wilden clung to the dark beast's writhing back, one hand outstretched while the other tightly gripped one of the embedded scythes. Sindri held out his small hand as he came close, and Wilden gripped it tight.

"Oof!" His ascent suddenly stopped, Sindri flipped over onto his back—on top of the dark beast itself. Up there no wind seemed to stir, and Sindri's hair fell in tangles over his shoulders.

Rolling over to his hands and knees, he felt the dark beast's flesh. It was rubbery and soft, squishy between his fingers. It was as though the creature were covered in some sort of transparent skin that contained its swirling black bulk.

"Wow," Sindri said, kneading the doughy flesh with his fingers. "What could have made this?"

"Sindri," Wilden said, pulling his scythes free and attempting to stand. "Maddoc told me you needed to be up here, that you could attack better. We—"

The flesh at Wilden's feet rippled, as though it were a lake into which a stone had just been tossed. The rippling flesh shuddered and pulsed—and then surged out as a tentacle burst into the air.

Silver flashed as Wilden swung one of his scythes. It sliced neatly through the tentacle, sending it flying through the air. The stub puckered and closed, then pulled back into the beast's flesh.

The creature roared, sending vibrations running up Sindri's bones. All around them the flesh rippled as the black, glassy eyes surged toward them.

Scythes at the ready, Wilden crouched down. "I'll hold the tentacles off," he said. "Whatever you plan to do, do it fast."

Sindri nodded. At that moment the first tentacle shot up, followed by another. Sindri leaped back, fumbling in his pocket for the golden dragon scale. Wilden darted, his moves swift and practiced, slicing at the tentacles as they rushed to envelop him.

They fell, dissipating into black smoke, as Wilden struggled to maintain his footing on the beast's bouncy body.

A tentacle surged in front of Sindri's face, like a tree suddenly sprouting from the ground. With a shout, Sindri's hand shot forward. The pointed end of the scale met the flesh of the tentacle, slicing in as easily as a stick in mud. As the creature's flesh was pierced, gold light burst from the wound. Sindri squinted and saw the edges of the tentacle's flesh shriveling and blackening, the swirling cloudy insides shuddering with the power.

The beast shrieked in anguish and pulled the injured tentacle back into its body. Where it was sucked in, the flesh rippled, forming a new appendage to grab Sindri.

"Argh!" Wilden cried out in anger behind Sindri. Spinning, Sindri saw that dozens of the snakelike tentacles had risen to overtake the renegade hunter, surrounding him like the bars of a cage. Wilden spun around with his scythes, cutting through as fast as he could, but more tentacles grew in their place.

The eyes milled about Sindri's feet, seeming like stepping stones in a stream. Sindri stomped on one, and the eye exploded into a mass of tarlike goo. Again the beast roared.

"Sindri!" Wilden bellowed. He chopped through another tentacle, but he wasn't fast enough. He was enveloped.

"Wilden!" Sindri cried back.

The rippling flesh sprouted, tentacles rising like deadly weeds. Sindri ran, bouncing on the beast's rubbery body as he zigzagged through the flailing forest. He had an idea, but he had to get to a clear area first.

Farther along the body, tentacles had yet to sprout. Forcing his short legs to go even faster, Sindri raced forward. Then, with one giant bounce, he leaped.

"Yaaa!" he cried, an expression of pure exhilaration. He landed farther down the beast. More skin crinkled into the bubbling ripples as the remaining eyes coursed after him like flesh-eating fish in a sea of black.

Holding his hoopak under his arm, Sindri clutched the golden dragon scale in both hands and raised it above his head. One stab of the thing's power had been enough to make a shudder of pain roil through the beast's body. Sindri's power was apparently close to that of the scale. The two of them together . . .

Sindri brought the scale down with a shout. It cut into the creature's flesh easily, sending forth a burst of magical golden light. Then, pulling back with his full weight, Sindri let himself fall down the side of the beast, the scale still stuck in its flesh. He descended down the beast's side the same way he and Tayt had made it down the tapestry in the great hall, clinging to the scale as it sliced the beast.

A giant gash opened in Sindri's wake, the edges of the flesh shriveling as though burned. The creature's insides, which smelled of dead pig, roiled as it screamed in pain and tried to buck Sindri free. Distantly, Sindri heard Wilden cry out as he was tossed from the creature's back to the hard courtyard below.

Sindri dug into the creature's side with his boots, stopping his descent before he fell. Down here the winds were fierce, raising up dust that made it hard to see, but he didn't care. He was close.

Clinging to the singed edges of the shrieking creature's gaping wound, Sindri stuck a hand into the cloudy mass. It was thick, a viscous liquid, and warm to the touch. Sindri felt the unusual magic once more roiling deep inside his gut. It burned with power, waiting for him to use it.

"Aaaargh!" Sindri let out a determined scream as he forced the power up through his chest and into his arms. A bright golden light blazed from his fingertips, incinerating the insides, turning the roiling mass into ash.

All around Sindri tentacles sprouted to flail uselessly as the creature shuddered, caught in the throes of death. A wail echoed through the sky as more of it burned away.

"Sorry," Sindri said through gritted teeth, even as he forced more of his power free. He felt weak, drained of every last bit of energy he ever had, but he couldn't stop. He was so close.

The tentacles fell limp, falling uselessly to the beast's bulky side. The winds fell away as the dark aura dissipated like a heavy mist burning off in the sun. The eyes drifted past Sindri lazily, no longer under the creature's control.

With one last cry, the creature collapsed to the courtyard.

Gasping for air, Sindri pulled his hand free and clutched at the dead creature as it landed. A thunderous boom overtook the entire courtyard as its heavy bulk crushed the brick. Dust billowed into the air.

Exhausted, Sindri found he couldn't stand. He was tired, so tired. And the beast's body was so soft.

But no, it wasn't over, not yet. As the booming died away, Sindri's sensitive ears picked up the sound of a rumbling deep beneath the courtyard. A roar, like a torrential waterfall, overtook him as the ground began to shake.

"The tunnels," Sindri whispered. "We're falling into the tunnels. I hope everyone got away all right."

The last thing Sindri saw was the courtyard collapsing into the caverns that coursed beneath all of Cairngorn Keep. Grand towers of black stone and a wall that had protected the keep for hundreds of years crumbled into the tunnels below, sending magical artifacts and furniture flying through the air.

Certain that he was about to go on the next great adventure—death—Sindri closed his eyes and let the darkness of unconsciousness overtake him.

CHAPTER

22 A Journey Begins

I'm coming for you!" Sindri screamed in his dream. "You won't escape!"

In front of him, a black-robed wizard ran down a dark hallway. Her robes billowed out behind her like a giant cloud covered with eyes and flailing with tentacles.

Sindri raised his golden scale and smiled. "That won't work twice," he said. "I know how—"

"Kender man!" a voice called out, pulling Sindri from his dream. "Kender man, you wake?"

Groaning, Sindri opened his eyes. He blinked once, twice, then finally made out the furry, triangular head of Rizzek staring down at him. The little lizard creature blinked its wide blue eyes, then poked at Sindri's cheek with a black claw.

"You hurt?" it rasped.

Sindri sat up, sending Rizzek leaping down from his chest, and looked around. He seemed to be in some kind of giant hole. All around him the ruins of the towers and the brick courtyard were piled in heaps. Setting his hands down, his fingers met rubbery flesh.

Standing, Sindri peered down at his feet. The dark beast had deflated. What little insides it had that weren't incinerated by his magic oozed through broken, transparent flesh. The stench was like uncooked pork left out to rot for several days.

"Wow," Sindri whispered. He found his pack and his hoopak lying unharmed in the rubble. Patting his pockets inside his purple cloak, he made sure the golden scale was still there. It was.

Bobbing its head, Rizzek darted over the dark beast's body, trailing behind Sindri. Hand on his hip, Sindri studied the ruins, trying to find the best way to get out of the hole.

Overhead Sindri heard the screech of a falcon. Shielding his eyes from the glare of the late-afternoon sun, he saw the shadow of a bird circling overhead. Its feathers seemed strange, as though they were drifting away, but it was far away and Sindri figured he just wasn't seeing it well.

"He's alive!" a voice called. "In the hole, he's alive!"

Up above, at the edge of the ruins, someone looked over the edge. Backlit by the sun, at first Sindri couldn't tell who it was.

"Sindri is alive!" the voice called again, its tone deep, regal, and commanding—Maddoc.

Others appeared at the older wizard's side—Wilden, then Tayt. Sindri sighed with relief to know they were all right.

Rizzek bounced around at Sindri's feet. "Up!" it said. "Up!"

"All right, all right," Sindri said with a laugh. As he stepped on top of the nearest fallen block, he tilted his head and looked down at Rizzek. "Where did you run off to, anyway?"

The little lizard creature ducked its head, as though sheepish. "I run, I hide," it rasped. "Dark thing come, I not stay to help. I sorry."

Sindri shrugged, then reached for the next block. Straining to pull himself up, he called back, "It's all right. We managed to kill it. See? We beat Anica—I mean, 'black eyes.' "

Thick tail whipping behind it, Rizzek landed on a block right above Sindri's head. "I see! I knew kender man could do it."

Sindri heaved himself up, landing with a grunt on the next highest block. "If you knew I'd do it, why'd you run?"

Rizzek flicked its furry tail and cocked its head. "Safe, not sorry?"

Sindri laughed. "Never been my motto, but I suppose it's a good one!"

With Rizzek darting ahead, Sindri climbed the rubble. As he neared the top, Wilden held down a hand and helped pull Sindri up. He landed on his stomach on a pile of soil, then pushed himself up.

"Wilden!" he cried, patting the man on his lower back. "And Tayt!" Sindri ran forward and hugged her around her middle. Startled, the girl didn't seem to know what to do at first. She gave him a tepid hug back.

"The man who kidnaps you gets a greeting, but not your master?" Arvin asked in his weaselly voice. Looking past Tayt, Sindri saw Maddoc standing there, stoic, hands behind his back. Arvin—the Goblin Man—peered around his back and let out a deranged giggle.

Maddoc said nothing despite Arvin's comment. The older wizard simply raised an eyebrow.

Sindri took a deep breath and went to stand before Maddoc.

Beyond the wizard was the crumbled wall of keep, and beyond its rubble was the open forest.

"I am glad you are all right," Maddoc said with a nod of his head.

Sindri wasn't sure how to react. His first instinct was to run and hug the man, his mentor, his surrogate father. But he still couldn't forget how it felt to find his scale in the fireplace, how it felt to realize that the man he'd trusted most had been lying to him, just as everyone had said.

"Me too," Sindri said at last. He brushed his windswept hair out of his face and looked down. "I saw you cast the spell to help me. Thank you."

Maddoc sighed. Coming to stand before Sindri, he placed a gloved hand on his shoulder. "Look around, Sindri," he said, waving to the destruction. "Do you understand my actions now? I was trying to protect you from this."

Sindri turned to look past Wilden and Tayt, who both stood quietly as Rizzek darted between their feet. Beyond the massive sinkhole from which Sindri had just climbed lay the heaps of black stone that had once made up Cairngorn Keep. Bookcases lay shattered on the ground, their books scattered and ruined. Armor and tapestries and antique furniture were crushed and torn. Beyond, hundreds of trees had disappeared into the earth where all of the caverns had collapsed, leaving lines of destruction sliced into the once stoic scenery.

Somewhere beneath all the destruction lay ancient rooms and magical artifacts. The time room and its many clocks, the gallery that could draw one into an imagined world, Maddoc's revered study—it was all gone. The keep and all its secrets were lost forever.

"I'm sorry, Maddoc," Sindri whispered. "It's my fault all of this happened. The beast was sent after me."

Maddoc sighed and shook his head, his blue eyes old and tired as he looked over his decimated home. "I wanted to keep you from this."

Pulling free from Maddoc's grip on his shoulder, Sindri turned and walked backward to stand at Tayt's and Wilden's sides. "But you couldn't, could you?" Sindri said. "The best way to protect me is to help me learn about my powers so I can protect myself, not hide me from it. You saw what I did to the dark beast. If I hadn't known about the scale or what it meant, it probably would have killed everyone."

No one said anything, not even the deranged Goblin Man, as the older wizard continued to stare over the remains of Cairngorn Keep. Maddoc's gray hair fluttered behind his head on a soft breeze that seemed so wonderfully peaceful after the onslaught of the dark beast.

"You're right," he said after a moment, his voice low. "At least about helping you learn about your powers. My notes are lost, but I can remember what they said, and everything else we can figure out as we go. However, you are wrong about this being your fault." Maddoc's jaw clenched. "The one responsible is the wizard who sent this thing after you."

"Anica," Tayt said. She seemed to shrink under Maddoc's steely gaze, but she clenched her pack tight to her chest and elaborated. "Anica, she's my old master. Sindri and I figured out it was her who sent the dark beast. She may be working with someone."

Maddoc nodded. "Anica," he said. Peering back over his shoulder, he met Arvin's eye. "Would be her, wouldn't it?"

Arvin strummed his fingers together and grinned. "Oh yes,"

he said. "She and you, always the best. It would figure she'd end up this powerful."

Sindri stepped onto a stone block to meet the older man's eye. "Anica?" he said. "You know her?"

Maddoc nodded, a dark look coming over his eyes. "Oh yes, I know her. She is the blackest of black-magic users, Sindri. She's been doing many illegal studies for years—kidnapping members of other races to force them to help in her 'experiments,' making alliances with dark forces." Maddoc clenched his fists. "She will pay for what she did to me."

"Yes, she will." Wilden stepped forward, brushing his blond hair out of his face. Despite a few scratches along his cheek and the gash on his chin, he seemed mostly unharmed by his earlier trials. "From what you and Tayt have said, and with this beast as evidence of her vile nature, it's clear that there's a bigger threat to the Conclave than Sindri and Tayt." Nodding toward Sindri, he smiled. "Guess you were right after all, Sindri. Still want me to come with you to Khur?"

Sindri grinned back. "Of course! You were pretty amazing when you leaped on the beast."

"You weren't so bad yourself." He winked.

Standing away from the others, Tayt looked down, pack still clutched protectively. Tilting his head curiously, Sindri leaped down from the stone block.

"Tayt?" he said. "Are you all right?"

Nodding, she looked down at the sinkhole, at the body of the dead beast. "I don't know, Sindri," she whispered. "Anica . . . " She shook her head.

Sindri tugged gently at her arm. "Hey," he said. "Remember what I said? About running forever? It was only when you and

I ran toward the dark beast that we were able to stop it. Maybe that will be true of Anica too, and then you can be free forever."

Tayt's gray eyes darted up to look from Wilden, to Maddoc, to Arvin, then to Rizzek, all of whom stared at her.

"You can lead us there," Sindri urged. "With your help, we can stop her. Between you, me, Maddoc, and Wilden, she won't stand a chance."

Smiling grimly at Sindri's confidence, Tayt felt at her neck, where her gem still hung beneath her tunic.

"All right," she said. "I can do this. You know, Sindri, you're the first person I ever met who got me to do things like this. What is it about you?"

Maddoc answered, "It's just his way."

"Oh, mustn't ask me to come!" Arvin said, scrambling forward to stand at Maddoc's side. His eyes bulged yellow as his ears reddened and stretched into points. "I know I wouldn't be the least bit of help. Look how I messed up today! Oh, such a tragic waste of space I am."

"Arvin, did you want to—" Sindri started to say.

The Goblin Man clapped his hands. "I'd be delighted!" he said, then let out another of his unusual chuckles. Tayt gave him a look but said nothing.

Sindri looked around the group—five wizards of various powers up against a single wizard backed by superior dark forces. Sindri liked any odds, but these seemed better than he could have hoped for.

"Thank you," he said. "All of you. We're going to get to the bottom of this and stop this woman if it's the last thing I do—though, I hope it isn't, since it'd be no fun to learn about my powers and not get to use them."

Wilden laughed and Tayt's lips twitched into a smile she couldn't hide. Sindri looked up at Maddoc to see his reaction only to find the older man's blue eyes locked onto Wilden. His look was one of hatred.

Rizzek leaped, landing on Sindri's shoulders and curling around his neck. "We go?" it asked in its raspy voice.

"Yes," Maddoc said, tearing his gaze from the renegade hunter. "We should go before night falls. The surviving servants and guards have fled, and we should do the same. Ravenscar would likely provide somewhat adequate lodgings for tonight."

Sindri stuck his hoopak staff in the ground and nodded. "Then tomorrow," he said, looking at each of his companions in turn, "we begin our journey."

With one last look at the ruined keep, the rubble casting long shadows in the light from the setting sun, the new companions headed west into the woods.

Tayt came to Sindri's side as they walked, and she whispered into his ear, "Sindri, be careful. You can't—"

"I know, I know," Sindri whispered back as he looked at Maddoc walking in front of him, regal black robes billowing behind his tall frame. "I can't trust Maddoc. I know."

Sindri tore his eyes away as they left the crumbled courtyard and started through the grass and underbrush. It was not the time to worry about Maddoc's true intentions. Whatever they were, they'd be revealed in due time.

His journey was about to begin. The truth of who and what he was would finally be revealed.

And he wasn't going to look back.

Later that night, as Sindri lay on an understuffed bed with a thin blanket pulled tight around him, Rizzek paced. The lizard creature could not sleep, so it trotted back and forth over the wooden floor of Sindri's room, the silver and red light from the risen moons casting the room in pale pink light.

The kender is not destroyed, a voice whispered in Rizzek's head. The voice was female, aged and commanding. *But it doesn't matter.*

Rizzek darted up to look at Sindri, then quickly tore its gaze away. Even from her stronghold far away, its master was able to see through Rizzek's eyes, hear through its ears. It was always her way.

I feared you had gone against me, the voice went on, Rizzek the only one who could hear her words. *When the man spoke to you of the scale, of the map, and I could not see or hear properly, I feared you actually listened.*

Rizzek could almost see the thin-lipped smile of its master, floating in the darkness. *But you led the beast to him anyway. You showed me the temple meant only for the kender's eyes, revealed to me the ancient words I was not meant to see. If I didn't know better, I'd suspect all of this was done on purpose.*

Claws clacking against the wood floor, Rizzek curled in the shadows under the end table next to Sindri's meager bed. The kender snored peacefully, completely unaware of the conversation happening in Rizzek's mind. The lizard creature curled into a ball and trembled.

"No, Master," it whispered. "No, please."

The voice ignored Rizzek's pleading. *Since your efforts worked out in the end, my dear familiar, I suppose your punishment for going against me won't need to be as severe. But oh, yes, there will be*

punishment, Rizzek. For you and for everyone you've allied yourself with.

Images of the woman's blank black eyes floated in Rizzek's mind, her stare full of cold, calculating malice.

You can count on it.

The story continues in . . .

THE EBONY EYE

SUNCATCHER TRILOGY, VOLUME TWO
by Jeff Sampson

Everyone knows kender can't do magic. But Sindri Suncatcher—the greatest kender wizard in the world—can.

Now that Sindri knows who has been trying to kill him, he sets off on a mission to find out why. But the friends who accompany him have confusing motivations. The black robed wizard Maddoc has lied to Sindri one too many times. And the renegade hunter who once vowed to imprison Sindri now acts like a true friend.

As Sindri and his friends break into a mechanical maze guarded by a frightening gorgon, the kender apprentice must tackle a grave lesson: how *not* to trust.

Available March 2007

Find out how it all began in . . .

TEMPLE OF THE DRAGONSLAYER

by Tim Waggoner

Acknowledgments

Thank you to the usual suspects: Shivam Bhatt, for the discussions on the nature of Sindri's power; Elsbet Vance, for her perceptive eye and friendship; Nina Hess, for giving me the chance to start the story; and Stacy Whitman, for seeing me through to the end.

**THE NEW
ADVENTURES**

A Practical Guide to Dragons
By Sindri Suncatcher

Sindri Suncatcher—wizard's apprentice—opens up
his personal notebooks to share his knowledge of these
awe-inspiring creatures, from the life cycle of a kind copper
dragon to the best way to counteract a red dragon's fiery
breath. This lavishly illustrated guide showcases the wide
array of fantastic dragons encountered on the world of Krynn.

The perfect companion to the Dragonlance: The New
Adventures series, for both loyal fans and new readers alike.

Sindri Suncatcher is a three-and-a-half foot tall kender,
who enjoys storytelling, collecting magical tokens, and
fighting dragons. He lives in Solamnia and is currently
studying magic under the auspices of the black-robed
wizard Maddoc. You can catch Sindri in the midst of
his latest adventure in *The Wayward Wizard*.

For more information visit www.mirrorstonebooks.com

For ages ten and up.

THE NEW
ADVENTURES

THE TRINISTYR TRILOGY

The Trinistyr
Ancient holy relic
Cursed symbol of power
Key to Nearra's future . . . or her destruction

WIZARD'S CURSE
Christina Woods
Imbued with vestiges of Asvoria's power, Nearra is convinced
she can restore her magical heritage. Will Nearra find
the strength to break the wizard's curse?
September 2005

WIZARD'S BETRAYAL
Jeff Sampson
Betrayals come to light. New powers arise. And a startling
revelation threatens to destroy Nearra, once and for all.
January 2006

WIZARD'S RETURN
Dan Willis
Can the companions stand together and fight the final battle
for Nearra and Jirah's future?
May 2006

Ask for **Dragonl ance: The New Adventures**
books at your favorite bookstore!

For more information visit www.mirrorstonebooks.com

For ages ten and up.

THE NEW ADVENTURES

Want to know more about the Dragonlance world?

Want to know how it all began?

A RUMOR OF DRAGONS
Volume 1

NIGHT OF THE DRAGONS
Volume 2

THE NIGHTMARE LANDS
Volume 3

TO THE GATES OF PALANTHAS
Volume 4

HOPE'S FLAME
Volume 5

A DAWN OF DRAGONS
Volume 6

By Margaret Weis & Tracy Hickman

For more information visit <u>www.mirrorstonebooks.com</u>

For ages ten and up.
Gift Sets Available